Advance Praise for *The Pearl Plot*

"In this gripping tale of love and death in the remote badlands of northern New Mexico, Vicky Ramakka captures the magic of the desert Southwest's plants, animals, and unpredictable weather. Once I started reading The Pearl Plot, I was taken right along for the ride. I particularly enjoyed the multicultural aspects of the story and loved every minute with Millie."

—Scott Graham, National Outdoor Book Award-winner and author of *Saguaro Sanction*, Book 8 in the National Park Mystery Series

"I thoroughly enjoyed The Pearl Plot. The story combines knowledge of the Four Corners and all its cultures with suspense and a compelling murder mystery."

—Cindy Yurth, Navajo Times Assistant Editor and Reporter, Retired

"The Pearl Plot is intriguing and informative. It presents BLM resource specialists and managers as people, working as a team. As a BLM resource specialist for over 30 years, I perceived my fellow specialists and managers as family—working side by side to implement Congressional mandates for conservation and preservation.

Vicky's rendering of the BLM and its challenges and humanity is as accurate as I have found in print. It's a story that sparks inquisitive minds and reflects the complexity of public land issues. It was hard to put down."

—Kristie Arrington, BLM Colorado State Office & San Juan Field Office, Durango, Retired

Praise for *The Cactus Plot*

"We meet a variety of characters that ring true... Yes, there is a cowboy and even a love interest. ...There are themes that we all recognize, the role of the BLM in the West, protection of rare and endangered plants, cactus theft, and appreciation of the beauty of the vast vistas of the West."

Cathy King, Utah Native Plant Society Sego Lily Newsletter

"This is a delicious, layered Cozy Mystery/Women Sleuth paperback. ...it's an informed cultural and ecological immersion rolled up in a mystery."

Phaedra Greenwood, Enchantment Magazine

"This book is for any native plant enthusiast, murder mystery fan, pet lover, or supporter of the great southwestern outdoors."

Shirley Nilson, Colorado Native Plant Society Aquilegia Newsletter

"...a scientist-as-hero in the process of discovering her strength, ultimately using her botanical training and professional curiosity to crack the puzzles at the heart of *The Cactus Plot.*"

Kathleen Hall, Cactus & Succulent Society of New Mexico The Xerophile Newsletter

"Readers will not only find out who done it but also learn a lot about desert plants."

Sandra Dallas, The Denver Post

"...a pleasing story with convincing descriptions that celebrate the important conservation work done in public agencies. It will certainly be a good resource of education and entertainment that will engage readers who are scientists and the ones who are not."
Aline Rodrigues de Queiroz, Plant Science Bulletin

"...takes the reader onto isolated BLM land in the Four Corners Country... Millie, the botanist protagonist from the East, rejoices in the variety of plants—even though some species are directly involved in ghastly murders."
Anne Hillerman, New York Times Best-selling author of the "Chee-Leaphorn-Manuelito" series.

"Vicky is very descriptive in her mention of Navajo places and events, such as the Shiprock Flea Market. You can just imagine the colorful items, the smells in the air and hear the children wandering among shoppers."
Elaine Benally, Director, San Juan College West

"Vicky Ramakka's page-turner, *The Cactus Plot* does an excellent job at capturing the sense of place and people of Northwestern New Mexico."
Jonathan Thompson, environmental journalist and author of *River of Lost Souls: The Science, Politics, and Greed Behind the Gold King Mine Disaster*

The Pearl Plot

Murder at the Old Homestead

By

Vicky Ramakka

Artemesia
Publishing

ISBN: 9781951122621 (paperback) / 9781951122638 (ebook)
LCCN: 2023934317
Copyright © 2023 by Vicky Ramakka
Cover image copyright © 2023 by James Ramakka
Chapter header drawings by Trudy Thompson Farrell

Printed in the United States of America.

Artemesia Publishing
9 Mockingbird Hill Rd
Tijeras, New Mexico 87059
info@artemesiapublishing.com
www.apbooks.net

Epigraphs at the beginning of chapters from copyrighted materials used with permission of publishers and/or copyright holders:

Gobernador by Marilu Waybourn with Paul Horn, 1999, © The Paul B. and Dorothy M. Horn Living Trust, Farmington, New Mexico.

The Lost Communities of Navajo Dam Volume 2 by Patricia Boddy Tharp, 2020, © San Juan County Historical Society, Aztec, New Mexico.

Crimes of the County, Northwest New Mexico 1876–1928 by Marilu Waybourn, 2013, © San Juan County Historical Society, Aztec, New Mexico.

Time Among The Ancients by Bruce Hucko, 2007, © Impact Photographics, Inc., El Dorado Hills, California.

Some quotes found on Wikiquote.org and Braineyquote.com.

**Dedicated to James Copeland,
Bureau of Land Management archaeologist, retired.**

In recognition of his professionalism and life-long
dedication for protecting and educating about the
cultural resources of the Four Corners region.

Jim's motto: "A bad day in the field beats a good day in
the office."

Ledges Ruin

Lejos Canyon, Rio Arriba County, New Mexico

August, 1913

Rosalinda Florez de Peralta surveyed the inside of the cabin and nodded. Everything was in place to greet José when he returned from tracking the mountain lion that had been attacking their sheep.

She had done her best to make a home in the cabin José spent the two previous summers building. She went to the small mirror over the table he'd built and straightened her braid of black hair that hung over her breast. Her hair was what José said he loved best when he was courting her. On their wedding night two months ago, she let it fall loosely around his face. That's when he began calling her *mi querida Rosa Linda*, my sweet, beautiful rose.

Before turning away from the mirror, she picked up her sewing basket and placed it on the bottom shelf, then straightened the two remaining objects on the table. She opened the cover of a thick book, *La Guia Practica de la Salud*, the Practical Medical Health Guide, a wedding gift from José's older sister, Margarita.

Rosalinda lightly traced her fingers over Margarita's carefully printed *Felicidades*, wishing the new couple happiness. The book's hundreds of pages held vital information for the young couple moving to their own homestead in the unsettled northwest corner of New Mexico. Rosalinda dreaded the time when she would need to consult the medical guide for a broken bone or a case of the croup in

1

the children she knew would soon be coming. It comforted Rosalinda knowing Margarita lived only a few miles away. Margarita and her *novio* had moved to Lejos Canyon three years earlier. The day after their own wedding, José and Rosalinda made the same move. Unlike the long-settled upper Rio Grande valley, this corner of the newly created state offered the opportunity to obtain free land. José and Rosalinda believed they could turn the wilderness into farmland. They would make a home, till fields, plant trees and vegetables, and raise livestock. In five years, they would prove to the government that they had accomplished all this and obtain permanent ownership of one hundred and sixty acres.

Next to the book lay Rosalinda's most precious possession, the rosary her mother gave her. She turned and looked toward the front door. *José should be back by now.* She picked up the rosary and moved to the kitchen window to gaze at the rose bushes she'd transplanted from Taos and tended so carefully. She prayed for José's safe return.

As she prayed, she fingered the rosary's shimmering pearls, strung on a cotton cord, ten in a row, a space, a larger bead, another space, until she had circled around all five rows. She slipped her hand under the silver cross attached to the rosary and recalled the scent of her mother's perfumed powder and her solemn words just before they went to the church on her wedding day. "Keep this dear to you, *mi hija*. It has been in our family for many generations. It came with our family from Spain over the ocean to Mexico and now here to Taos. Someday you will give it to your own daughter on the day she weds." Her mother kissed the cross and placed it in Rosalinda's hands.

The rosary was beautiful, the pearl beads matched in size and shape, yet its silver cross seemed too large, more suited to be draped in the hands of a Virgin Mary statue in a church. She hefted the solid silver cross that extended from her wrist to the tips of her fingers. It was smooth except for Roman letters inscribed where the vertical and horizontal pieces met. The ends were elegantly scalloped. "This would buy many cows or the finest two-horse carriage. But no," she patted her stomach, "if you are a girl, this rosary will be yours. This cherished cross and rosary must stay with our family."

She slid the rosary into the pocket of her apron, settling the cross diagonally as it was just a little too big to fit inside. "This is a special day," she whispered, "the day I will tell José he will be a father. He should be back by now."

At the sound of a horse's hooves, she ran to the door. But it wasn't José she greeted. A stranger tied the reins of a half-starved horse to the clothesline post and strode toward her.

"Where's your man?"

Rosalinda looked in the direction of the sheep pen by the red sandstone cliffs. "He should be here by now."

He grunted, pushed her aside, and stomped into the kitchen. "What you got to eat, woman?"

"I have posole and beans on the stove, Señor," Rosalinda mumbled.

"Let's have it then." His voice held no hint of courtesy or gratitude.

The stranger had a matted brick-red beard, and his canvas pants looked like they carried dirt from sleeping on the ground and the blood of animals skinned for food. He smelled like his shirt had not seen the benefit of a wash tub for a very long time.

Rosalinda had never seen such a big man, not like her kin back in Taos. With shaking hands, she dished out the posole, put the bowl on the table, and retreated back to the stove. She looked out the window across the rose bushes. Only Molly, the old carriage horse, and the milk cow stood in the corral. *Where is José?*

The man wolfed down the food and said, "What else ya got?"

She reached into the warming oven at the top of the stove and pulled out a bread pan. Rosalinda sensed the man's brutish presence behind her. Instead of reaching for the bread, he grabbed her arm. "You're a pretty little bitch, aren't you."

He yanked her across the cabin and threw her onto the bed.

The monster stood next to the bed, leering at her, showing yellowed teeth. "Now for dessert."

Rosalinda's hand went to her pocket.

He knocked her hand away, pulled out the rosary, and dangled the cross above her face. "Ah, that's a pretty piece of silver you've got there."

Rosalinda clutched at the rosary and gagged as he lowered himself onto her shaking body.

Pearls scattering on the floor were the last thing Rosalinda heard.

***

José stepped down from his saddle, slung the rifle scabbard over his shoulder, and tapped his good riding horse on the rump. The horse would go to the corral where José would unsaddle and feed him later, after saying hello to Rosalinda. He was eager to tell her the sheep would be safe now.

He stopped at the open door and called her name. He went into the kitchen and saw one empty bowl on the table and the bread pan on the floor. He called again for his *Rosalinda*.

At the bedroom door, José bent double as if hit in the stomach by the devil. He moved to the bedside, dropped to his knees, touched his beloved's cheek, and bawled. In time, he stood, backed away, and bellowed in outrage, "Dios! ¿Por qué? ¿Por qué?"

José staggered to the corral, harnessed Molly to the wagon, tied his saddle horse to the back, and drove to the front of the cabin. He wrapped a blanket around his dead wife and carried her to the wagon, murmuring to the horses to settle. They swished their tails at the strange sight and smell of death.

José went back into the cabin. He picked up dish towels from near the sink, found the broom and dustpan, and went back into the bedroom. He covered the darkening blotches on the bed with the towels.

Squeezing tears from his eyes, he collected the parts of the rosary that were still intact. He touched to his heart the jagged end where the cross should have been. He would not leave Rosalinda's most treasured possession, now defiled, in this place of violation. He swept under the bed as best he could and put the pearls into the dustpan.

Speaking to the horses to stand and wait, he carried the dustpan far away from the cabin and gently emptied the pearls on the ground. On his knees and using his hands, he pushed newly tilled dirt over them.

He kept his eyes on Molly's ears as he climbed onto the wagon, glanced one last time at the home he had built with his own hands, and jiggled the reins. The horses knew the way to his sister Margarita's house.

Pack Rat Nest

Lejos Canyon, Rio Arriba County, New Mexico

Present Day

1. First Pearl

Stand on the rimrock high up on the mesa... Gaze up and down the canyon. The fragments of habitation visible today mask the long and eventful history of the area. Echoes of the past resound.

— Marilu Waybourn with Paul Horn, *Gobernador*

"Millie, come here, I've found something."

"I'm not wading back through all that cow manure to look at another piece of blue glass from some old bottle," Millie shouted back.

"This is different. You've got to see this."

The excitement in Lydia's voice intrigued Millie. She walked to the corner of the orchard where a blue tarp, pegged to the ground, served as a work base. She laid her clipboard face down so a breeze wouldn't ruffle the site recording forms. With long strides, Millie followed the path through the sagebrush that connected the orchard to the abandoned cabin and outbuildings.

Millie ducked under the weathered lintel of the old homestead's door opening. The door had disappeared long ago. She looked around the middle room, somewhat larger than the kitchen area in front and the much smaller room in back that had probably been used as a bedroom. The roof was still intact, held up with sturdy ponderosa pine vigas brought from the high country, crisscrossed by narrower juniper latillas, and covered by a thick layer of adobe. Cows had found this shaded room a fine place to loaf on hot summer days. Millie picked her way around the dried manure piles toward the corner where Lydia was squatting next to a pack rat's nest.

"What did you find this time?"

Lydia snapped a photo then set her camera on a nearby clipboard. She used the hem of her T-shirt to rub dirt off a small object and held it in a shaft of sunlight coming through a crack between the wallboards.

An iridescent spark flashed from between Lydia's stubby, calloused fingers.

"It's round, like a bead," Lydia said, without taking her eyes off her newest discovery. "Look, there's a hole in each end like a string would go through. It's a bead, that's what it is. Look at the way it shimmers. I think it's a pearl."

Lydia dropped the pearl in Millie's outstretched hand. It was about the size of her fingernail and tapered slightly into an oblong shape.

"It's beautiful, almost glows. What would it be doing in here?"

"There's a story here," Lydia mumbled, accepted the pearl back from Millie and resumed rolling it around in her palm, mesmerized.

"That's what you archaeologists do, right? Figure out the stories of how people lived a long time ago."

This seemed to snap Lydia back to her job of documenting the cabin and outlying buildings. As project botanist, Millie was focused on identifying the site's vegetation, both native and remnants of the cultivated plants. The homestead was once home to Hispanic settlers who migrated from communities north of Santa Fe to unclaimed land in northwest New Mexico. The site had recently come under Bureau of Land Management care as part of a land swap with the homesteaders' descendants. They traded 160 acres of this sparse canyon land for 23 acres of crop land where the family could grow vegetables and the lucrative green chile.

Millie and Lydia were assigned to survey, record, and produce detailed documentation of the 160 acre parcel. Building on the survey conducted under the National Historic Preservation Act prior to the land exchange, their work would form the basis of a management plan for the entire site. If successful in representing its special features and cultural connections, their report would be used to nominate the homestead for the National Register of Historic Places.

Lydia stood up, reached into her backpack slung on a peg in the wall, and pulled out a small white cloth bag. She dropped the pearl into it, pulled the drawstring tight, and felt for the round treasure inside the cloth. She tied the drawstring into a double knot, taking no chance of losing this surprising artifact. She filled out its tag with date, location, and description, then tucked the little bag in the front zipper pocket of the pack.

"Let's see if there are any more curiosities here." Lydia got down on both knees and began whacking a black chunk of dried rat droppings with a trowel.

Millie eyed the three-foot-high jumble of sticks piled in the corner. "You think digging through that rat crap is going to do you any good?"

"Yup. Pack rats are an archeologist's friend. They drag food for themselves and their young into nests like this. Sometimes generations of them. They keep piling on sticks, conifer branches, seeds, bark shreds for nesting material, even small animal bones. And bless their little pea brains and sharp eyes, they are curious, adventurous creatures. If they see a button, something shiny, anything out of the ordinary, they carry it back to their nest."

"I'll leave you to it. I'm going back out into the sunshine." Millie picked her way back around decaying manure piles, ducked out the door, and threw her arm up to shield her eyes. She tugged her wide-brimmed hat lower on her forehead, pulled her ponytail to one side to free the sunglasses' string, and put them on. She surveyed the view that the people who built and lived in this humble structure would have woken up to every morning. The corral twenty yards to the south would have had many more logs between the posts. Now, only the tops of gray, wind-whipped posts were visible above the overgrown rabbitbrush and Russian thistle. Next to the corral, a low shed was almost overtaken by weeds. One end of the roof was still held upright by 10-foot, round posts, but its other end had collapsed and sagged to the ground.

Millie walked halfway along the 50-yard path that led from the cabin to the dirt road that ran the length of Lejos Canyon. When the homestead became federal property, the BLM had outlined a small parking area next to the road with a split-rail fence. Beyond the road, red sandstone cliffs blocked the sky to the west. Millie estimated it would take less than a fifteen-minute walk to reach the base of the cliffs, but that had to wait for another day.

She turned a complete circle. Beautiful, rugged, lonely. What was it like to live in this remote place? Blazing hot in the summer, freezing in winter. Leaving your family and venturing to an unsettled land two hundred miles away. The quiet. Husband off tending sheep. Not seeing another human being until taking horse and buggy to church on Sunday.

Millie herself was two thousand miles from her family. It had taken her three days to drive to New Mexico from New Jersey. It would have taken about that long for this family to travel from Taos by horse and wagon, packing supplies and essential goods, starting a new life. What high hopes they must have had, building, planting, making a home. What happened to make them leave?

Lydia's humming and thumping on the pack rat's nest filtered through the disintegrating walls of the cabin. The sun's glare off their Bureau of Land Management vehicle parked by the road made Millie again throw up an arm to shield her eyes. Each evening, she and Lydia drove the 45 rough miles back to town for a shower and soft bed. The sturdy Suburban with the triangular BLM logo on its door was reassurance that working in this lonely outpost was only for the duration of the survey of the Peralta Homestead. She turned back and followed the path between the cabin and corral to the orchard.

Millie stopped by the first apple tree, not much taller than herself. Two blooms lingered on this tree, labeled #1 on the diagram she'd sketched the first day of her survey. This one, Millie was pretty sure, was a Jonathan apple tree, probably planted by some later caretaker of the property in the 1930s or 1940s. Not as old as some of the specimens in this historical fruit orchard. Likely it was planted to replace one of the original orchard fruit trees that didn't make it through a harsh winter.

It had taken Millie three days to locate the nearly 100 original orchard plantings, eight rows spaced roughly twenty feet apart, each with a dozen trees zig-zagging back toward the wash and red rock cliffs on the far side of Lejos Canyon. Some of the trees were now no more than stumps two or three feet high. Others still had gnarled branches that sprouted leaves each spring, produced a few blooms, and amazingly enough, fruit. It was these survivors that were the sought-after heirloom varieties. Valuable because of their genetic makeup that somehow suited them for survival in the extreme hot and cold seasons of the high desert. Valuable and vulnerable to poaching for grafting on temperamental, newer varieties.

The sound of a car door slamming brought Lydia out into the sunshine. Millie left the orchard and joined her by the cabin's doorway. A medium-height man waved and walked toward them, his scuffed hiking boots lifting puffs of dust from the sand.

2. Root Cellar Chill

Avoid inquisitive persons, for they are sure to be gossips, their ears are open to hear, but they will not keep what is entrusted to them.
— Horace, Roman Poet, 65–8 BC

This was the first visitor to the site since they'd started surveying three days ago. The stranger called out in a gravelly voice, "What are you ladies doing out here?"

Lydia met him halfway, shook his hand, and started up a conversation as if she hadn't seen another soul for weeks.

By the time they reached Millie next to the cabin, Lydia knew enough about the visitor that she was ready to introduce him. "Gavin, this is Millie Whitehall, the botanist on our project. Millie is recording the fruit orchard and vegetation on this homestead site."

"Hi, I'm Gavin McIntyre." He pulled two business cards out of his shirt pocket and handed one each to Millie and Lydia.

"Ancient Ones Adventure Travel," Lydia read aloud, "and your logo looks like a Phase Three Puebloan trade-ware pot."

Gavin's eyes narrowed, his head tilted to one side. "How would you know something like that?"

Lydia sighed. Sounding as if she'd been challenged by such questions too many times, she said, "I'm the archeologist on this project. I'm doing the documentation on this homestead."

"Is that so? I've never met a Black, um, African American archaeologist before."

"Well, now you have." The tone of Lydia's voice made it clear that any further questions would get him nowhere. "We'll be writing up a proposal to have this place added to the National Register of Historical Places."

Millie fingered the grubby, ragged-edged card that apparently had been in Gavin's pocket for some time. She glanced toward his van parked along the road, an eight-passenger carry-all. It had a banged-up bumper and mud-splattered windshield. The same elegant bowl shape was painted on the side door.

"Yeah, now I have." Gavin flashed a no-harm-intended smile. "I thought I was at the right place when I saw the government vehicle parked here. I do jobs for various cultural resource contractors helping on archaeological digs, driving my van for their crews, fetching equipment, that kind of thing. Whenever they need an extra field person, they call on me. In between those jobs, I use my van for tours. That's my favorite thing to do, take people around to places like this."

Millie wondered why a man who looked to be in his

late forties didn't appear to have a steady job. Yet, his creased, tanned face and field clothes backed up his claim of doing outside work in the desert southwest.

Gavin's head swayed as he took in the cabin from end to end. "Interesting," he said. "I've driven past this place, but never took the time to look around on this side of the road. I usually go right to the Lejos Canyon rock art site, over there." He pointed toward the cliff across the road, then snapped his fingers as if remembering why he stopped. "I'm scheduled to take a van load of university graduate students on a week-long tour of northwest New Mexico archaeological sites. It would work out just right to bring them by here the morning we come off two nights camping at Chaco Canyon. That would put us in Wellstown just about supper time."

Lydia was nodding her head, but Millie cut in before she could speak. "That'll depend on how we're doing on this survey. You'll need to check with the BLM office in Wellstown." Millie wasn't ready to give away a half-day's work to entertain this man's tours.

Millie ignored Lydia's scrunched-up face. Millie was the lead on this project, having all of one season with BLM under her belt and familiarity with working in the Piñon Resource Area's remote backcountry. Lydia was new to the BLM agency, though she had more years doing historic archeological work.

Undeterred, Lydia addressed Gavin. "Well, anyway, have you ever seen the inside of one of these old places?" Lydia patted the doorpost, ready to usher their visitor inside the cabin to see her pack rat nest excavation.

Gavin made no move to step into the dim interior. "'Course I have. I've spent years poking around these canyons." He had a deep, strong voice, the kind that carried far, an appealing asset for leading tours. "You know this place is haunted, don't you?"

"What?" Millie and Lydia said simultaneously.

"Everybody around here has heard the story that this place is haunted. Legend has it that the couple who home-steaded here, well, the wife was murdered. The body's buried in that old cemetery about twenty miles down the road, or it's buried somewhere on this property. I've heard it both ways."

Lydia's raised eyebrows pulled her eyes wide. "A murder? Here?" Then she shook her finger under the much taller man's face. "Ah, you're fooling with us."

Millie turned, put a hand on each side of the door opening, and leaned inward. "I don't see any ghost." She turned back and nailed Gavin with a hard stare. "I don't appreciate hearing tales, either. We're doing authorized research here. Not interested in stories you might feed to tourists."

Gavin folded his arms, and his face took on a deeper tan. "It's not a story. That's why nobody's lived here ever since the family that built it."

Lydia jumped in, "Un-uh, that can't be. There's been a fire in that cast iron stove way later than that. I poked through the ashes and saw some bits of tin foil."

"I know why that could be," Gavin said. "The hands from Turley ranch used to stay here once in a while when they were rounding up cattle. I had my load of tourists at the Devil's Claw café a few years ago. A half dozen or so cowboys came busting in for lunch after delivering cattle to the big transports that pick them up at the mouth of Lejos Canyon."

Millie crossed her arms and gazed upward, noticing for the first time the spindly needle and thread grass that had taken root in the cabin's sod roof. The distinctive twisted projection with pointed end lent to its nickname of needle and thread grass. Lydia had not taken her eyes off Gavin.

"Those cowboys claimed they saw the ghost, well maybe they said they just heard the rattling and moaning. They were all sleeping outside, of course. Nobody's going to bed down in that rat infested shack, but they used the stove to heat their supper. They were pretty quiet, so the waitress said, 'Out with it, boys, what happened?' One of the fellows finally fessed up they'd heard some strange things coming from the kitchen around midnight. I guess they were being quiet about it because not one of them had braved up to go inside."

Gavin pointed to the dark interior. "It's my thinking that those cowboys just heard pack rats or something scrambling around in there. But the story goes that the wife's ghost comes back here, dressed as a bride, still waiting for her man to come home. Rumors go around every so often about somebody passing by on the road thinks they see a figure in white at the door, this door here. Who knows?"

Gavin shrugged, gave a chuckle, and turned to look across the property. "You ladies found the root cellar yet?"

"Haven't located it so far," Lydia said, "but I know most of these homesteaders put in a root cellar. Had to store up food to last through the winter, being so far from town out here."

Gavin nodded toward a slight mound that extended about twenty feet from the cabin before it slanted back into ground level. "I always like to check out a root cellar. I found a, well, I'll just say, something valuable, in a tobacco can once. Wouldn't mind taking a look in that one over there."

"Bless my soul, why didn't I see that?" Lydia grumbled. "Let me get my camera and clipboard." She ducked into the cabin's dark interior and rejoined Millie and Gavin, carrying a meter stick in one hand. "Let's check it out." While settling the camera strap around her neck, Lydia headed toward the mound, but a tangle of raspberry brambles stopped her when she got closer to the door. Gavin skirted around her and stomped through the tangled thorns with his heavy boots.

Millie, nearly a foot taller than Lydia, saw where the patch of raspberries, planted long ago, petered out. "Over here, Lyd, come this way."

They rounded the end of the old garden with Millie in the lead. Gavin was standing in front of a door overgrown with bindweed. Three stone steps led down to the door made of wooden planks, now weathered and gray. The door had two panels that met in the middle, with a rusty hasp holding them together.

Gavin moved back from the door and motioned to Lydia, "Let's open 'er up."

"Yeah, that's in the movies, where they smash through a wall and find a skeleton." Lydia placed the meter stick against the door. "First, I'll document this opening *in situ* before we even touch it." The stick's 39-inch top came even with the hasp and another two feet of planking extended above it. Lydia took eight steps back, clicked the camera, moved to the left, clicked some more, and did the same from the other side. Then standing on the top step, she turned and aimed the camera back toward the cabin. "Later, I'll measure the distance the homesteaders had to walk back and forth every time they needed supplies for a meal."

Millie wasn't too keen on seeing what was behind the decaying door; it looked like the entrance to a crypt. She turned her gaze toward the rock cliffs across the road. Maybe a rock would roll off, something, anything to keep her occupied while waiting for Lydia to finish.

Gavin swiped sweat off his forehead but said nothing. Finally, when Lydia lowered the camera, Gavin said, "Go ahead, open it, just like the archaeologists in the movies who open up a king's tomb."

Lydia set the meter stick aside and pulled out the wooden peg holding the hasp closed. This jiggled the rusty hasp loose and Lydia caught it just before it fell to the ground. "Well, that was easy," Lydia said, squeezing her fingers into the crack between the weathered doors and lifting upward. Nothing moved. Lydia pushed in, still nothing. She tried prying the doors apart with the broken hasp.

Gavin took a step closer and said, "Look at the bottom. Sometimes they put another latch at the bottom to keep snakes and mice out."

Lydia reached behind the tangle of bindweed on the bottom step. They could hear a scrape as she pushed the bottom latch aside. The two doors dropped inward revealing another set of steps down into the root cellar.

"That latch didn't do much good keeping critters out." Lydia turned sideways so Millie could see. Bits of snakeskin, a desiccated horned toad, and the skull of a small mammal littered the steps.

"I ought to take photos," Lydia muttered, but curiosity superseded her scientific training. She used the meter stick to sweep back and forth to clear a way through a curtain of cobwebs and eased down the steps.

Millie, on the first step outside of the root cellar, bent low and looked over Lydia's shoulder. Lydia stiffened.

"Oh my God." Lydia backed up the steps, hands over her mouth, and pushed past Millie.

"What?" Millie took a couple more steps down and ducked through the door. She breathed out short puffs of

19

breath to push away the floating dust and earthy smell, letting her eyes adjust to the dim interior. There was an upside-down bushel basket, a dented washtub, and a broken crock on the wooden shelves that lined both sides of the root cellar.

Then Millie saw it. A crumpled form tucked under the lowest shelf on her right. Bones inside a flannel shirt and tan slacks gave shape to a human form, dried out by desert heat. Tufts of hair still clung to the back of a partly bare skull.

"Oh, gawd," Millie groaned, "I don't want to deal with another dead body. This happened to me last summer."

Millie retreated back into the sunshine. She knew the look of horror on Lydia's face likely matched her own. She put a hand on Lydia's shoulder for support as they breathed out dust and disgust.

They both turned toward the sound of the van's engine starting and watched Gavin back onto the road and drive away.

"What's going on with him? Yellow-belly just turned tail and ran," Lydia grumbled.

"We've got to call Robby," Millie whispered. Then answering the quizzical look on Lydia's face, added, "Robby Ramirez. She's the Law Enforcement Officer for the Piñon Resource Area."

3. Magnet For Trouble

The Homestead Act of 1862 has been called one of the most important pieces of Legislation in the history of the United States. ...this Act turned over vast amounts of the public domain to private citizens. 270 millions acres, or 10% of the area of the United States was claimed and settled under this act.

— National Park Service History & Culture

The next morning, Millie arrived at the BLM office later than usual. She had been awake half the night trying to assimilate what she'd seen and the confusion afterwards. Sheriff's officers keeping gawking oil and gas hands at bay. Robby leading the Medical Investigator down into the root cellar. Her relief when her boss, Area Manager Wirt Hernshaw, arrived to field questions about why BLM staff were at the homestead. It was nearly dark by the time Wirt said she and Lydia could leave the site.

Millie yawned, dropped her shoulder bag on her desk, went down the hall, and looked in the area manager's office to see if he was there.

Wirt Hernshaw looked up from behind his desk and motioned her to the straight-backed chair squeezed in between the desk and the bookcases that lined the office wall. "Are you a magnet for trouble or what?" He stood up and leaned toward her, both palms resting on the pile of papers in front of him. "Dang it, I said I never wanted to see another situation like that, after what we went through last summer."

"Sorry sir, I never wanted to see another dead body again either."

He sat back down and let out a slow breath. "Tell me exactly what happened."

"Lydia was working in the cabin, and I pretty well had the old orchard mapped. I would have started on the garden area if that Gavin guy hadn't shown up."

Wirt nodded, "We'll get to Gavin McIntyre later. Keep going."

"He started spinning tales about the place being haunted and then he wanted to go look in the root cellar. Guess he got our curiosity up, too. We found the root cellar. Lydia took some photos and opened it up. She went in first, cobwebs all over." Millie shivered, remembering how she'd snatched a spider out from inside her collar after she got the call through to Robby.

"Lydia came barreling back out. I looked in and saw why. Wish I hadn't." Millie shook her head, still unnerved by the previous day's discovery. "I should have braved up and taken a better look, so I could have told Robby more details when I got through to her. But I got the heck out of there just like Lydia."

She'd seen her boss rub his eyes whenever it seemed he didn't want to hear what he was hearing. He was doing that now.

"What did this Gavin fellow say?"

Millie gave a slight laugh. "He didn't say anything. I don't think he even looked in there. He just took off."

"But you said he was the one who wanted to look in there in the first place," Wirt commented. "And then he just took off? I wonder why?"

Millie shrugged. At the time, Gavin was not their main concern. "We had to drive a few miles back toward Wellstown before getting a cell phone signal. After I told Robby what we saw and where we were located, we drove back to the homestead. I went back in the root cellar, well, just down to the lowest step. Lydia stayed outside and I told her to make sure those doors stayed open. It was dark in there. What I remember seeing was, um, sort of a deflated bag of clothes. The corpse was under a shelf, on its side, back facing me. I could see sort of leathery skin on its neck and an arm draped over the back. The arm looked strange, not a natural position, and the hand hung out of the sleeve, fingers showing mostly bone. The shirt looked yellowish."

Wirt leaned back in his chair, his eyes downcast, seeming to be re-living the gruesome sight himself. "At least you knew enough this time to call Robby right away. You and Lydia were still pretty shook up when I got there. Good thing Robby was close by, checking on that cattle trespass. She took control, being the homestead is now federal property. She got the sheriff's deputies to keep on-lookers from stomping all over, especially around the root cellar."

"When can we get back to doing the survey?" Millie asked.

"Don't plan on working there for at least a couple of days," Wirt cautioned. "Robby and Detective St. Claire from the sheriff's office will be going over that place with a fine-tooth comb. Robby tells me that Detective St. Claire has a reputation for solving cold cases. She'll be on this like a barn cat on a mouse. Although it's my guess that body has been there a lot of years, so it's not likely there'll be any evidence show up outside of the root cellar."

Millie had an urge to go wash her hands. She just wanted this interruption to be over with, to resume her work and enjoy the peace and quiet that surrounded the homestead.

"Robby said she'd be meeting somebody from the medical investigator's office to oversee removing the body this morning. She'll be back later this afternoon and can tell us more about the procedures. I'll call you in when Robby shows up. Lydia, too. You two trouble-makers need to hear what the situation is at the homestead." Wirt almost smiled, to Millie's relief. At least, they weren't dealing with finding a dead colleague this time.

Wirt stepped from behind his desk and stood by the open office door. "You get any sleep after I sent you home so late?"

Millie got up and said, "Sure, slept like a baby. Not."

"Hang in there, Millie. I'll have Momma Agnes buzz you when Robby gets back."

Beckoned by a chunky hand motioning with a come-here gesture, Millie veered across the reception area just outside Wirt's office and over to the information desk. Mrs. Agrippina Maria Galleagos-Martinez's official title was Front Office Supervisor, but Millie thought of her as office matriarch and mother hen. Everybody called her Momma Agnes. While waiting for the portly woman with short, wavy black hair to finish with a phone call, Millie inspected the front and back of a sand-painted name plate spelling out MOMMA AGNES in glittering blue turquoise. Nothing that happened in the area manager's office escaped her attention, nothing in the whole office of a hundred staff, for that matter.

Finally, Momma Agnes wrapped up the phone conversation, punched a button to transfer the caller, and hung up. She glanced toward the area manager's door and took a quick breath. "I can tell you what that ghost story is about. It's true."

"You're saying that Gavin guy wasn't just trying to scare us off or something?"

"Well, all I'll say is a lot of my relatives won't go near that place. I'm related to half the Hispanic families that settled in Lejos Canyon back in the late 1800s and early 1900s. Most were young people from Tierra Amarilla, Abiquiu, and other parts of Rio Arriba County. There was still government land being doled out through the Homestead Act at that time. Anybody willing to build permanent structures and farm for five years could get their one hundred and sixty acres of land for free. Of course, the Navajos who had lived there for a few centuries weren't so keen on all that. But by then, the Navajos had mostly migrated farther west because of raiding by the Utes, and because early Spanish explorers sometimes took children as slaves, lots of reasons."

"Yeah, Lydia filled me in on some of this from the research she did on the site before we started our survey."

"Hon, this doesn't come from reports on paper. I know from family stories passed down for generations. Such a shame about that young woman." The phone rang and Momma Agnes reached for it. "I'll tell you later what happened at the Peralta Homestead."

Millie resolved to follow up with Momma Agnes about

Ramakka

the rest of this so-called ghost story.

4. Pocket Notebook

Life is the desert, life the solitude, death joins us to the great majority.
— Edward Young, English Poet, 1683–1765

It was late afternoon when the call came from Momma Agnes that Robby Ramirez was back in the office and to gather in the conference room in fifteen minutes. Millie bookmarked the PDF file on her computer screen, saving the spot where she was reading about heirloom fruits in the 1910 *The Old Farmer's Almanac.*

Always a little more than punctual, Millie thought she was the first person to enter the conference room until she saw Robby already seated at the table, resting her head on crossed arms.

"Are you all right, Robby?"

Robby pushed herself upright. "Yeah, just dog tired."

Millie took a seat opposite the window side of the conference room and looked into the enforcement officer's dark-rimmed eyes. Wisps of her shining black hair, usually tied in a neat bun at the back of her neck, had escaped to hang over her ears.

Lydia arrived, took one look at the officer, and wrapped her in a busty hug. The two could not be more opposite in physique. While both were not much more than five feet tall, Robby had the muscular body of a weightlifter. Lydia, on the chubby side, could have made the model for a Norman Rockwell painting of Mrs. Santa Claus. Lydia nearly smothered Robby with her hug, then held on to her hand while plopping in the chair across from Millie.

Robby pulled her hand away. "Geez, do I look that bad?"

Wirt entered, pulled out a chair next to Millie, saw Robby, and said, "You go home after we're done here, get some rest. Looks like you've been up all night."

"Just about," Robby said. "I stayed at the scene until nearly midnight and got back out there at dawn so I could take a good look around before the others arrived. The sheriff's office big bomber of a crime scene van came about eight. The medical investigator arrived not long after." Robby's usual trim, spotless uniform shirt had ground-in dirt on each elbow, as if she had been crawling on the floor of the root cellar.

Robby flipped open her stenographer's notebook. "This is what we know so far. The body was that of a Caucasian male, approximately six feet tall, impossible to tell exactly after the desert sucked all moisture from him. Same with his age, hard to tell, my best guess is forties, maybe early fifties. He was wearing blue jeans, Vibram-soled hiking shoes, and what looked like a button-down shirt, but that was fairly deteriorated. We could see that it was long-sleeved, and best thing is, the shirt pocket had a little notebook. Sylvia, I mean Detective St. Claire, bagged that. Didn't open the notebook in case there might be any identifying traces that show up with a closer look under a microscope. If we're lucky, it'll have notes that are still readable."

"What about a wallet?" Wirt asked.

"No wallet, no keys, no coins, jackknife, no other identifying objects. Once the medical investigator got done taking pictures and was ready to move the body, he had me and a sheriff's officer slip a canvas sheet under the body in order to pull it out from underneath the wooden shelf."

Lydia shifted in her seat. "Archaeologists sometimes get to deal with human remains. At least, I've had my share. The museum I worked at in Mississippi went through the NAGPRA process for repatriation of three ancient skeletons to the Choctaw Tribe."

"You got involved in a NAGPRA situation?" Wirt broke in. "Lucky you. I hear that's a complicated process."

"Uh-huh. You wouldn't believe the paperwork required to meet all those Native American Graves Protection and Repatriation Act requirements. I was involved in the process of preparing the remains and related funerary objects for the transfer. But this is different. Those remains were hundreds of years old. What I saw there, pushed back under that shelf, still had hair on the skull."

"Lydia, the way you came sprinting out of there," Millie chided, "it's a wonder you saw even that much. I saw the hair and how the hand and part of an arm dangled over the back of the shirt. Unnatural position was my impression."

"Well, you didn't spend overly long down there yourself, Miss Millie." Lydia wasn't going to take any guff from a botanist. "And you told me three times to keep an eye out for anything that moves when you went back in there the second time."

"You did the right thing, not disturbing anything until we got there." Robby studied her notes for a moment, then looked up. "Brace yourselves, here comes the grisly part. When we pulled the canvas out, we got a good look at the side that had been facing the sod wall. Front of his skull was cracked wide open. Somebody hit him with an axe or something. I'd never seen a dried-up brain before."

Lydia gasped and Wirt was rubbing his eyes. Millie fingered the scar on her forehead, obtained during her previous summer's field work when she'd confronted a murderous cactus thief.

"So, we know the body is from the current era, not one of the Ancestral Puebloans that pot hunters are so fond of digging up." Wirt said. "Lydia, do you think the state archaeological office needs to be notified?"

"Definitely. I don't believe they'll have much interest in this corpse, but when we go to nominate the Peralta Homestead as a National Historic Site, we've got to have endorsement from the state office first. I'll talk to them about this situation. It'll at least make them aware of what we are doing."

Robby laid her notebook down on the table. "The medical investigator said he'd give me a call in a couple days after he inspects the body. And I should hear anytime now from St. Claire about that little pocket notebook."

The area manager took a couple deep breaths, appearing to be sorting these facts in his mind. "Thanks, Robby. Keep us apprised as soon as you hear anything." Wirt turned to Lydia. "Make a courtesy call to the state archaeological office. See if they want to follow up. We need to be proactive on this. Might avoid any complications later if word gets out about finding a corpse in Lejos Canyon, and word *will* get out."

Wirt stood, ready to get back to his office, but stopped by the door. "Oh, I forgot to tell you earlier, this Gavin McIntyre you met, he contacted me a week ago, before all this happened. He's bringing a group of Northern Arizona University graduate students on a field trip to cultural sites in northwest New Mexico. I told him about the survey work you two had going on at the old homestead."

"That's right." Lydia snapped her fingers. "That explains why he was there. Remember, Millie? When he first got to the cabin, he said he was bringing a field trip through. But then he started talking about the cabin being haunted."

Wirt nodded. "He asked whether there were any archaeological digs occurring on the Piñon Resource Area. I told him where the homestead is and to check it out to see if it would interest the students. He said he could find you with no problem, that he's traveled the Lejos Canyon road many times. He showed me the trip description from the university and asked permission for the class to visit."

Millie groaned. "You told him to come yesterday? Now you're saying he's coming back, with a bunch of students? It'll take half a day to tour them around the homestead. We're already behind."

"Yes, I okayed it. He said he'd get back to us when he's got the final schedule for the field trip. I'll have Momma Agnes let you know when he contacts us." Wirt turned to Lydia, "It'll be a good opportunity to cover the BLM's responsibilities for managing cultural resources." He looked at Millie, his lips tight together, and left.

5. Lucked Out

Most of the earliest settlers were Hispanos coming primarily from Chama River valley of New Mexico or the San Luis Valley of Colorado. The majority had roots in the Abiquiu area. Often, they were related and migrated together.

— Patricia Boddy Tharp, *The Lost Communities of Navajo Dam Volume 2*

Millie didn't mind the half-hour commute home from the BLM office in Wellstown. Traffic was a snap compared to the crazy, crowded freeways she'd learned to negotiate around her New Jersey hometown. The drive was unwind time, shifting her mind from work to the laid-back pace of her current neighborhood. But after the last two days, she was especially thankful to pull into the driveway of her quiet casita rental.

She got out of the new-to-her 2018 Honda hybrid car and eased the door shut. Maybe she did baby it a little. It had taken most of her savings from last summer's job to replace her old rustbucket Ford Explorer that was more suited for hauling cleaning supplies than traveling wide-open western highways.

She looked for Ragged Ear. The cat was not curled up in his usual spot on the porch bench next to the front door, nor strolling over for a head-rub. When he trotted out from under the lilac bushes in the side yard, she let out her breath. "I should have known you wouldn't get lost, you old skank. You haven't forgotten your stray cat wandering days, but you're too attached to the pop of a cat food can to wander off, aren't you?"

She reached down to pet the cat but yanked back. Something dangled from Ragged Ear's mouth. It wiggled. The cat had a look of bliss on his face. "Let it go, now!" He trotted toward the front door. "Oh no. You are not bringing that lizard inside." Seeming surprised that his gift was being spurned, the cat darted back under the lilac bushes.

"Let it go," Millie called again, shrugged, and stepped through the front door. She took a deep breath, savoring the earthy smell of adobe brick walls mixed with a hint of wood smoke. Happiness and contentment seemed to emanate from the walls.

***

Millie had lucked out finding this place just one day after arriving in New Mexico from a dreary, anxious winter stay in her parents' New Jersey home. She didn't mind helping out with the family's janitorial business, but she had chewed her fingernails down to nubbins while maneuvering through the interminable federal hiring process.

When word finally came in late April that she was top candidate for the permanent botanist position at the Piñon Resource Area BLM office, Millie was delighted. Her experience the previous summer working in New Mexico's high desert as a temporary seasonal hire had reinforced her commitment to a career in botany. That experience had taught her that protecting endangered plants on public land had its dangers but also a sense of achievement.

After accepting the job, it took Millie only a day and a half to pack, put Ragged Ear in his carrier, and head west. Before leaving New Jersey, she had researched rentals in her price range and found three that appeared likely. When she arrived in Wellstown, she began tracking down a place to live. The first rental on her list was located in a small town twenty miles from the BLM office, a considerable drive, but it was on the road to Lejos Canyon where she would be working. She called the landlord and arranged a time to look at the rental. When Siri's voice directed a turn onto a dirt lane, she double-checked the address and continued bumping along until she heard the reassuring "you've arrived" message. The place looked older but settled into a comfortable retirement after years of sheltering a series of occupants.

An elderly man was sprinkling fertilizer on a row of rose bushes in front of a large, handsome hacienda-style house next door. He waved, placed the fertilizer bag in a wheelbarrow, and walked toward her. He introduced himself as the owner, Antonio Gaspar.

"This was our first real home," the landlord related as he led her through the spotless casita. "Della and me, we'd always lived in a trailer before that, moving from one construction site to the next. We were so happy to settle in this place. We pretended we were newlyweds. I carried Della over the threshold, even though we had four kids by then. I almost tripped over the youngest. The two boys had this bedroom, the girls were here, and..."

The casita was just right, Millie decided, even before Mr. Gaspar finished the tour.

"The kids have all gone their own way now. Della sometimes threatens to move back in here, says the house we built next door is too big to take care of. What do you think, Miss? I can let you have it for seven hundred a month, all utilities paid. I've got somebody coming this afternoon to look at it."

Millie's upbringing taught her to squeeze a hundred and ten pennies out of every dollar bill. "I like it all right, sir, but I'm starting my first full-time job with the Bureau of Land Management. I'd be a good reliable caretaker of this place if the rent were six hundred a month."

It took a little convincing of her potential landlord that yes, she really was single at her age, and yes, she had a steady job and would pay rent at the first of each month. After a little more dickering back and forth, they struck a deal, and moved out to the driveway. Millie got out her checkbook, diligently printed 650 in the proper space, and handed the check to her new landlord. Mr. Gaspar stuffed the check into his shirt pocket and asked, "What's this new job you're starting?"

"The site I'll be surveying is called the Peralta Ranch, an old, abandoned homestead in Lejos Canyon." Millie did not notice the astonished look on his face while she tucked the checkbook into her pocket,

"Did you say Peralta Ranch? In Lejos Canyon?" Mr. Gaspar almost shouted. He turned away and hobbled back toward his house, calling out, "Della, Della, come here! Listen to what this young lady is doing!"

Millie stood, open-mouthed. Had she said something wrong?

The Gaspars' much-larger, stuccoed home was encircled on three sides by an inviting veranda, festooned with hanging plants and massive, bright-colored ceramic planters. Mrs. Gaspar came out the side door, wiping her hands on a dish towel. The portly woman met her husband halfway to where a puzzled Millie waited.

"What has you all in a tizzy, Antonio?"

"Listen, listen. You'll never believe it." The old man shoved his hand under her arm, and hustled his wife over to stand in front of Millie.

"Tell her, tell her what you're going to do to our family's homestead." Before Millie could say a word, Mr. Gaspar gushed on, "She's going to be at the Peralta Ranch, going to make it a historic place or something. It's government now, it's going to be kept up, taken care of. Isn't that wonderful?"

"I know it's government now. They gave us those acres down by the river three years ago in exchange for it. You said back then you'd rather see rows of chile growing than watch the old place fall down." Mrs. Gaspar took a step back, looked up and down at the five-foot ten-inch-tall young woman, and honed in on Millie's eyes. "Is it true? The BLM is going to do something way out there? Take care of it?"

Millie hoped her next words would result in having a place to live rather than being dismissed as some meddlesome government worker. "That's what I'm here to do. I'll be working with an archaeologist to survey and document the house, the orchard, and all the property around it that's called the Peralta Homestead. Do you know about it?"

"Know about! Of course, we know about it. Antonio's family came from there. He will tell you. Come with us." The woman extricated herself from her husband's arm, motioned to him to bring Millie along, and bustled back to her house.

The next thing Millie knew, she was rocking in the big swing on the Gaspars' veranda and tasting fresh-baked bizcochito cookies for the first time. The long-time married couple, now in their eighties, sometimes talked over each other, but mainly Mrs. Gaspar let her husband tell the story. His ancestors emigrated from Old Spain to Mexico, then traveled *El Camino Real* trail north, landing in Taos. As that area became more settled, one branch of the family ventured to Lejos Canyon where land could still be had for the taking. It was Antonio's great uncle who built the ranch that Millie hadn't even seen yet.

The old man's eyes misted over. Mrs. Gaspar suddenly got up and started gathering the dishes. She turned to Millie, shielding Mr. Gaspar, and said, "Please excuse us. Reminiscing about the homestead's past is a little sad. We are so happy you are here. I will have a fresh batch of bizcochitos for you tomorrow when you move in."

Millie shook her new landlady's hand, gave a slight bow to Mr. Gaspar, and took her leave. She was baffled and disappointed. Just when it seemed like she was going to hear a first-hand account of life at the homestead, everything shut down. Would renting next to the Gaspars be like that? A series of ups and downs, tantalizing bits of history but never the complete story?

***

Today, Millie was especially grateful she had her own adobe retreat. It was bad enough hearing Robby's grisly description of the body this afternoon, but that didn't compare to the shock she had felt when she realized that shape in the root cellar had once been a living, breathing human being.

By the time Millie changed out of jeans and cotton blouse into shorts and T-shirt, Ragged Ear was perched on the top of the porch bench and peering into the living room window. Millie held the door open. "Okay, come on in. Hope that poor lizard got away." The cat lashed his tail against Millie's legs and trotted to the kitchen.

Millie plopped a half can of yucky-smelling pâté in her buddy's bowl and checked his water dish. Ragged Ear demolished his supper, sat down, and proceeded to lick his paws and rub his face. Watching the cat's methodical maneuvers eased Millie's dark thoughts.

Ragged Ear strolled to the front door and gave a demanding yowl. Millie followed him out to the porch but caught her breath when she saw Mr. Gaspar pushing his wheelbarrow toward the row of roses, a rake and long-handled clippers balanced inside. He spotted Millie, let go of the wheelbarrow with one hand long enough to wave, and continued on.

Millie let out her breath. News of what happened at the Peralta site had not gotten out yet. He must not know or he would be asking her about it. She settled onto the bench and relaxed, extending out her sun-deprived pale legs and studying the logs and vigas that made up the porch roof.

When Mr. Gaspar's humming and clipping stopped and he called her name, she jolted upright. He was waving the long stem of a deep red-colored bud and motioning her over.

Doing her best to act nonchalant, Millie ambled in his direction. Using her loudest voice for the semi-deaf man, she called out, "Mister Gaspar, how are your roses today?"

"*Bonitas, como siempre*," he replied and presented her with the rose as if it were a precious jewel.

Millie clasped both hands around the bud and lifted

it to her nose. "Ahhh, it's beautiful. It smells like cinnamon. *Gracias.*" Millie towered over her neighbor-landlord. Probably never much taller than five and a half feet, his age and stooping due to a bad back put him eye level with Millie's shoulder.

"My roses will be the prettiest ones at the church when they are in full-bloom. Now they are just beginning to awaken." He caressed a tender, shiny leaflet with his gnarled fingers, scarred and nicked from decades of hard work.

The old man hobbled to the bush farthest from his house, motioning Millie to follow. It was smaller than the others and had a thick, stubby central stem. Its spindly branches teemed with closely-spaced, vicious-looking tiny thorns. "This rose you see, *Señorita* Millie, it came from the Peralta Ranch that you are studying. I dug it up many years ago and planted it here. It's not very pretty, but it survives. Just like me."

Millie had trouble seeing the tumbled down buildings and weed-covered site as a functioning ranch.

"You know, sometimes when I go there, not so often anymore since my legs don't walk so good, I go over to see the petroglyphs, the rock art on the cliffs. I have followed that path to the sheep pen many times." The old man's voice held a wistful tone.

"A sheep pen? That would be part of the ranch structures that Lydia needs to inventory. I plan to start the vegetation inventory over there once I get the cabin surroundings completed. That side of the road all the way over to the cliff is part of the protected area that BLM wants to make a National Historic Site."

"If it's history you want to see, you must walk across the road and follow the old trail to the cliff. When you see the sheep pen, look up and walk along the cliff to the north. People have lived in Lejos Canyon for many centuries. Those rock carvings show their history just as much as words printed in a book. Long before my ancestors came there, the Navajos settled there, and before them, the Anasazi people. Wait, I shouldn't say Anasazi, the lost ones, anymore. A better name is Ancestral Puebloans because the Pueblo people are not gone. They live in many New Mexico and Arizona communities."

"I think you are a pretty good historian, yourself, Mr. Gaspar." Millie's regard for her landlord grew with every conversation she had with him.

"Ah, no, I am just a humble farmer." He lifted his broad-brimmed hat and made a sweep of the surrounding well-tended fields, Millie's rental, and his spacious hacienda-style home. "And, maybe too, I was a foreman for the El Paso Natural Gas Company. I supervised the laying of hundreds of miles of pipes that gather natural gas from the wells you see in many parts of New Mexico." He stood a little taller.

Millie remembered the lesson she learned the previous summer. In the Land of Enchantment, never gauge a person by their clothing or what they tell you when first meeting them.

"Miss, look out."

Millie ducked.

The old man's hat sailed toward the pasture fence. "That damned goat."

Millie watched the octogenarian hobble toward the bleating nanny stuck halfway through the fence.

The distracted man called back to her, "Remember, when you see the sheep pen, walk only to the north."

Millie strolled back to her porch and sat on the bench for a while, sniffing the rose bud and stroking Ragged Ear, relieved that she had the weekend to escape from the previous days' chaos. She resolved to keep busy catching up on field notes and taking long walks to acquaint herself with the village. And she'd call Lydia and tell her about the sheep pen.

6. Sheep Pen

Archaeological sites and historic landscapes give us important insights into the ways human activities and the land have been linked together through time.
— Bureau of Land Management Cultural Resources Program

Millie looked at her watch and stepped beyond the driveway to see if Lydia was coming. At last, the tan BLM Suburban came into sight, Lydia's head barely showing above the steering wheel. Most days, she picked Millie up and they rode together to the study site. Lydia rented an apartment in Wellstown, and it was easier for her to check the vehicle out from the BLM motor pool. And most days, Lydia was late.

Millie climbed in, lobbed a scowl at her tardy chauffeur, and took a sip from her travel coffee cup. Usually on the drive to the Peralta site, Lydia gave a running commentary on the weather, what she packed for lunch, a stray dog she saw on the way, whatever. Today, it seemed she didn't want to touch on anything that might stir up thoughts of the trouble they'd endured the previous week. Millie broke the silence with, "Let's go over to the cliff as soon as we get to the site and find the sheep pen Mister Gaspar told me about and look at the petroglyphs."

"I'm all for that." Lydia was quick to give her wholehearted agreement. "Rock art, cool. I've only seen southwest rock art in pictures. And I want to see that sheep pen, estimate what I need to do to incorporate it in our report."

Lydia's eagerness, Millie figured, matched her own because they could explore the rest of the proposed area to include in the Historic Site and delay going back by the root cellar.

"My baby boy called last night. Said he got a raise." Lydia was back to her usual chatty self.

"Is that the baby boy that's a software engineer in Dallas?" Millie endeavored to show interest.

"No, this is the younger one, the one that's still trying to 'find himself.' I bet I could find him a job in a New York minute that pays better than what he's doing. But, no, he's now being a barista, learning the important art, according to him, of making flower designs on lattés. I told him..."

Millie, resigned to Lydia's narration, slumped down in her seat and took a gulp of lukewarm coffee.

***

Lydia parked and, instead of going to the cabin, they turned toward the tall rock cliff to the west. It took a few minutes of walking back and forth along the road until Millie spotted the age-old trail that her landlord had described. She led the way through sagebrush, rabbitbrush, and scattered juniper trees.

"There's the sheep pen," Millie called out. She waited for Lydia to catch up. Being a head shorter than Millie, Lydia was struggling to push her way through the brush. "Watch out for nails sticking out of those boards."

Lydia, puffing a bit, joined Millie in front of the mostly fallen-down gate. "Well, look at that. They sure knew how to take advantage of natural features."

Fence posts, cut from juniper trees, leaning every which way, outlined three sides of what had been a corral about the size of a double-car garage. A few boards remained nailed to the posts, but most had fallen to the ground. The cliff made up the back side of the pen. Sturdier posts driven tight against the rock wall had once prevented any escape by livestock. The cliff towered over the sheep pen. It was at least four times higher than the tallest tree in Millie's New Jersey hometown and consisted of tan, red, orange, and sepia-toned sandstone strata with an occasional layer of gray clay.

Millie maneuvered around a rusty wire sticking out from a post and stepped over two flat boards still attached across the bottom of the pen's gate.

Lydia followed but took only a few steps into the corral. "Gawd, these weeds are awful."

"Yeah, that's what happens when the ground has been grazed down to nothing, then left to nature. Weeds invade."

"It would have been mostly sheep," Lydia said. "From my research, most of the homesteaders in Lejos Canyon raised sheep to supply the government with wool for World War One uniforms. Can you imagine wearing an outfit made of scratchy wool?"

"Maybe not a whole uniform, but it's a fall ritual in places like I come from to get your wool coats and jackets out for winter. Nothing better to keep you warm in drizzly, cold rain and snow."

Millie bent down, and with a slight tug, pulled up a tender-looking plant, roots and all. "This pretty green stem with its purple stripes at this time of year will turn into those prickly brown bushes by the end of summer. Those hard, brown ones are last year's growth, or the year's before, or before that. It's prickly Russian thistle, a nasty invasive weed that came from Central Asia. Your classic tumbleweed."

"Really, tumbleweed, like the old cowboy 'Tumbling Tumbleweeds' song?" Lydia felt the young, flexible plant. "This turns into these big, prickly bushes?"

"Yup. It's fun to watch the wind tumble them along, but they are scattering seeds along the way. They have specialized cells that allow for the stems to break loose when the seeds are mature. That's how they've spread all over the West."

Millie tossed the weed toward the middle of the corral and ran her foot over a patch of grass.

"We're walking on another invasive weed, cheat grass, the bane of the American West, Canada too. It's shallow-rooted and outcompetes native vegetation for moisture. I'll be adding both non-native and native species to the plant list for this site."

"This tender-looking grass, it's bad?" Lydia asked. "It's all around here, looks kind of nice."

"You won't think it's very nice in a couple of months when it's dried out. The awns on the seeds poke into your socks, shoes, clothes—they're awful. But worse is that cheat grass just takes over. It crowds out food for wildlife and wildfire burns through it fast as a racehorse. Oh, look over there, another pack rat nest for you to investigate."

They climbed back over the gate and went around to

get a closer look at the pile of sticks. Several generations of pack rats had assembled a nest tucked against the cliff and corner fence post. It was nearly four feet high. The collection of sticks and dried cactus pads was topped off by a long-decayed rabbit carcass.

"Oh, Millie, another treasure of amberat for me to dissect," Lydia whispered as if she were gazing upon the Taj Mahal.

"Treasure of... What did you say?" Millie asked.

"Amberat—it's a special name for those hard chunks you see stuck against the rock. Pack rats, or woodrats some people call them, urinate on their nest piles. It hardens over time, trapping and preserving everything that was in the nest."

"Seriously? There's a name for rat pee that's turned hard?"

"Uh-huh, I worked on a contract our museum had back in Charleston, South Carolina. It was one of those big old plantation mansions that was being restored. Inside some of the walls, there were a couple of woodrat nests. Instead of the way they piled up sticks here, they used bits of cloth, mattress padding, paper, all kinds of stuff they could steal from the house and grounds. There were buttons, a couple of human teeth, a silver fork, tongue of a shoe. It added a lot to interpreting how people lived then."

Lydia stepped closer to the nest, bent at the waist, and wiggled what looked like another stick. "Ha, already found something. A pencil." She held out the stubby, yellow pencil with a broken point for Millie to see.

"That's a real treasure, all right." Millie made no move to touch the scuzzy object. "I can see some bits of paper, too. Wonder how pack rats found paper over here."

Lydia placed the pencil next to the bottom of the nest pile and brushed her hands together to get rid of bits of black dirt from the pencil.

"Maybe you'll find another pearl, Lyd. And I see another treasure for you." Millie lifted a long-handled, blue enamel dipper from a peg on the corner post. A couple spots of black showed where a scale of enamel had flaked off around a dent on the rim.

"That's been used for a long time," Lydia said. She looked it over and hung it back on the peg. "What's this?" She lifted a thick rounded wire, hooked on both ends.

"Oh, I've carried enough mop buckets to know what that is," Millie said.

"I've got it. This is the handle off a bucket, maybe for water or feeding the sheep. Proper name is bail. A pail bail, so to speak." She giggled and put it down in the same spot. "Glad we came over here. It's these kinds of artifacts that tell the story of how the homesteaders lived. I'll have to come back with my camera and field book to record this as a feature linked to the site."

Millie was looking up along the cliff. "Mister Gaspar said go north from the sheep pen and look for rock art."

"Oh, wow, I see something," Lydia said, pointing above Millie's head. "Up there, it's a..., I don't know what it is."

"That's a carved petroglyph, for sure. Now we go north, this way." Millie stepped sideways to the right, never taking her eyes off the cliff face. "I see a sun over here." The circle was about one foot in diameter and almost perfectly symmetrical. It had lines extending from the rim at the top, bottom, and each side, mimicking the four cardinal directions. The outline was a couple feet above Millie's head, chiseled into the sandstone a half inch deep and as wide. The cut lines looked lighter than the surrounding stone, easy to spot once they began looking.

Lydia nodded, "That's a better sun than I could ever hack out on stone. Something below it. Kind of looks like an arrow pointing downward. There's a line looping back and forth down it, like a doctor's caduceus emblem."

"Here's a row of little people, holding hands." Millie reached out at shoulder height, and began tapping each figure, counting, "One, two, three..."

"No, no, Millie. Not good to touch these. Even the oils on your fingertips can change the composition of the surface. There are ways to determine the age of rock art by chemical analysis. None are terribly reliable. Archaeologists pay more attention to what artifacts are found nearby, like stone tools or fired clay pots to get an idea when designs were made, either painted or carved into the rock surface."

Millie pulled her hand back. "Oh, I didn't know that would matter." She continued counting. "Nine people in a line, including two smaller ones. Maybe children? Maybe it's a family portrait?" Millie stepped back and pointed upward toward a smooth rock face. "Look at this one. Big upside-down triangle, with a head and thin arms and legs sticking out. A smaller one beside it."

"That humanoid figure is typical of Ancestral Puebloan age rock art, about nine hundred to thirteen hundred years before present." Lydia sounded excited.

Millie looked at Lydia's sparkling eyes, happy to share the excitement of discovering the ancient site. "How'd you come up with that 'nine hundred to thirteen hundred years before present' anyway? You said you lived your whole life in the southeast, never been west of the Mississippi before you got hired here."

"University course on 'Indigenous Peoples of North America.' I've only seen pictures in books of this kind of rock art, but we archaeologists pay attention to dates. Might forget our own birthday, but ask me when the Mound Builders inhabited the Mid-west."

Millie continued walking. "Wonder what that one is—looks like a person with long hair streaming to one side, as if standing in a strong wind."

"Looks more like a cloud or fog," Lydia said. "From what I've read, that's how the early Navajo portrayed dreams or visions."

"Hey, that fits. See that plant against the cliff, the tallish one, about three feet high? People call it jimsonweed. Its scientific name is *Datura wrightii*. Hallucinogenic as all get-out. Notice how there's more plants growing next to the base of the cliff? A little more moisture collects there from rain and snow melt. The sagebrush we walked through to get here is taller than farther down the road, too. That means there's better moisture here. I suspect there's a hardpan layer below the ground here, probably a layer of clay that hinders drainage. That's why people chose this particular site to live, from the Ancestral Puebloans to those homesteaders that built the cabin."

"We make a good team, Millie. We each recognize aspects of this site that help piece together its story."

"I'm glad we are exploring together, too. We could wonder about this rock art all day. I'll ask Ben if he knows someone who could tell us what these figures mean."

"Who's Ben?" Lydia asked. "Oh, is that your cute boyfriend from last summer that Momma Agnes told me about?"

Millie shook her head in disbelief. "Momma Agnes told you that, huh? Ben Benallee is not my boyfriend. She's just full of gossip, isn't she."

Millie put a hand up to shade her eyes and peered down the rock wall. "Looks like this is where the petroglyphs end. Let's just cut out to the road from here, that'll be shorter than going all the way back to the sheep pen."

Lydia made a bee-line toward the road but slowed to

detour around a massive boulder about the size of a small house. "Ooh-whee, check this out, Millie." Lydia plunked both hands over her mouth, but giggles spilled out anyway. "Some sheepherder must have been pretty bored or missing his sweetheart."

Millie moved to stand next to Lydia and followed her pointing finger to a life-size, nude female figure chipped into the side of the boulder. "Mister Gaspar didn't tell me about *that*," Millie sputtered, and shaking with laughter, put a hand on Lydia's shoulder to steady herself. "That... that is downright, um, graphic."

Millie leaned closer to the chiseled letters beneath the voluptuous silhouette. "Look, the guy even signed his name. I see an A, then a G-A-S-P—can't make out the rest of the letters. Then a two, a six, *Marzo*, then looks like a one, nine, another two, and four. That would make it March 26, 1924, if I remember my high school Spanish. About a hundred years ago, somebody named G something must have spent a lot of time engraving this. Looks like a sheepherder watching over a grazing flock found something to do."

"Especially the boobs, must have taken a lot of time." Lydia snickered, sending them into another fit of laughter.

"Look how squared and even and ornate these letters are, like old-time Spanish script." Millie whispered the letters that were still decipherable "Gasp...hmm, that could be Gaspar, my landlord's name, his family name. I bet it is. I've got something to ask Mister Gaspar about next time I see him. He said there are layers of cultures here and they all left their mark on stone, first the Ancestral Puebloans, then there's Navajo symbolic figures."

Millie stepped back to take in the whole figure. "Then some Hispanic fellow decided this boulder made a good place to leave his mark as well."

"I have an idea," Lydia said. "Let's get back and just

take a walk around the cabin and orchard. I don't know about you, Miss No Cute Boyfriend, but I've got to get my mind back onto what I was doing before that Gavin guy showed up."

"I'm with you there. But we're not going to open the root cellar, right?"

Lydia shivered at the thought of having to open those creaking doors again. "You got that right, girlfriend."

***

On the way home with Lydia driving, Millie let her head drop back against the headrest. Their deliberate walk around the site seemed to help dim the anxiety of getting back to work. Lydia had even called it "making peace with the site."

For the next couple of days, Millie was able to return to her routine of working the orchard area while Lydia focused on the cabin.

On Wednesday morning, shortly after they got to the site, Robby arrived, called hello to Lydia, waved to Millie, and disappeared into the root cellar. When Millie looked up later, Robby was outside of the root cellar, pacing ever-widening circles around the area, eyes to the ground, apparently looking for anything that might be relevant to the long-ago crime.

Near noon, as Millie and Lydia walked toward the road to get their lunches out of the Suburban, Robby caught up with them. "Nothing here that I didn't see earlier. Guess I wasted the morning, but I had to make sure."

Millie wasn't going to say it out loud, but that was good news, meaning no more disruptions at the site.

"Did you bring a lunch? If not, I'll split mine with you," Lydia offered.

"Can't stay. I've got some good leads on that body.

Should be getting more info this afternoon from Santa Fe. This was no ordinary local yokel who got himself killed." Robby headed toward her pickup. It had the BLM triangle on the doors, along with red flashers attached to the roof and an antennae sticking out that looked like it could pick up a signal from Mars.

Just as Lydia started digging into her oversized lunch container, Robby stopped and took a couple steps back toward them. "Almost forgot. Momma Agnes said to tell you guys that university field trip will be here tomorrow."

Pueblo Sun Petroglyph

7. Lydia Lectures

Discovering, studying, and understanding the evidence of past human uses of the land gives the BLM and the public critical background as we consider how to use and manage the same land today and in the future.

— Bureau of Land Management Cultural Resources Program

"Here they come," Lydia pointed to the dust cloud a half mile down the road.

"Let's get this over with," Millie said and tossed a sandwich wrapper, water bottle, and yogurt container into her lunch box.

They had found a cone-shaped hill thirty yards from the homestead cabin that made a pleasant spot to break for lunch. Sandstone rocks shaded by a piñon pine provided adequate seats. From this vantage point, they could see over the fringe of juniper trees surrounding the base of the hill and across the canyon beyond the cabin. They were about level with the mid-point of the tall red cliffs to the west.

They hustled down to the Suburban and put their lunch boxes on the back seat. Lydia pushed the glove compartment button making it clunk open. She pulled out a stack of index cards.

"I've got my notes all ready." Lydia fanned the cards, ignoring Millie's you-can't-be-serious look. "I worked until midnight last night. I've got the whole shebang of archaeology laws and regs right here." She snapped off the top card, glanced at Millie, and read, "The 1988 amendments to the Archaeological Resources Protection Act require federal land managers to, and I quote, 'establish a program to increase public awareness of the significance of the archaeological resources located on public lands and Indian lands and the need to protect such resources.' So there, Miss Workaholic, that's why Wirt said to be nice to these students. It's an area manager's job to 'increase public awareness' of cultural resources on BLM."

"You're not going to go through *all* of those cards, are you?"

Lydia stuffed the index card into her jeans pocket, which took a couple of tries since there was little room to spare in the already snug pants. "Just nineteen more to go." She waved the remaining stack.

They watched the Ancient Ones Adventure Travel van rumble toward them. Gavin McIntyre gave a wave and parked alongside the Suburban. He hustled around the van and slid the passenger side door open with a resounding thunk. Eight students clambered out, stretching and massaging various parts of their anatomy rattled by two and a half hours of bumping over rough, unpaved roads.

A petite young woman with raven black hair, except for dense bangs dyed turquoise, was the last to climb out. "Gawd, if I have to ride in that rickety van over roads like this for the rest of the week, I'm going to need a three-day massage."

Gavin stepped next to her and said, "Okay, Bailee, you get to sit up front on the way to Wellstown."

Lydia and Millie waited in front of the vehicles while the students arranged themselves in a semicircle, eager to hear about an active historical site investigation. Gavin began introductions, "Folks, this is Lydia Hamilton, archaeologist on this project, and Millie Whitehall, the botanist working on the plant inventory. I'm sure these specialists will be happy to answer any of your questions." He looked at the student next to him, "Why don't you introduce yourselves and say a little bit about what you're studying? Jake, you start."

Jake pulled his lanky body together from an extended stretch and settled his Indiana-Jones-style hat on his head. He described his research specialization as interpreting LiDAR data on Chacoan roads. "I've been to Chaco at least a dozen times, but never came through here. I'd like to..." He finished by describing what he was hoping to learn on this tour.

One by one, the students gave enthusiastic descriptions of their graduate research projects.

Millie thought back to her time in graduate school, stuck in foul smelling labs, peering into microscopes and dissecting flower parts until her eyes burned. How delighted she had been with any compliment from a professor, making her feel her research was important. And how she had to put on her imaginary tungsten cloak the minute she got home to deflect her mother's grumbles about why Millie couldn't help more in the family business.

From her mother's perspective, college was good for Millie up to the time when her headstrong daughter changed from a business major to botany. Millie's eyes roved toward the red cliffs crowned by endless blue sky, reinforcing to herself once again that she was in the right place, that she did the right thing to escape to New Mexico.

The last to speak was the student who'd had enough of dusty adventuring. "I'm Bailee Fernandez, and I'm the exception in this class. I'm majoring in cultural tourism and took this Southwest Archaeology course because of the field trips. I need to see these ruins and stuff so I can get a job with a Santa Fe marketing company. Santa Fe is full of ways to make money off tourists."

She sent a polished-toothed grin toward Gavin. "This is the place I really wanted to see, ever since Gavin said we would be making a stop in Lejos Canyon. I did a summer internship at the Palace of the Governors archives in Santa Fe. It was a project tracing the route that pack-mule caravans took from Santa Fe to Los Angeles. The first one in 1829 took twelve weeks. Ha, I can drive that in a day." Bailee stood on her tiptoes and pointed beyond the cabin, across the canyon. "The mule trains came through here, well, not just where we're standing, but somewhere between this side of the canyon and over there."

The students shuffled aside a step or two in order to see past Lydia and Millie and take in the view across the broad canyon floor to the cliffs on the other side.

Bailee wasn't yet done with telling about her plans for the future. "I'm thinking about starting a business taking people on mule trains, just like in the old days. Cultural tourism is getting popular, adventure tourism, too. I figure there's a way to make money off this stuff."

"Yeah, sure, Bailee," Jake said, "I can just see you driving a mule train. You've been whining about this road just riding in a van."

"Maybe I'll hire you, Jake, when you can't find a job in archaeology. Lots of people pay good money to sleep on the ground and be uncomfortable." Bailee didn't seem a bit intimated by the much taller young man. "You don't have enough imagination to figure out how to monetize what you're studying. The Old Spanish Trail was designated a National Historic Trail twenty years ago. Lots of people want to trace their heritage, how their ancestors traveled from Santa Fe to California. And I'm one of them." She flicked her head, making her hair sway.

Lydia was nodding all the way through Bailee's spiel. "You've got the idea—connect people to their history. That's why my specialization is historical archaeology. We focus on what happened after European settlement on this continent. Most of you guys are probably a lot more into prehistoric research."

Lydia worked a hand into her jeans front pocket, pulled out a small white cotton bag, and took out the pearl she'd found in the pack rat's nest. She held it up and rolled it side to side so that it shimmered in the sunlight. "This, for example. What's the story behind this? It came from there." She pointed a thumb over her shoulder toward the cabin. "When my people were brought here, all family heritage was lost. We don't even know which African country our ancestors came from. For this site, it's different, because the Spanish settlers have records going back centuries. I know somehow, somewhere there are written letters and diaries that will tell me the story of this pearl."

"Cool," Bailee thrust a thumbs up in Lydia's direction.

"Now come this way, and I'll introduce you to the Peralta Homestead." Lydia was nearly walking on air.

Millie waited while Gavin grabbed a water bottle from his van and they walked side by side the fifty yards to the cabin. "How long are you guys going to be here?"

"We've got all afternoon here."

"All afternoon, huh? So, not like last time? You peeled out of here like crazy and left Lydia and me staring at a dead man."

"I figured you'd bring that up," Gavin muttered. "That wasn't one of my best days."

"Yeah, wasn't mine either."

Gavin looked away, toward the root cellar, and didn't say anything. Millie stepped in front of him, forcing him to stop and look at her.

"Guess I owe you an explanation," he said. "I've had a couple differences in the past with the New Mexico State Police. If they saw me here, I figured I'd lose my commercial license to drive the van. I gotta be able to drive groups—that's how I make my living. At least the murder happened years ago. I've been following it in the Wellstown newspaper."

The whine in his voice didn't engender a speck of pity from Millie.

When he didn't say anything further, Millie stepped aside and they continued following the group. "We're not going to talk about it with the students, right?"

When Gavin didn't reply, Millie asked, "Will they want to go down to the orchard?"

He was quick to answer this time, apparently relived at the change of subject. "I, for one, want to see what's growing around here. Might help for my talks on the tours I give."

Millie started making a list in her mind of plants she had documented that the settlers had planted or used.

They joined Lydia who had positioned herself in front of the cabin door. Gavin motioned his flock to gather around. Lydia, clutching her index cards, beamed at her audience. "We estimate this cabin was constructed in 1911. Estimate because some records from its original occupants have gone missing. But we do know the land claim was filed in 1910 under the Homestead Act with the name of Peralta, and proved up in 1915."

Gavin broke in with, "Lydia, you'd better explain 'proved up' because these students probably know more about prehistoric cultures than how this area was settled."

Lydia gulped, appearing as if she hadn't anticipated this question. She rolled her eyes upward for a moment and recovered with aplomb. "The Homestead Act was passed way back in 1862, signed by Abraham Lincoln himself, and was used for decades thereafter by people to claim government land. A person could file a claim for one hundred and sixty acres. Then they had to live on the land, build a home, and farm successfully for five years. If they could prove they met those requirements, if they 'proved up,' they'd get a deed of ownership. That's what happened here and it's how much of this area was settled."

A female student, nearly as tall as Millie, tossed her head, crossed her arms, and said, "Yeah, that's what happened all right. Except we've got to remember that it wasn't really the government's land to give away. The land was stolen from Native Americans, my people."

Millie nodded to the student and said, "Of course, we recognize that now. That Manifest Destiny thing kind of got out of hand."

This affirmation seemed to satisfy the student, allowing Millie to add a bit more to the homesteaders' story. "That original paper deed would have had Woodrow Wilson's signature on it. Deeds were always signed by the president. It's something families hang onto, kind of a record of their past."

Millie's attention to detail provided one more tidbit

to share. "Odd thing, though, was that the name on that first claim was José Manuel Peralta de Martinez. The name on the deed five years later was M. J. Peralta de Martinez. You wouldn't think that on such an important document, initials would be reversed. All the same, I guess. How we know that is through the BLM General Land Office Records. That's a huge public database on the internet that you can research by people's names, location, or year of issue." Millie directed the students' attention back to Lydia with a nod.

Lydia peeled off the next card and read, "Many people say the most important law is the Antiquities Act that was passed way back in 1906 because it was the first law that did anything about protecting archaeology sites. The Antiquities Act allowed the president to designate national monuments. Before that, precious places like Mesa Verde were being looted and vandalized. The most desirable pickings were, ahem, *appropriated* by scientific organizations. It was absolutely *the* thing for big museums back East to have showy pots, stone tools, even a skeleton or two on display for the edification of visitors."

The tall student who spoke earlier muttered, "Barbarians."

Lydia said, "You're right. It was despicable. I'm with you on that. Even European museums sent expeditions to the southwest to add ancient Native American artifacts to their collections. Thank heavens, Teddy Roosevelt signed the Antiquities Act to put a stop to that. Except it didn't really put a stop to it at all. Illegal looting and collecting continues today."

Lydia slid the top index card off her stack and started on the next one. "The best-known places got designated as national monuments, that was all well and good for those places, but greedy looters just moved on to lesser sites. Not until 1979, did a more enforceable law come along that carried criminal penalties—the Archaeological Resources Protection Act. People call it ARPA for short. ARPA added protection on *all* federal lands. But a lot of damage had already been done. Most archaeological sites on federal lands all over the west have had some sort of looting or collecting or just outright malicious destruction. And most perpetrators have never been identified. It's a travesty."

Lydia fanned her face with the index cards, stretched as tall as she could, and said, "The Archaeological Resources Protection Act is, in my opinion, the most important law because it really put teeth into protection of cultural resources." Lydia coyly held the index cards in front of her lips and whispered, "I'm saying it's the most important because I probably wouldn't have this job otherwise."

Bailee called out, "How'd you get this job, anyway?" Lydia had the rapt attention of her audience, probably because they all knew how seldom archaeology jobs turn up.

"Miss Bailee, the answer to your question is two things got me here. During the 1960s and 70s, legislation was passed that required federal agencies to identify historic resources and take care of them. So, the BLM is responsible for protecting this site as part of our cultural heritage." Lydia swept the group with a big smile. "The other thing is, thank the Lord, government hiring looks at what education and experience you have. This job specified experience with documenting historical sites, which I had plenty of. Being a veteran didn't hurt either. Nowhere on the application did I need to mention that I happened to be a Black woman in her fifties, who barely reaches five feet, and takes size twenty jeans. But that's me and here I am."

The students laughed. Someone called out, "You go

girl."

Lydia let the chuckles peter out, shuffled to the next card, squinted at it, and held it out at arm's length. "ARPA gave a specific, legal definition for archaeological resources." She gave a teacher's probing scan of her listeners. "Who can tell me what 'archaeological resources' means?"

Jake, making air quotes with his fingers, dropped his voice to a drone, and said, "Archaeological resources means any material remains of past human life or activities which are of archaeological interest, and at least one hundred years old." Returning to his normal voice, but with a hint of boredom, he added, "To me, that means anything that helps understand past human behavior and cultural practices. We know this stuff already. Had it in undergraduate classes."

"Ah, but did you know that historic sites more than fifty years old qualify for protection under other federal and state laws? The 1966 National Historic Preservation Act defines 'historic property' as eligible to be placed on the National Register of Historic Places, if they meet certain criteria. We believe this site by far and away meets those criteria."

"Hmm, I see," Jake said, nodding in understanding. "The 1979 ARPA covered what we think of as the older archaeological sites, and the 1966 National Historic Preservation Act was aimed at buildings, battlefields, and such, that more or less represent the previous two or three centuries of human endeavor."

"There you go, Jake, you've got it." Lydia took a deep breath and pulled out another index card, but a plaintive voice interrupted.

"Can we look inside?" Bailee was miming a big yawn. Her words brought vigorous nods from the other students.

Gavin moved to Lydia's side. He shrugged and said,

"Guess you're talking to the choir here, Lydia."

This gave Lydia time to regain control over the group. Undaunted and drawing on an experienced mother's bag of tricks, she used the art of redirection. "I can't wait to show you what we've discovered already. But there's just one more thing you'll want to hear about first. Your turn, Millie."

This brought Millie's attention back to the group. She had been wondering about the diamond stud in Bailee's left nostril. *How does she blow her nose with that?* She noticed the students shuffling their feet and glancing this way and that. "Well, I was going to talk about what we're doing to put the Peralta Ranch on the National Register of Historic Places. That process takes a lot of documentation and coordination with local communities, especially the Hispanic families that settled this area. But you've been standing here long enough. Let's go to the orchard and I'll show you how homesteaders provided for themselves when the nearest grocery store was a day's drive by horse and wagon."

8. Fruit Trees and Roses

Like any heirlooms passed from generation to generation, the vintage varieties of garden plants that we still grow today have lasting value. Some old types of vegetables have been kept alive within families or communities by succeeding generations of seed savers.

— National Agricultural Library, *Vegetables and Fruits: A Guide to Heirloom Varieties and Community-Based Stewardship*

Millie took five strides toward the orchard, glanced back, and saw only Gavin and Bailee following. Some students had disappeared into the cabin. Others had scattered farther out, eyes on the ground, voices exclaiming, "look at this," and, "I found a piece of crockery."

Millie stopped, and Bailee almost bumped into her.

Hands on hips, Millie surveyed the situation, laughed,

and said, "Okay, first we'll spend some time exploring the site."

Bailee, almost in Millie's face, said, "Well, dammit, I want to go to the orchard and hear about how this place connects to the local Hispanic community. And when are you going to talk about the ghost and the body you guys found?"

"Gavin, you didn't tell them about the body and that crazy ghost story, did you!"

"Yeah, he told all of us last night at supper." Bailee moved over to Gavin's side and linked an arm through his.

Gavin grimaced, looked at the ground, then threw his head back. "Guess I did. Well, why not, it's been in the newspapers."

"You could have told me that earlier." Millie glared at Gavin. "I thought this was supposed to be a professional observation of a working site survey. Not a looky-loo for ghosts and corpses."

Voices from inside the cabin were pelting Lydia with questions. The other students were prowling the site, opening the screechy outhouse door, peering into the partially fallen-down barn. Two walked by, talking about looking for the midden.

Gavin said, "Let's go to the orchard. Those guys can find the trash pile, the rest look well occupied." He seemed to be trying to regain control of the situation.

"Okay, let's move on." Millie resumed walking. When they arrived at the blue tarp that Millie used as a base to keep equipment, she still had only Bailee and Gavin with her. "You can see the flag markers I put around the perimeter of this orchard, and there's a marker at the beginning of each row."

"How come it's so far from the cabin?" Bailee asked.

"Did you notice how we walked downhill to get here,

almost halfway to the wash? The wash, or some people call it an arroyo, is the lowest place between the north and south canyon walls. In the spring or after a big rain, it's likely to have running water. But it usually dries up in the summer. There's more moisture in the soil as we get closer to the lowest part of the canyon. Just enough to keep these fruit trees alive."

Millie pointed toward the petroglyph cliff. "There's evidence that people have inhabited this site for centuries. Lydia and I looked at a whole string of rock art on the canyon wall over there. I believe this particular area holds moisture because of a hardpan layer of clay not far below the surface."

"Interesting," Gavin said. "That rock art site over there is one of the stops I make on my archaeology tours, but I never connected it to this old homestead for why people settled here."

"The rock art and the buildings are the obvious signs that people have lived here, but the plants tell us that just as clearly," Millie said. "Over by the cliff, there are plants that the ancients used such as coyote tobacco and jimsonweed. And here we have these cultivated plants the homesteaders planted."

"This is great." Gavin seemed just as excited as the students in learning about the site. "When I take my tourist groups to archaeological sites, I try to give them a complete picture of the area—geology, history, Native American culture, all of that. I'm going to add that bit about a soil difference. I've got a tour for Jolt Journeys coming up next month. I always take this route through Lejos Canyon on the way from Chaco to Wellstown."

"This is your regular tour route? What's Jolt Journeys?" Millie asked.

"It's a tour company based in Santa Fe. Jolt Journeys

is one of my best customers. They cater to California types that want the, ah—'ultimate awesome experience.' That's their slogan, honest, 'the ultimate awesome experience.' You know, those New-Agey-seeker-types that go on retreats to connect to their true soul, meditate at ashrams, want to hug the earth spirit, that kind of thing."

"The 'ultimate awesome experience'—you're kidding," Millie said. She never had any travel experience, ultimate or otherwise, growing up in New Jersey in a hard-working family. Their custodian business did not stop for vacation days. The best breaks she ever had were occasional trips to the seashore on a holiday weekend. She mulled this over for a moment, and said, "Guess I'm on the other end of that spectrum. I get to be at these ultimate awesome places and get paid for it at the same time."

"Back off, you guys." Bailee folded her arms and tossed her head, setting her hair swaying again. "I came up with 'ultimate awesome experience' myself. That internship in Santa Fe I told you about, I wasn't just sitting in the archives all day. I made contact with some of the travel agencies, checking them out to see which one I wanted to work for. Jolt Journeys liked that I was a homegrown California Gen Z'er. They paid me to toss around ideas with them. They put me in touch with Gavin to help on some of his tours with those," her voice took on a mocking tone, "New Agey types."

"So, you two knew each other before this university trip. I thought you were all grad students."

"I am a graduate student. I'm a Lumberjack fan, not that I'd go watch a NAU football game if they weren't free for students. Raised in California, educated in Arizona, going to work in Santa Fe. That's my plan."

Millie scanned Bailee's face, trying to decide whether she liked this brash young woman, ought to believe anything she claimed, or what. Yet she couldn't help but envy Bailee's self-confidence, having a life plan all worked out. Millie hoped she could just get through her first year working as a professional botanist.

Gavin stepped forward, putting himself between Bailee and Millie. "I'll show the Jolt Journey group this old homestead. I can talk about how the environment— soil, location—influences how people lived here over the centuries." He looked toward the cliff. "The jimsonweed, now that's something that would interest the Jolt Journey clientele. Was it by that old sheep pen? I'll tell them about the other plants you said, too, of course."

"Yeah, where was it?" Bailee chimed in.

Millie stared hard at the pair. "Why are you so interested in jimsonweed?"

"No reason. I've just heard that people can get high on that stuff." Bailee winked at Gavin and pointed to a decrepit-looking tree. "How come you're marking these broken-down old trees. Who cares?"

"I care, lots of people care," Millie shot back. She was losing patience with this girl. No, not a girl. Bailee was just a few years younger than herself. So why did she feel resentment toward this young woman? Was it Bailee's self-assurance or the way she seemed to know more about what's going on? And why would she want to "monetize" this beautiful, remote location?

Millie took a deep breath and lowered her voice, tying to minimize the exasperation she felt. "First of all, seeds and cuttings from these heirloom specimens are non-GMO. Modern farmers catering to organic food markets know they'd better guarantee their produce is not genetically modified. These fruit trees, well, the ones still alive, not that one you're standing by, have survived the hot summers, cold winters, and scarce rainfall we get here."

Bailee shrugged, "So what. Most of these trees are just about dead."

Millie treasured plants of all kinds, whether thriving or past their prime. Maybe relating to dollar signs might appeal to Bailee. "These are the kind of tough specimens that gardeners and horticulturalists collect seeds from to hybridize with weaker varieties. They pay high prices for these heirloom plants. They also take cuttings to graft onto other trees. The aim is to produce cultivars more resistant to pests, that need less irrigation water. Who wouldn't want that?"

"They still look scuzzy to me," Bailee said.

"I guess you've only seen those massive, intensely cultivated California fruit orchards." Millie tried another approach to get through to Bailee. "These heirloom trees produce fruits that are a little smaller and have a different color, but they often have better flavor."

"I've got a question," Gavin said, moving them on, ambling toward the center of the orchard. "Which ones are oldest? I suppose those are the ones people want to graft from the most."

"It's more the peach trees that are the rarest, because not so many people planted them," Millie said. "The first rows are apple trees, these two rows on either side of us are pear trees, and the rest are peach trees." She continued walking, leading them toward the farthest corner of the orchard. She stopped by a waist-high stump and tapped its rotted top. "Not many of the peach trees were hardy enough to survive decades with no attention. That one that Bailee is standing beside with leaves and buds coming out, is more tolerant of weather extremes of freezing temperatures and drought."

Bailee tore a pink bud off a low branch, sniffed it and held it out to Gavin. "So this is what's going to make a peach."

"Not that one, not now anyway," Millie grumbled. "Let's head back. I'll show you what's left of the family's vegetable and herb garden, even some rose bushes that I bet the wife dug up from her family's garden in Taos and brought here by horse and wagon."

As they strolled toward the cabin, Millie was careful not to glance toward the tangle of raspberry bushes that hid the root cellar. She stopped at the back corner of the cabin, next to one of the three rose bushes that still put out a few spring leaves. "I like to imagine that the wife who planted these roses put them just outside the kitchen window here to have a reminder of her home. My landlord dug up one of these roses and transplanted it to his place in Blanco. He says the flowers have a gold color like no others."

"I know where you live, Millie." Bailee had a Cheshire cat smile as if she knew a secret.

Millie's eyebrow raised almost up to the scar on her forehead. The scar, an unwanted souvenir acquired at the end of last season's field work, was a reminder that some people encountered on her job are not who they seem.

Bailee giggled at Millie's surprise. "My mom's family lived in Taos. She married a lineman for the telephone company. He got sent to California when the big Northridge earthquake hit in 1994 to help put power back on for, like, half the state. They liked California, there was plenty of work 'cause so many people were moving there, so they stayed. But way back, part of Mom's family in Taos split off and moved to Lejos Canyon. Guess who my great-great uncle is?"

Millie looked at her watch. *Not much longer until these guys will be out of here.*

Gavin nudged Bailee's shoulder, "Spill it, tell Millie

why you're so interested in this place."

"Tony Gaspar is my great-great-uncle. I've been to their house lots. When I had that intern job in Santa Fe, I came up here on weekends. Aunt Della makes bizcochitos to die for."

Millie looked at Bailee's glinting eyes beneath her turquoise bangs, "You're just full of surprises, aren't you?"

Bailee went to the kitchen window, joining Jake who was leaning inside, head and shoulders twisted upwards. "What 'cha looking at?"

"Tin cans, the tops of tin cans nailed all along the rafters." Jake pulled back and stepped aside for Bailee who took the same twisted position.

Lydia came around the corner with three students trailing behind. The three took turns peering upward at the row of tin covers.

"Why would they do that?" one student wondered.

"In the trash pile," another student spoke up, "I saw remains of Calumet baking powder cans, tobacco cans, and cans of salted fish—that's what those tops are from."

"Yup, you're a genuine archaeologist," the first student said, "rooting through trash middens."

Lydia was still in her teacher mode. "Before electricity, what did people use for light?"

Someone said, "Candles and lanterns."

"It's my guess that the those rounds of tin reflected candle light. What do you guys think?"

Jake was quick to answer, "Looking at this site makes me think how tough it was to homestead way out here and how smart they were to use everything they had."

By then Bailee had moved off. She held her phone in one palm, tapping it with her other hand, then smacked it. "There's no signal here." Her voice conveyed disbelief and aggravation. "I'm ready to go."

Some of the students were already drifting to the van, having explored the site, inspected numerous remnants of the homesteaders' lives, and taken selfies with the cabin in the background. Millie and Lydia walked to the van with Gavin, who called to the rest to gather.

Gavin slid open the door to the van and the students climbed in, with comments of "thanks," "neat place," and "glad we came here." Lydia handed her stack of index cards to Jake in the middle seat, telling him to pass her notes around to anybody who wanted to review them. Millie wondered if Gavin would be bringing his next load of tourists to interrupt their work.

Gavin backed up the van and turned toward Wellstown. Bailee, in the front seat, waved out the passenger side window and shouted, "See you at Uncle Tony's birthday party."

9. Treasured Family Heirlooms

As a whole, the library's holdings provide insights into the history and culture of New Mexico and the American Southwest, from pre-European contact to the present.
— New Mexico History Museum, Chávez Library Building, Fray Angélico Chávez History Library

The next week passed with no more interruptions—no more desiccated bodies, no law enforcement people prowling the grounds, and no students pestering them with questions. By Friday, it was time to spend a day in the office catching up on field notes. Millie planned to get all the plant species she had located so far into one Excel sheet. It would take time to verify the spelling of species names. Spelling was always a challenge for Millie and more so when she had to argue with the computer's spell check about correct scientific names. Lydia had a collection of clipboards holding copious notes to type up and organize.

But shortly after Millie arrived at the office on Friday morning, she received a call from Momma Agnes. "Wirt wants to meet in the conference room at nine o'clock. Robby Ramirez has an update on the information she's gathered from other law enforcement agencies and reading what she called, 'egghead stuff that made her eyes water.'"

So much for catching up on the week's work. Millie was beginning to dread meetings in the conference room. She hung up the phone and lightly caressed the name plate on her desk. It was a little over a year ago that Momma Agnes had used the "moccasin telegraph" to contact a Navajo artist to make this sand-painted name plate, like many others that graced the desks of BLM staff. Momma Agnes had requested the name plate be customized with plants, appropriate for Millie's botanist position. She treasured the result. It had a piñon tree drawn with many shades of fine lines from tan to brown to charcoal and a sagebrush image made of shades of green-colored sand. The letters MILLIE were formed of black sand outlined with glistening turquoise.

Last year had been different. She was just a summer temporary, the target of low expectations, especially by the local college professor who didn't believe she had discovered an unrecorded location of an endangered cactus. Her love of the job would always be shadowed by knowing her discovery had contributed to the murder of Herb Thompson, the beloved former botanist on the Piñon Resource Area. She would never outlive the horrific memory of the murderer's evil stare as he threatened her life for information on the cactus location. The sound of crashing glass that left the scar on her forehead still echoed in her mind.

Her hand drifted to the scar, gently tracing what had been a bleeding gash from eyebrow to hairline. She was proud that her accurate species identification and knowledge of plant ecology had led to the capture of the cactus thief-killer. That was the turning point for her gaining credibility and being hired in the permanent botanist position, the same one that had been held by Herb Thompson. Now she carried the responsibility of making recommendations for managing all plant habitat on the Piñon Resource Area, an expanse of public land that covered much of northwest New Mexico. While she shared Herb's love of the land, could she ever be as capable of replacing him in protecting this valuable resource in a multiple-use agency tasked with balancing the many demands on public lands?

Now here she was, summoned again to the conference room to deal with another murder when she just wanted to get on with her job. Not fair. She hoped Robby would give a nice, tidy wrap-up, putting the mysterious body to rest and leaving her and Lydia to their work. She yanked a drawer open, took out a pad of paper, and headed for the conference room.

Millie was the last to arrive and took the chair next to Lydia. It wasn't fair that Lydia was tangled up in this mess either. As soon as they were all seated, Wirt asked, "How'd that field trip visit go?"

"Great," Lydia said, "the students loved it."

Millie nodded. She didn't see a need to mention their lack of interest in the biological aspects of the site.

Robby, sitting next to Wirt, flipped open her ever-present stenographer's notebook and looked at Millie and Lydia seated across the table. "I figured it was time to update you all on the latest information on your body."

"Oh, gawd, don't call it that," Lydia whined.

"Sorry. Let me backtrack. I told you in our last meeting that the victim was a Caucasian male, approximately six feet tall, in his forties, maybe early fifties. We've got a lot more info on the victim now. A picture is starting to emerge on what he was doing at the Peralta Ranch and how he was killed. There's still nothing on who killed him or why."

Millie leaned toward Robby, wanting to hear her report, yet not wanting to think about the grisly start to this field season.

"First, info from the medical investigator's office. Cause of death was a severe blow to the front of the head. Not just a strike, but a real whack that carved a four-inch fissure into the skull. Other than that, no evidence of injury, except abrasions on the skin, indicating the actual deed probably occurred outside the root cellar and the body was dragged down into it. However, per the autopsy report, that is speculative because the epidermis was extremely hardened."

Wirt said, "It looked like saddle leather to me."

Millie shrank back in her chair from this macabre discussion. *Why is Robby going through this again?* Lydia was studying her fingernails.

"Here's where it gets interesting." Robby flipped over a page. "The little notebook that was in his pocket, the one I said was bagged at the crime—full of notes. Pages and pages with dates, places he made them, and what he was doing. All written in pencil. The pencil marks were pretty faint, but the crime lab was able to enlarge and darken the writing.

"The notes stop in 1996. It took some tracking down, but having the year gave us a starting point. Searching missing persons databases and comparing dental records led to identification of the body as a Doctor Sterling Bernnard. Doctor, as in professor of Latin American History at the University of Texas. That's when the man disappeared. Neither his family nor the university department ever heard another thing about his whereabouts. The car he was driving, a new Ford Bronco, his clothes, his papers, nothing ever turned up. He just flat out disappeared. After seven years, he was declared dead by a Texas court."

"Good call on their part, he was dead, that's for sure," Wirt said.

Robby ignored the flip remark. "Here's a full copy of every page that had a mark on it. Not every word was decipherable. Hell, I can't even read my own notes sometimes when I jot things down in a hurry."

Robby opened a folder in front of her and pulled out two sets of 8 ½ by 11 sheets, approximately 30 pages each, stapled at the corner. She handed one set to Wirt and the other to Millie.

Millie put it between herself and Lydia. They almost bumped heads as they scanned the sheets. Wirt was doing the same. Robby waited while they flipped through the pages.

After the first few pages, Millie's eyes adjusted to the small, neat printing. Some of the penciled letters and numbers were too faint to read. Her mind collected the words, *... mi hija mayor... un rosario... this archaic Spanish is difficult to understand... Wellstown motel... x by x.* It seemed like nosing into someone's diary, yet it revealed the path the man had taken during the last days of his life. Headings on the first pages began with 1996, early June dates, and the letters, 'FACHL.' These notes contained what looked like lines copied word for word from references because a multi-digit document number appeared after each quote.

The headings on the last few pages began with Wellstown and subsequent dates.

"What in the world does FACHL mean?" Lydia asked.

"I bet you'll know when you hear the rest of this. The university department's records show he was on sabbatical leave for the semester. He filed a plan of study before he left. It supports what you see in those notes."

"I still don't know what FACHL means," Lydia said.

Robby chuckled. "Fray Angélico Chávez History Library. He was at the New Mexico History Museum in Santa Fe that houses the Fray Angélico Chávez History Library archives."

"Of course," Lydia bopped her forehead with the palm of her hand, as if the words just penetrated her brain. "The renowned Fray Angélico Chávez History Library. I need to go there sometime this summer to look for materials related to the Peralta site, beyond what I've already dug out from government documents."

Wirt asked, "How does that relate to him ending up in the root cellar, for... for what, nearly three decades if those notes go back to 1996?"

"He must have been doing research," Lydia said. "That place keeps maps and documents from way back before New Mexico became a state, when it was part of Mexico, and even before that—part of Spain. The early explorers and mission priests sent reports back to Spain, their mother-country."

"That's what he was doing, all right. And...," Robby made a dramatic pause, "I can also tell you just what he was looking for."

Millie held her breath, her mind working to align these pieces of information, to organize them in a logical way. Instead of Robby winding up the investigation, freeing her from being involved, Millie was being pulled in deeper.

Robby flipped to the next page of her notes. "Seems the really old, irreplaceable materials are located in the Fray Angélico Chávez History Library. To get access to them, a researcher has to sign in, request specific items, and use them under supervision. When they sign out, they have to open bags and briefcases to show they aren't carrying anything other than what they came in with."

"I know that for a fact," Lydia affirmed. "For that historical mansion I worked on back in South Carolina, I had to do a lot of research at the state museum. If you think there's anything meaner than a junkyard dog then you've never seen an archivist tackle a patron trying to sneak out a document."

"We know that Doctor Bernnard spent four full days at the PoG. That month's sign-in sheets show he checked in a leather satchel every day at ten minutes after eight and checked out just before five o'clock. The archives people were able to send us a photocopy of the documents he requested, believe it or not."

"I believe it," Lydia said, "archivists keep everything."

Robby pulled the sign-in sheet out of her folder, held it up so Wirt, then Millie and Lydia could see the lines filled in with time, Doctor S. Bernnard, and item numbers. "They told me that, based on the items he requested, he was reading letters, diaries, and journals of aristocratic families who traveled the *Camino Real* from Mexico to Santa Fe. These, of course, were in Spanish. Those elite families were the most likely to possess the most valuable religious articles."

"I noticed where he wrote that archaic Spanish was difficult to read and interpret," Millie said. "No wonder, it's hard enough to read old-fashioned handwriting, let alone in another language."

Robby said, "Yeah, I should know formal Spanish

myself, being Hispanic and all. But my parents were of that generation that desperately wanted to adopt the American lifestyle whole hog. They discouraged us kids from speaking Spanish even at home. What words I did learn came from the Tex-Mex I heard at school, which doesn't help much.

"Anyway, the last couple of days, he was tracing descendants of a family that moved north to Taos." Robby glanced at the sign-in sheet. "He seemed to be narrowing in on one family in particular—Peralta."

Wirt sprang up, walked around his chair, and sat back down. "By gawd, that's why he was at the Peralta site. He was tracking the family all the way back to Mexico."

Robby countered with, "Actually, he started from Spain and tracked one of the aristocratic families to Mexico, then north here to New Mexico." With a great flourish, Robby pulled out another piece of the story.

She held up a copy of an article from a research journal and pointed to the title. She read, 'Religious Relics: Most Treasured Family Heirlooms,' by Sterling Bernnard, Ph. D. But look at this second page, it's a chart of—"

"No way," Millie's loud interruption grabbed the others' attention.

Millie had continued flipping through the reproduced pages of the notebook. She was at the last page.

"Lydia, does this look familiar?"

"O-M-G, that's a diagram of the homestead site." Lydia pulled the page closer.

"Yup, that's a reproduction of a page from his notes of the Peralta ranch," Robby said.

Wirt flipped to the last page of the set Robby had given him. "That's it all right. Damn good job drawing the place from what I remember of being out there."

The diagram on the letter-size paper was greatly

enlarged from the little notebook that had fit in the professor's shirt pocket. A rectangle outlined the cabin itself, other carefully placed lines, circles, and dashes showed locations of the corral, root cellar, and outhouse, labeled 'privy,' on the map.

Wirt turned his page sideways. "That's about as accurate a layout of the place that a person could draw."

Millie turned the page sideways, as well. She glanced up to see if Lydia minded, then leaned in to study it closer. The meticulously drawn diagram plotted the orchard fruit trees with rows of x's. Lightly-penciled dashes showed the trail to the cliff. A small square marked the sheep pen. There was a lopsided T with a question mark next to it on one side of the sheep pen and an arrow on the other side pointing to the word 'petroglyphs.'

"Look at that," she said. "He even put in the orchard and the trail over to the sheep pen. You'd think he'd be most interested in the cabin, but he explored the whole site. I wonder why."

"What sheep pen?" Robby asked.

"It's across the road but still a part of the homestead. My landlord told me about it. He said I ought to go look at the rock art on the cliff, that it starts by an old sheep pen. We found the sheep pen last week, then looked at the rock art."

A sly smile spread across Wirt's face. "Is that, by any chance, the rock art place they call the 'Dolly Parton' rock?"

Millie's face went red from held-in laughter, mixed with dread about what her boss might think about them ranging way beyond their survey site. Lydia tried to smother giggles, clamping both hands over her mouth.

"What? What are you guys talking about?" Robby looked bewildered.

"That's it, isn't it!" Wirt shouted. "You found that big

boulder with the nude on it. Sheep pen, good excuse. I didn't connect it with the Peralta Ranch since it's up the road a little ways and on the cliff side of the road."

"What are you talking about?" Robby demanded.

"It's a popular place, Robby," Wirt said. "One of the finest Navajo and Ancestral Puebloan petroglyph sites on the Piñon Resource Area."

"Well, I know that. I've seen vans parked along the road there. I usually walk over to the cliff and give them a little spiel about respecting cultural sites. So, what are you guys smirking about?"

Millie tried to redirect the conversation. "Seriously, Lyd and I were looking for the sheep pen."

Lydia joined in with, "The pen's mostly fallen down, but it's part of the homestead site, so I need to take measurements and record it."

"We walked along the cliff for a ways, looking at rock art figures, then went out to the road." Millie looked to the ceiling. "We did happen to pass by a big boulder."

Robby said, "Guess I better have you show me that sheep pen. I didn't know to look over there when the corpse was being removed. Maybe we can find this 'big boulder' you're talking about."

Lydia's giggles turned into squeals of laughter.

Robby sounded a bit peeved at being interrupted and out of the loop concerning the boulder the others continued to snicker about. "Once you all are done ogling that diagram, I'm going to tell you why the professor was at the homestead and why you two need to be on guard out there."

10. Tracing Precious Artifacts

Spanish influence permeates New Mexico. From the dawn of the 16th century, supplies and communications came into the area along El Camino Real, the Royal Road stretching 2,000 miles (3,220 kilometers) from Mexico City to Santa Fe.

— New Mexico Secretary of State Office, New Mexico History

Millie forgot about her dread of conference room meetings, overlooked Robby's blasé description of Doctor Bernnard's brutal end, and almost forgot to breathe. Nothing could tear her away from the information the law enforcement officer was about to dole out.

Robby rapped her knuckles on the desk, but she didn't need to, she had their full attention. She was still holding the research article she was about to show them before

Millie spotted the professor's diagram of the site.

"Seems Professor Bernnard specialized in religious art objects brought from Spain by the early explorers and settlers. He traced and documented how these became dispersed throughout Central America and the south-western US."

Robby flipped to the back page of the research article and, holding it with both hands, thrust it forward. "See all the references here? Most are things he published himself, like 'New Mexico Santeros Stay True to Spanish Motifs.' Here's one that appeared in *New Mexico Magazine*, 'Dead Ends and Disappointments–Tracing Precious Artifacts.' Catchy title, except it turned out to be a little too true." She looked up with a smirk. "It's my opinion that the professor wasn't at a dead end when he went to the Peralta Ranch, but that's why he ended up dead."

Robby looked so smug with her play on words that Wirt laughed, Millie wagged her head, and Lydia rolled her eyes.

Robby turned to the first page of the article and read the title, "Religious Objects Constituted Wealth and Status for Immigrants." She flipped to the second page and turned it around so the others could see. The top third of the page featured a painting depicting what looked like a statue of a saint. The painting may have been vibrant at one time but was now darkened with age, perhaps from exposure to candle smoke. The frame was ornate with intricate floral carvings covered with gold leaf. In places, white plaster showed through a few nicks in the gold leaf. The saint's head was bowed, his hands folded over his chest were eye-catching because they were so pale against his black robes. In his hands, pressed against his heart, was a silver cross. This object of veneration was the same length as the saint's slim, delicate hands. The surface was smooth, except for Roman letters inscribed where the vertical and horizontal pieces met. Three scalloped lobes graced each end of the horizontal piece. The cross gleamed and seemed to float above the canvas, a tribute to a master artist.

Robby's voice broke their contemplation of the image. She tapped the caption under the painting, "This says 'The only known depiction of the Maltese-style cross which disappeared from La Iglesia Sagrada in 1694.'" She skimmed farther down the page. "And down here somewhere, it says... here it is... 'legend has it that the stolen cross had been carried by the Crusaders in the twelve hundreds.'"

Wirt picked up the professor's photocopied notes and plopped them back on the table. "That's all very interesting, but what's it got to do with Doctor Bernnard ending up in the Peralta Ranch root cellar?"

"I'm getting to it. Here's where it really gets interesting." Robby turned over two more pages and squinted to read the fine print at the bottom of the page. "The caption for this chart is, 'Spain's famous lost Iglesia Sagrada Silver Cross handed down through matrilineal descendants.'" She gave the article to Wirt, who studied the page, passing a finger back and forth and from top to bottom of the page. He pushed the article across the table.

Millie and Lydia peered at the chart. The top left of the genealogy diagram began with "Arrival in Mexico City – 1754." A cascade of women's names angled downward to the right, culminating in the box labeled "Rosalinda Carmalita Florez de Torres, m. 1912 - José Manuel Peralta de Martinez."

"I don't see where you're going with this," Wirt said.

"I do." Millie's almost photographic memory clicked. Robby's lead-up all tumbled into place—the archive's sign-in sheets to Doctor Bernnard's research topics. She picked up the photocopy of professor's notes. "I saw it in here somewhere, when he was at the Fray Angelico Library." She thumbed through the notes and stopped about halfway through the pages. "Found it."

Millie pushed a page over so Lydia could see and moved a finger beneath a meticulously copied line.

Le dio mi rosario de perlas a mi hija, Rosa Linda, el día que se casó.

Doctor Bernnard had noted its source as "Rosalinda's mother's diary, June 1912."

Stumbling over pronunciation, Millie did her best to translate. "Mi rosario—my rosary, gave my rosary to my daughter—mi hija Rosa Linda, el día que se casó—the day she married."

Lydia said, "That Spanish class you took in high school keeps paying off."

Millie looked up, "The caption under this chart says the cross was handed down through matrilineal descendants. Mothers gave it to their oldest daughters on the day of marriage."

Lydia picked up the chart. "That would make it kind of a dowry. Nope, nope, I take that back. A dowry is something that the bride's family contributes to the couple, and the husband gets control of it. That's a fine point, but Doctor Bernnard's chart here shows the rosary stayed completely with the female descendants."

Millie pointed back to the line from Rosalinda's mother's diary. "The cross was passed to Rosalinda, the oldest daughter, on her marriage day. Except the diary says 'me rosario de perlas,' my pearl rosary."

"Okay," Wirt said, drawing out the word. "The rosary goes to the oldest daughter. Doctor Bernnard was at the Peralta Homestead looking for a silver cross. Connect the dots for me here, Millie."

"A rosary would have a cross. See? Doctor Bernnard figured it out. The silver cross he was looking for is on the rosary. The mother gives it to her oldest daughter, Rosalinda, on her marriage day. Rosalinda marries José Manuel Peralta—that's the name on the homestead claim papers. It's the Peralta Ranch."

Lydia grabbed onto the story. "It wasn't uncommon for immigrants to hide valuable items they brought from the old country. I can see why the family might attach a valuable cross to an everyday item like a rosary. No doubt every Spanish family carried a rosary or two or three as they traveled across the ocean, through an unfamiliar country, then north on *El Camino Real*."

"That's got to be it, Lydia," Millie almost shouted. She loved solving a puzzle. "Somehow, at some point in time, for some reason, the cross that disappeared from Spain's La Iglesia Sagrada, the holy church, was attached to the rosary. Doctor Bernnard tracked the famous Iglesia Sagrada Silver Cross to the Peralta Ranch."

"Well, I'll be," Wirt said. "So, the professor found the last mention of this cross and went looking for it at the Peralta Ranch. You two make a good pair of sleuths."

"It was Robby who did the foot work and found that article." Millie shied away from being the center of attention.

Robby sat back, arms crossed, looking smug.

Lydia was bouncing in her chair. "Ooh-wee, that cross would be worth a fortune today. Just the pure silver in an item that size would bring a pretty penny. The cross looked to be about six inches long in that painting." She put her hands together in a prayer position to mimic the saint's hands. "But that's not its real value. Historians would seek it out just for the prestige of finding such an antiquity. Legends build up around something like that. Carried by the Crusaders, maybe attributed to saving them in a battle. Stolen in the middle ages. Ha, that's the kind of thing treasure hunters would kill for."

She slapped both hands over her mouth and mumbled through her fingers. "Oh my gawd! What did I just say?"

Millie recoiled in her chair. A grisly image floated in front of her eyes. Blood dripped from the cross in the saint's hands. She shook her head. This had to stop. How did she become entangled with a centuries old artifact when all she wanted to do was deal with plants, to protect the botanical resources of the Piñon Resource Area?

Open-mouthed, Wirt stared at Lydia until he turned to the law enforcement officer. He tapped the photocopied notes in front of him. "When you came in here, Robby, you covered the latest info from the medical investigator's office about how the professor was killed. Then you said there's still nothing on who killed him or why. Now, we know the why."

Lydia tapped the tips of her fingers together. "I wonder if he found it—the silver cross."

"Who knows?" Robby shrugged, "I told you there was no identification or anything with the body."

Wirt slapped a hand down on the photocopied notes. "I bet whoever killed him knows where that cross is."

No one said anything for a moment. Robby remained leaning back, arms crossed. Wirt rubbed his eyes. Millie thumbed through the photocopied notes. Lydia sat in The Thinker statue pose with her eyes closed.

Wirt was the first to speak. "Who'd know that the professor would be going to the Peralta Ranch?"

"I asked the Palace of the Governor's person who provided the sign-in sheet. She had no idea, didn't think anybody working at the archives back then would still be around. And I looked through his notes to see if there might be mention of which Wellstown motel he stayed at. No luck, and probably no chance anyway of finding motel records that go back that far."

"He was in the root cellar," Millie observed, "or got put into the root cellar. Who'd know to hide something there? It was so overgrown that we didn't even find it until Gavin showed up."

Wirt ran his finger down the genealogy chart that Robby had passed around. "All these names look familiar, same as the Hispanic families that now live in Wellstown or Blanco and surrounding area. Many of them have connections to the homesteaders in Lejos Canyon. Any of the old-timers would know those places have root cellars."

"Gavin seemed to know. He's the one who wanted to look in the root cellar," Lydia grumbled. "He got out of there darn fast after I pulled that old door off. A yellow-bellied thing to do, leaving Millie and me with a dead body."

"You're right about that. The day he came with the field trip, while you were talking to the students, I asked him why he took off like that. He told me he'd had problems with the New Mexico State Police in the past and was worried that he might lose his commercial license to drive the van."

Robby jumped on that piece of information. "Problems, huh? Why don't I find out just what kind of problems? I'll run his name through police records. Wirt, can you have Momma Agnes make me a copy of his field trip visit request."

"Will do," Wirt said, "but keep in mind anybody might have been poking around and seen that root cellar. You can see the cabin from the road. Photographers, tour groups, archaeology clubs from all over stop there to look at the rock art panels."

Robby gathered her papers and put them back in the folder. "I'll make a copy of the journal article if anybody wants it."

"I do, for sure," Lydia said. "I love tracking family histories. That's the best part of my work."

"I'd like one," Millie added. "I'll compare it to the Government Land Office Records and see how the names on that chart connect to names on the homestead claim filing papers."

Robby stood, taking a commanding stance. "I'll be making regular checks on your site, keeping a presence out there. It was a long time ago, but somebody took offense to that professor poking around there, kind of like what you two are doing. I don't want to be pulling your dead bodies out of that root cellar."

11. Tamales and Empanadas

Tamale-making is a ritual that has been part of Mexican life since pre-Hispanic times, when special fillings and forms were designated for each specific festival or life event.
— Wikipedia

Millie stood by the conference room door, her hand hovering over the light switch, and waited for Lydia to leave. Wirt and Robby were walking down the hall, going back to their offices, but Lydia was glued to her seat.

"Did she really say that? Somebody out there might kill us?"

Millie walked back and sat down next to Lydia. "I know how you feel. I was in your shoes last spring when I started working for the BLM. On my very first week, Wirt said something at an all-employees meeting that stuck with me. He said, 'Be careful out there. The 'bagos are out, don't pass them if you can't see around them, keep an eye out for mares sneaking away to drop their foals, and rattlesnakes are crabby this time of year.' That makes me laugh now, because he was so wrong."

"Rattlesnakes and 'bagos make you laugh? They're not something to worry about? What are 'bagos anyway?"

"He meant Winnebago camper-trailers. But a much bigger menace was operating on the Piñon Resource Area that summer." Millie pushed her hair back and pointed to the scar on her forehead. "I got this just for doing my job. The Resource Area is a big piece of land that a lot of people use—for recreation, oil and gas, cattle and sheep grazing, and on and on. Everybody I met working in the field was super nice, except for one really bad actor."

Lydia's eyes grew wide, a look of concern sweeping across her face.

"Sorry, Lyd, I don't want to scare you. That bad actor was a greedy thief and murderer and he won't be seeing the outside of a prison for the rest of his life. What I'm telling you is, we'll pay attention to what Robby said, but you know that expression 'lightning doesn't strike twice'? I figure that kind of bad luck can't happen to me again. We'll be okay."

Millie added a silent, *I hope.*

The solid conviction in Millie's voice was enough to release Lydia from her chair. They left the conference room and walked side-by-side down the hall. When they reached the reception area, Momma Agnes spotted the subdued-looking pair. "Looks like Robby put the fear of God into you two. Robby's been in law enforcement so long that she sees everybody as a crook until they prove otherwise."

Millie admired the office manager's knack for reading

people and saying just the right thing.

Lydia's chin trembled. "I need a hug, Momma Agnes."

To Millie's amazement, Momma Agnes was out from behind the counter in a flash and had Lydia wrapped in a hug. "Oh, darlin' come here."

The hug seemed to work. Lydia extricated herself, threw her shoulders back, and said, "I believe you, Momma Agnes. You, too, Millie. Bad stuff happened at the Peralta Ranch but that was nearly thirty years ago; lightning's not going to strike twice. I guess I miss seeing my kids, the smell of magnolia flowers, the southern cooking I'm used to. Everything's just so different here."

Lydia's words plunged Millie into a funk, as well. She recalled the many times she'd fought off homesickness her first field season in the Land of Enchantment.

Momma Agnes patted Lydia's arm. "I know just the thing to take your mind off these troubles. It's family and good food that you're missing. You can just come and help make the best food you'll get in New Mexico. My second cousin Tony's *cumpleaños* is this weekend. We always celebrate Antonio's birthday, but this one is special, he'll be eighty-five. We'll be cooking all day Saturday for the big fiesta on Sunday. Millie's going to help. You can too."

Millie threw up her hands and landed them on her hips. "Why didn't I know you'd be related to the Gaspars. You already knew that I was asked to help make tamales, didn't you?" Mamma Agnes seemed to know half the people in the county and their circumstances.

"I help my *primos* get ready for the big party every year." Momma Agnes lowered her voice to a whisper. "Don't let Della show you how to fold the tamale, hers always fall apart."

Lydia's eyes sparkled in anticipation of a homecooked meal.

***

When Millie knocked on the Gaspars' side door, a woman that could be Mrs. Gaspar's twin opened the door. "I'm Amalia, Della's sister, come on in. We're all in the kitchen."

Millie knew the way, but only needed to follow the aromas of frying pork, roasted green chile, and hints of anise to find the kitchen.

Mrs. Gaspar called out to Millie, "*Hola, Señorita*," and kept pushing chunks of pork and onions around in a humongous cast iron frying pan, charred black from decades of use. "Will you please help *mi hermana* make the empanadas?"

The kitchen was a hubbub of banging pots and a medley of Spanish and English. Amalia introduced Millie to two more helpers bustling around the three butcher block-style tables that occupied the center of the huge kitchen.

Amalia led Millie to an unoccupied table and pointed to ingredients already assembled there. She said, "I'll be right back," and went into a pantry off the kitchen. The portly woman returned with a five-pound package of hamburger and plunked it down next to a bag of onions on the table. She motioned to a smaller, second stove. "Once you get the hamburger and onions fried, stir in the ingredients I've gathered here and keep stirring until they're all well blended."

Amalia began to walk away but Millie's panicked voice brought her back. "Wait, what do I do with these?"

"Just put in whatever seems right and taste it. You'll know. Come and get me when you're done and we'll start mixing the dough next. The meat mixture and the dough will go into a refrigerator overnight and we'll do the frying last thing before the party."

Millie pushed each component into a line that she thought might, possibly, hopefully, be the correct sequence to add them. Large cans of tomato paste first, then cloves, cinnamon, salt and pepper, cumin, chile powder, and lastly, dried currants. Having no idea what empanada filling should taste like, Millie tipped a few currents into her hand, rolled them into her mouth, and scrunched up her face at the sweet then tangy flavor. She looked at two large skillets on the stove and knew she was in for a long morning.

One of the helpers glanced out the window and said, "Della, there's somebody over at your old place." Mrs. Gaspar put down her wooden spoon and hustled over to the window.

"I don't know who that is," but after a moment, she called to Millie, "Is that your friend, Millie, the one you work with at the Peralta Ranch? She's standing in your driveway, looking this way. Cousin Agnes called last night and said she invited someone else from work, but she never said she was... ah, African American."

It hadn't occurred to Millie that Mrs. Gaspar may not welcome Lydia in her home. Where Millie grew up, most gatherings included a mixture of ethnic groups.

Millie rushed over to Mrs. Gaspar. "Yes, that's Lydia, she's the archaeologist on our project." Millie stood breathless. *Now what's going to happen.*

"Well, go get her. We need all the help we can get."

Amalia added, "Many hands make light work. I'll watch your stove."

Millie let out her breath and trotted outside.

Lydia headed her way and they met by the rose bushes. Lydia said in a tentative voice, "I wasn't sure just which door to go to."

"Come on, they want your help. We'll go in the side

door."

Lydia smiled and they walked to the house. As they neared the kitchen, Lydia sniffed the mouthwatering aromas of frying onions and roasted chile and started rolling up her sleeves.

Mrs. Gaspar looked the newcomer up and down and, apparently recognizing a good cook when she saw one, ushered Lydia to the big stove. In no time, they were deep in conversation about the nuances of concocting enough traditional posole to feed forty people. Although every time Mrs. Gaspar added another pinch of red chile to the pot, Lydia's face crumped up and she grabbed a handkerchief out of a pocket and sneezed.

Millie got busy at her table making the empanada filling. Peeling the onions made tears puddle in her eyes to the point where she had to turn away from the commotion that arose when Momma Agnes stepped into the kitchen. Wading her way through hugs and *holas*, Momma Agnes put an arm across Millie's back and said, "You're not still upset with finding that dead man in the root cellar, are you, hon?"

The women, caught in mid-stir or mid-measure, turned toward the pair, faces sympathetic but hopeful to garner more details about what happened at the Peralta Ranch.

Using one arm to wipe her eyes and runny nose, Millie waved a knife with her other hand toward a mound of chopped onions. "Onions, Momma Agnes, I've been chopping onions."

"Oh, I thought you needed cheering up because I know something that will."

Millie could hardly keep her stinging eyes open but could see a big grin on Momma Agnes' face. "Guess who stopped by the office?" She paused for effect. "Ben

Benallee. I invited him to tomorrow's fiesta."

"Ben! I thought he'd forgotten about me. I haven't heard a word from him since I left last year at the end of my summer temp job."

"Yes, your Ben. He's been out-of-state for his job."

Lydia appeared next to Momma Agnes and filled the kitchen with an "Ooh-wee, is that the cute boyfriend you had last summer?"

Millie's face turned the color of chile powder. She spluttered, mumbled, and wiped her eyes again.

Momma Agnes saw the laughing women and headed off further embarrassment for Millie. "Amalia, what are you doing, making this young one do your job? You take over here. You know everybody's going to ask for your empanadas. I'm going to teach these two easterners how to make tamales."

With Momma Agnes' coaching, Lydia mastered mixing the masa harina and lard to just the right consistency. All the while, they discussed how this pale, finely ground corn flour compared to the best corn meal for making grits. Millie worked with two of the helpers to flatten out the corn husks that had been soaking in water.

Next, Millie and Lydia were guided into the tamale-making assembly line. Lydia scooped up a palm-sized amount of masa and shaped it to fit three-quarters of the length of a corn husk held spread out by Millie. Next Millie spooned on a layer of the pork, lard, red chile, and onion mixture and pushed the corn husk along the line, where the master tamale-maker dominated.

Momma Agnes overlapped the long edges of the corn husk over the mixture, then folded the short ends inward. Her quick fingers seemed to move on their own, while Momma Agnes caught up on news about the helpers, their children, and neighbors.

Millie kept eyeing the finished tamales, expecting the corn husks to spring open. Not one did because the next-in-line helper scooped each one up and placed it, folded side down, in large rectangular baking pans, stacking the bundles in row after row.

By late afternoon, wonderful aromas emanated from ovens, conversation had slowed, pots and utensils were washed, and sweaty helpers released from duty.

As they walked to Lydia's car, Millie said, "Are you as tired as I am?"

"I could sleep all day tomorrow, but I'm not going to miss this party for all the grits in Mississippi."

"I've never done a mass cooking before. That was fun."

"All I'm going to be thinking about is tasting this authentic Mexican cooking that I helped make."

With a high-five and a wave, Millie watched Lydia back down the driveway and called out, "See you tomorrow."

When Millie got to her porch, Ragged Ear was waiting for his usual evening serving of cat food. Millie held open the door. As he passed, he brushed against her ankle and whapped her leg with his tail. "What was that for? So what if I spent the day in the Gaspars' kitchen. We cooked and laughed all day."

Without a whisker twitch of acknowledgement, the cat trotted to the kitchen. Millie placed his favorite cat food on the floor before Ragged Ear got to his sixth pitiful I'm-starving-to-death meow.

She loved to hear the cat's contented purr while he ate. "You can come tomorrow. We'll be in the backyard for the big party. But don't go jumping on tables, no matter how good the food smells. It'll be fun." *At least most of the time.*

When the Wellstown newspaper featured the news about an unidentified corpse discovered in Lejos Canyon,

Millie had gotten good at dodging questions from the locals such as "what did that body in the root cellar look like?" and "do they know who it was yet?" A couple more articles about the mystery followed, and interest petered out over the next few days. But tomorrow's affair would bring relatives from several states to the Gaspars' birthday celebration. *I better warn Lydia to resist nosey questions about finding the body. And definitely not to say anything that Robby told us about the professor's research on the Peralta family. Robby said to be careful; the killer might still be around.*

The cat seemed to sense her worry because he left his food, jumped up on the counter, and pushed his way into Millie's folded arms. "I'm okay, Ragged Ear. Like I told Lydia, lightning won't strike twice. And Ben is coming tomorrow. Remember Ben from last summer? He said cats are smart and can sense things that we can't." The cat rubbed Millie's chin as a pink flush crept up her cheeks.

12. Lydia Talks

An early-morning walk is a blessing for the whole day.
— Henry David Thoreau, American Naturalist, 1817–1862

Millie woke up early the next morning. Like Lydia, she couldn't wait to savor the dishes she helped prepare for the party. But the pleasant spring morning beckoned, and there was time for a visit to the awakening plants along the San Juan River. Millie wove her way among the big cottonwood trees that shaded the seldom used trail that curved along the water. She pushed her way into a stand of waist-high young willows, playing with their bright yellow stems, swishing them back and forth.

Moving on, she came upon a tangled clump of saltcedar bushes. The tallest ones extended just above her head and were surrounded by their prolific shoots, invading the river's banks. Millie broke off an elongated twig and sniffed its pink, fuzzy-looking flowers. No detectable scent. "You're a pretty bush, and the bees are very keen on collecting your pollen, but you don't belong here." Not native on this continent and considered an invasive species, New Mexico categorizes saltcedar as a noxious weed. Saltcedar pulls great amounts of water from the ground, outcompeting surrounding vegetation. Millie tossed the twig over her shoulder.

She approached the water's edge and listened to the late spring run-off splash against rocks on its life-giving journey from the San Juan Mountains to the Colorado River. She bowed to a Showy Milkweed and caressed the soft hairs on its top leaf, then bent over to sniff its cluster of eye-catching, pink flowers and shrugged. "You don't have much of a scent to attract me, pretty plant, but I know Monarch butterflies couldn't get along without you." Millie didn't hesitate to talk to plants, as long as no one else was around.

After an hour's meander, Millie returned home and enjoyed a refreshing shower. She patted Ragged Ear, who was stretched out on the porch bench, and headed next door. Lydia's car was already parked in the driveway.

Millie waved to Mr. Gaspar who were supervising the half-dozen men setting up tables and chairs in the backyard. At the side-door, she almost bumped into Mrs. Gaspar who was balancing a basket piled high with paper plates, cups, and utensils. "Oh good, Millie, you're here. Will you get the chips and salsa and bring them out?" Mrs. Gaspar already had beads of sweat on her forehead.

Millie greeted the other helpers in the kitchen and began parceling out a dozen baskets of chips and filling a dozen plastic bowls with homemade salsa. She found a tray large enough to fit four baskets and salsa bowls and headed to the backyard.

She almost collided with Mrs. Gaspar again at the door. This time Millie, balancing the tray, had right-of-way. Her busy hostess grumbled, "Such trouble that man puts me through every year. We cook for two days, and he sits out there entertaining his *compadres*."

Eight-foot tables spread across the backyard, and folding metal chairs were set up around each one. Millie stopped halfway to the first table. "I can't believe it. I should have known she'd invite Gavin," Millie mumbled. Gavin and Bailee were nudging their way into the group of men surrounding Antonio Gaspar. The Ancient Ones Adventure Travel van was parked on the side of the road. A chile-red MINI Cooper was double-parked next to it.

Mr. Gaspar sat at the head of a table with his friends, Carlos Lucero and Manuel Garcia, sitting on either side of him in comfortable-looking canvas lawn chairs. The men helping set up tables earlier stood nearby or lounged on chairs. They looked relaxed but attentively listening to someone sitting at Mr. Gaspar's table.

"...heard it from the BLM Law Enforcement Officer myself. The professor was tracing religious artifacts brought all the way from Spain to Mexico to here. His notes had a sketch of a precious cross stolen from a church. And he tracked down a rosary that ended up with the couple who built the very place where we are working."

Oh, no. Lydia, no. Millie gasped, sat the tray on a table, and hurried over to the group.

Lydia took a deep breath, about to add details, but a flurry of exclamations and questions erupted.

Millie's jaw dropped. *Didn't Lydia remember Robby's warning!*

"—so that was who they found in the root cellar."

"—a professor she said."

"—who'd be trying to find something worthwhile at that old place, been abandoned for years."

"—must have been important, he got killed over it."

Millie wormed her way among the men until she stood behind Lydia. Her eyes met Bailee's, who flashed a smile back. Gavin stood behind Bailee and nodded to Millie, then leaned in to listen to the next speaker.

Carlos Lucero stood up. Although in his eighties, he stood as erect and tall as a young man. With his trim form, pointed goatee, and iron gray hair that brushed the back of his collar, he could have been a character from the *Zorro* movies. "There was talk long ago..." He paused. All voices hushed. The *viejo* had much knowledge. He placed a hand on Antonio's shoulder, and said, "Yes, there was talk about a beautiful silver cross that came to Lejos Canyon with the Peralta family. But I tell you now, it is a fairytale. Why would such a poor couple have something so valuable?"

Gaspar laid his hand over his long-time friend's and gave it an appreciative squeeze.

Manuel Garcia, sitting on the other side of their host, made a dismissive motion with his skinny arm. "I disagree, my old friend. There was such a silver cross." Garcia's voice barely carried over the others. His withered body suggested he was even older than Antonio. "My grandson still grazes a few cows on our family's homestead, not more than ten miles from the Peralta Homestead. It was a sad thing that happened to the young woman there. They said José rode off with the one thing left from his dead wife—a silver cross. Something sacred like that has its own spirit. It would not leave the family that held it for many generations."

Gaspar cleared his throat and said in a gruff voice, louder than any other time Millie had heard him speak. "Listen to Carlos. He is right. It was custom to bury the dead with a treasured rosary or piece of jewelry. Let sleeping dogs lie. There is no need to look for such a cross anymore. The professor was wasting his time."

"Well, there was a rosary, for sure, a pearl rosary. That was in the family documents the professor found in the achieves." Lydia had a history story to tell and she seemed bent on telling it.

Millie had to stop her co-worker. She put her hand on Lydia's shoulder and squeezed, hard. "We've got to help in the kitchen." She pulled Lydia up from her chair.

The men made way for the women heading for the kitchen. Nobody wanted to delay the delicious meal they knew was coming.

Halfway to the house, Millie hissed between clenched teeth, "Don't you remember what Robby said? Whoever killed the professor could still be around."

Lydia stopped, hesitated a moment. "I... I guess I shouldn't have. Mister Gaspar asked how we were getting along on the Peralta Ranch and those fellows started asking questions."

"You've got to remember the Peralta site is a long way from help. We're on our own out there. We are doing the same kind of work the professor was. Maybe somebody still out there, or even here today, knows something about what Doctor Bernnard was looking for.

"I don't want us to end up in the root cellar." Millie's hand strayed to the scar on her forehead. "Come on. I've already been put to work on chips and salsa. I'm sure there's a lot for you to do, too."

13. Sad Story Revealed

An honest tale speeds best being plainly told.
— William Shakespeare, Richard III

When Millie came back inside after her third trip distributing the chips and salsa, she spotted Lydia and Amalia frying empanadas at the big stove. Lydia had managed to don an apron with a vivid sunflower pattern with World's Best Cook embroidered in red. Millie figured this was probably Lydia's favorite attire.

Lydia stepped back from the stove, wiped her forehead with the back of her hand, and grinned as Millie passed by. "Hey, sister, you're looking fly."

Millie giggled, tugged the front of her form-fitting turquoise blouse up a bit, and rolled her wrist back and forth so Lydia could see her thick silver bracelet's etched yucca pattern. "When in Rome, at least when in New Mexico, show off your silver."

More guests arrived, more crock pots, salads, and pies appeared on the veranda's food tables. Millie glanced often at the cars, SUVs, and pickups that filled the driveway and extended up and down the road. She helped Momma Agnes carry out the giant pan containing dozens of tamales. Momma Agnes was rewarded with cheers and whistles when she lifted the lid slightly to give a peek at the contents. Millie kept busy, trying to push away doubts that Momma Agnes was wrong about Ben coming.

When all the food was in place, Antonio and Della Gaspar stood side-by-side on the veranda and signaled for silence. Mr. Gaspar led a prayer of thanks for the bounty about to be received. He spread his arms in a welcoming gesture, "*Mi familia, mis amigos,* thank you for coming. Today, I am eighty-five years old. How could that happen?" He stopped, shrugged, and shook his head in apparent wonderment. "God has granted me many blessings. I am proud and honored that you are here to share the hospitality of the Gaspar house. Come, my friends, fill your plates."

After going through the food line, guests settled at tables with friends and relatives. This left Millie and Lydia to start their own table. When Millie saw Gavin heading in their direction, she scanned the other tables but did not spot any other seat to escape to. She ripped a tortilla into pieces, dropping them one-by-one into her posole bowl. Bailee flitted over and sat down next to Gavin. With a couple hellos and nods, the four tucked into their meal.

After making their way to each table, assuring all guests were content, Mr. and Mrs. Gaspar filled plates for themselves and stepped down from the veranda. Bailee patted the seat next to her, insisting her Tio Tony join her table. Gavin jumped up and held a chair steady while the elderly man sat down. He did the same for Mrs. Gaspar who gave a gratified grunt when she settled on the other side of her husband, this being her first chance to sit since early morning.

"Great story, Lydia," Bailee said, "what you said you found out about the cabin. Some professor looking for a cross."

Lydia continued meticulously peeling back corn husk from the tamale on her plate.

Bailee nattered on. "Awesome place, Tio Tony. Gavin let our class spend all afternoon looking inside the cabin and all around. Wild that anybody really lived in that little house. So cool they moved all that way from Taos, starting a new life and all."

Mrs. Gaspar leaned around her husband and said, "The young couple that lived in the cabin was José Manuel Peralta and Rosalinda Carmalita Flores. José's older sister Margarita is Tony's grandmother. That makes you related to the Peralta family too, Bailee. You can trace your mother's mother, and... and... maybe a couple more generations all the way back to Margarita. It was Margarita that raised Tony because Tony's mother died soon after he was born."

"Really? Do you know what happened, why they left?" Bailee's eyes sparkled.

Millie couldn't help but smile at Bailee's look of anticipation. *She really does care about her Hispanic heritage.*

"It's a sad story what happened there." Mr. Gaspar looked at Bailee. "It is time you know the truth. Before their marriage, for two summers, José rode from Taos across the wilderness to build a cabin and clear the land for his *novia*. He made a special place for a flower garden in front of the kitchen window because he knew she'd be lonely moving away from her parents and sisters and brothers. At last, in June of 1913, when he could be sure the snow would be gone from the Sangre de Cristo mountains, José brought his beautiful young bride to what he planned to be their home for years to come. The wagon was piled high, a mattress, chests of clothes, even an iron stove. And for her, he made room for a few rose bushes."

Millie caught Bailee's eye and they both nodded. They knew those rose bushes.

Mr. Gaspar's voice took on an intense, passionate tone. "José and Rosalinda married just that spring. Maybe it was because Rosalinda was lonely that she let a stranger into the cabin one day when José was away. This stranger, he took advantage of our beautiful Rosalinda, then he stabbed her—like a person bleeds out a hog."

The others at the table stopped in mid-chew and hovered forks over plates. Millie remembered the day she first met Mr. Gaspar and the way he suddenly stopped talking about the Peralta Homestead. He must have held in this horrific memory until it, just now, forced its way into daylight.

Bailee squeaked a drawn-out, "Jeez."

Antonio ignored his plate and folded his hands in his lap. Mrs. Gaspar laid a loving hand over his until he was ready to go on.

"When José got to the cabin and saw the terrible evil that happened, he did two things. He wrapped his beloved wife in a quilt and put her in the wagon. Then he tied his saddle horse to the back and drove the wagon to his sister's place."

While her husband took a few spoonsful of posole with a shaky hand, Mrs. Gaspar filled in. "That would be Margarita, Tony's grandmother—Margarita Joséfina Peralta. She lived with Alejandro Gaspar. They already had a homestead farther down Lejos Canyon."

Mr. Gaspar continued, "José was overcome by guilt for

leaving our beautiful Rosalinda alone that day and became bent on revenge. All that Margarita could get out of him was, 'take care of her' and 'I'm going to kill that bastard.' He rode off on the horse, leaving his sister to arrange the funeral. Margarita and Alejandro went to the homestead the next day. It was a bloody scene. They just closed up the cabin and went back home to make arrangements for burial. They caught three of the hens that had scattered and took the cow with them. Days later they noticed the sheep pen over by the cliff. Eight sheep died of thirst."

"That's a sad story, all right," Gavin said. "Tell me, Tony, was the wife buried at the homestead or not. I've heard it both ways."

A quiet gasp from Millie was echoed by Lydia's groan at Gavin's insensitivity. Bailee wrinkled her nose.

"It's that talk of the ghost bride at the cabin that you're really asking about, isn't it?" Mrs. Gaspar challenged.

"I never said there was a ghost." Gavin sounded huffy.

Mr. Gaspar half stood and leaned toward Gavin. "That's all hogwash. Our beautiful Rosalinda lies in the cemetery you pass a mile or so after you turn off the highway onto the Lejos Canyon road."

"Sit down, Antonio." Mrs. Gaspar turned to the others at the table. "My Tony, he talks of Rosalinda as if she is still with us, not some poor soul buried long ago. He visits the old Peralta Ranch every year on August tenth to honor what happened there. He's a good man, my Tony."

Millie noticed Ragged Ear slowly making his way among the tables, sniffing each pair of shoes: shined-up cowboy boots, sneakers, loafers, and sensible-but-nice-enough-for-church low-heeled shoes.

Lydia was so caught up in the story that she'd put her fork down and asked, "What happened to José?"

Mrs. Gaspar answered, allowing her husband to take

a few bites. "Margarita received some personal effects from him two months later. There was a short note. Tony still has it. Hard to read the printing but it just says 'Take care of the livestock. You can have the homestead. I won't be back.'"

"José killed the bastard. I'm sure of it." Mr. Gaspar's voice was stern. He turned to Bailee, "I hate to think it, sweetheart, but we've got a criminal in our family. José killed a man and was never brought to justice, even though the son-of-a-bitch deserved what he got. I believe José either rode on to California or joined the army and got killed in World War One. A year later, José didn't come back. Three years later, he didn't come back. That's when Margarita and Alejandro took over the claim."

Millie's face must have looked puzzled because Lydia asked her, "What's got you all knotted up?"

"I see, I see now how that happened. Remember when we talked to the students, you said homesteaders had to prove up in five years or lose the claim to the land." Millie raised her voice to make sure Mr. Gaspar could hear. "I said there was something odd about the Peralta deed. The claim application was made by José Manuel Peralta in 1910. Five years later, the final deed had initials M. J. Peralta. The first names were mixed up, José Manuel turned into an M and a J."

Mr. Gaspar chuckled. "Nothing gets past you, *Señorita* Millie. My grandmother filed the claim; she always kept her maiden name, Margarita Joséfina Peralta. Margarita and Alejandro weren't married."

"Shame on them, living together. No excuse for it."

"Now Della, they had no money back then. Can't blame others for doing what they have to do. I don't blame José for what he did, even though he'd be judged a criminal today. And don't speak bad about my dear grandmother.

Margarita and Alejandro did right by each other when the children came along, a son and two daughters. Her oldest, my father Faustino, he was grandmother's greatest disappointment. Even before he married my mother, he was drinking too much. When mother died shortly after she had me, he abandoned the family. Grandmother survived all that and lived to be ninety-three, bless her soul."

There was a quiver in Mr. Gaspar's voice. By Millie's calculation, he would have been well into his forties when his grandmother died. Still, even now in his eighties, the sentimental man mourned Margarita, a grandmother who became his surrogate mother.

"So, your grandmother and her husband ended up owning the one hundred and sixty acres in addition to their own?" Millie asked. "Who lived in the cabin?"

"Yes, they took over the land and pastured sheep and cows there. One of their kids bunked in the cabin every once in a while when they were taking care of the livestock, but nobody ever lived there."

"Uh-huh, that fits with what I've looked at so far," Lydia said. "The place feels so abandoned, as if the cabin is sad, that nobody ever cared about it."

"Sad, yes, but not cared for, that's wrong," Mr. Gaspar corrected Lydia. "My *abuela* Margarita loved her younger brother and his bride Rosalinda. She told me many times how beautiful Rosalinda was, how she was kind and good to José even though he took her so far from her family. Even though beautiful Rosalinda died twenty-three years before I was born, I feel like I knew her myself."

Bailee started tapping her phone awake but looked up when Gavin asked, "This morning, Lydia said that BLM ranger found out that dead man in the root cellar was a professor looking for a cross and rosary that went with the bride. What happened to that?"

"That's nobody's business." Mr. Gaspar groused in a menacing voice, pulled his plate closer, and started eating like a starving man.

Ragged Ear swirled against Lydia's leg and climbed onto Millie's lap. Running both hands along his furry sides, she could feel him suddenly stop purring. The cat looked across the table and leaped away.

Mrs. Gaspar nudged her husband and said in an apologetic voice, "It's hard for Tony to talk about the sad thing that happened and that maybe José—we don't really know—killed somebody. These past years, Antonio always goes to church to atone for the sin that taints our family after he pays his respects at the homestead."

Gavin stood up, his attention focused toward the road. "Somebody's limping up the driveway. Looks like he's been beat up."

Everyone at the table looked where Gavin was pointing. Millie jumped up, "It's Ben!"

14. More Than One Version

This northwest New Mexico locale has been under three flags – Spain, Mexico and the United States.
— Marilu Waybourn with Paul Horn, *Gobernador*

Millie reached the latecomer halfway down the driveway by the rose bushes. Ben Benallee ignored her outstretched hand and pulled Millie into a tight hug. He smelled of sage, sweat, and—good.

When they moved apart, holding each other at arm's length, Millie searched his face. "What happened to your eye?"

"Looks pretty bad, I admit" he grinned. "You should see the other guy. Not a guy really, it was a thousand-pound female."

"There's got to be a good story behind that." Millie dropped her hand to the thick bandage wrapped around his hand and wrist and said, "Come and get a plate of food. I helped make the empanadas. I'll introduce you to the Gaspars and you can tell us what happened."

On the way to the food tables, they detoured to say hello to Momma Agnes. She sat with her arms draped over two teenagers on each side of her.

Momma Agnes didn't blink an eye about Ben's appearance. She must have already learned Ben's story when she saw him at the office and invited him to the fiesta. Momma Agnes made introductions all around her table starting with Cousin Amalia, various other relations, and beaming with pride, finished with two nieces who were inspecting Ben with admiring eyes while revealing shiny braces.

They moved to the veranda where Ben swept along the food tables, munching bizcochitos while surveying the array of crock pots, warming pans, and trays of desserts. Even with a bandaged hand, he loaded one plate, laid two tortillas over it, balanced a second plate on top of it with more bizcochitos and two slices of pie, and filled a bowl with posole with his other hand. Millie got a can of Dr. Pepper out of a cooler for him and led the way to her table.

Ben set his food on the table and walked around, shaking hands with each person. When he got to Mrs. Gaspar, the young man laid a hand over hers and said, "Those are the best tasting bizcochitos I have ever had in all of my twenty-seven years." The dignified octogenarian giggled like a teenager.

Mr. Gaspar offered a curt nod, eyeing the newcomer with what looked to Millie like a suspicious expression, perhaps because of Ben's banged-up appearance or maybe he was wondering how often this Navajo ate bizcochitos.

Lydia wiggled in her seat, ready for her turn to fall under Ben's charm.

The others shuffled aside to make room for a chair

next to Millie's. Millie tried not to stare at the purplish bruise under Ben's eye. The shoulder-length, raven black hair that Millie remembered from last summer was gone. His hair still glistened in the sunlight, but the fringe touching the collar of his white oxford shirt looked ragged, as if trimmed by a clumsy friend.

Millie could stand it no longer and blurted out, "What happened to you?"

"I've been in Wyoming trapping buffalo. We brought back two bulls and three cows." He held up his bandaged arm. "Taking a ride to New Mexico wasn't their idea of fun. They don't trailer so well."

Dressed for a party and not in his official department uniform, Ben's explanation only brought stares from people around the table.

"What in the world were you doing with buffalo, young man?" Mrs. Gaspar's tone sounded both amazed and worried.

"Ben, you better explain what your job is before you go any farther," Millie said.

"I'm a wildlife biologist for the Jicarilla Apache Game and Fish Department. I'm Navajo, but the Jicarilla tribe hired me anyway. The tribe wanted to introduce some genetic variety in the buffalo herd it keeps. If they ever get the notion they need more buffalo, I'm going to look for another job. Working on an oil and gas drilling rig would be less dangerous than tangling with a buffalo in a squeeze chute."

Millie could see Ben was having fun entertaining his listeners, all the while hovering his fork over the heaping plate of food in front of him.

"Let this young man eat," Mr. Gaspar said. "Della, we have guests to visit with."

Bailee steadied her Tio Tony's chair while he straightened up with a grunt. Gavin zipped around the table and did the same for Mrs. Gaspar. The others half rose in deference to their hosts.

The way that Mr. Gaspar put his arm under his wife's and guided her toward the veranda reminded Millie of their first meeting when she'd learned of their connection to the Peralta site.

While Ben vacuumed up the food on his plate, Gavin chatted about a tour he had coming up. The clients were flying in from California, he would meet them at the Albuquerque Sunport, and drive the adventure seekers to popular archaeological sites in the Four Corners region.

"I've got the itinerary all planned. First, Chaco Culture National Historic Park, just the ride from Albuquerque into the park will make those California dudes think they're in the wild west. Then Mesa Verde in Colorado is the next must-see." Gavin glanced toward the Gaspars who were now well out of hearing range. He lowered his voice as if letting the younger people remaining at the table in on a secret. "After Mesa Verde, we always do an overnight in Durango. These New Agey types think Colorado has developed the best cannabis because it's been legal there longer. I swear, those dudes can drive you nuts arguing about the best mix or how much to tip their budtender. They do their part to contribute to the economy."

Bailee adopted the same conspiratorial tone, "Yeah, for sure, you'll give them the genuine ancient experience."

Millie turned to Lydia and saw she had the same *what the hell?* look on her face.

Gavin looked past Bailee and talked in a louder voice, "I need to give these dudes a good time. I hope they're generous with tipping their tour guide. If this trip hadn't come along, I'd be close to missing the next insurance payment on the van. And that van is how I make a living."

"What about taking them to the rock art site, the part you wanted me to help with?" Bailee asked. "When's that?" Gavin sent Bailee a look, as if she said something she shouldn't have.

"Uh, never mind." Bailee gave Gavin a contrite smile and swatted a fly away from her face, ruffling her turquoise bangs.

Bailee pulled out her phone, stood, and wandered away, tapping out and flicking away messages. Gavin excused himself to go in search of more dessert.

Ben said, "You know, that area surrounding Lejos Canyon is where my people, *Diné*, came from. We call it *Dinétah*, our homeland. My people lived there a long time ago before they got pushed farther west where the Navajo reservation is now. A few families still live there. Grandfather Sageman showed me some of the sacred sites on his collecting trips for medicinal and ceremonial plants."

"That's what makes the Peralta site so interesting," Millie said. "The mix of vegetation reflects the cultures that occupied the place. Over by a cliff with petroglyphs, there's jimsonweed, wolfberry, and wild tobacco that I think the early Native Americans selectively encouraged by spreading their seeds and removing competing vegetation. Then the homesteaders came with plants that helped them survive, fruit trees, vegetables, and herbs. The old orchard has some fruit trees that could be a hundred years old. Some of them still put out blossoms."

"What about that prickly tumbleweed in the old sheep pen? Nobody would plant that on purpose," Lydia said.

"Right, that's the current phase of human activity in Lejos Canyon. Seeds of invasive species show up in hay that ranchers truck in for livestock, and oil and gas traffic spreads weed seeds in tires. All that changes the flora pattern too," Millie said.

Gavin came back carrying two plates, a slice of pie and piece of *tres leches* cake on each. He sat down across from Ben and pushed one plate toward him.

While the men gave complete attention to the desserts, Lydia went into her thinking pose, elbow on table, chin resting on one hand. "Millie, we need to research and write-up a description of the pre-European contact occupation of that site. If we covered the story of the Peralta site going back centuries, it would be a shoo-in for the National Register of Historic Places protection."

Ben leaned around Millie and said to Lydia, "I know somebody that could help with that, Kenny Conroy. We were roommates in our undergraduate days at Northern Arizona University.

"Kenny's gone the academic route since then. He studies Pueblo migrations; their oral history goes way back in time. He says there's evidence of them in the rock art of Lejos Canyon. Kenny's from the Hopi reservation way over in Arizona, but now he's a professor of anthropology at University of New Mexico. He's been tracing what happened with the Pueblos along the Rio Grande when the Spanish invaded the second time."

"The second time?" Gavin asked. "I thought the Spanish moved north from Mexico and spread all over the southwest."

Ben nodded and said, "They did make settlements along the Rio Grande starting in the fifteen hundreds. They dominated the native Pueblo people and treated them pretty bad, really bad in fact. So, the Pueblos staged a revolt and drove the Spanish out in 1680. But they came back twelve years later, making what's called the second Entrada or reconquest. I've heard Kenny call it an invasion." Ben took the last bite of pie and started on the cake.

"I've read about that." Lydia said. She balanced both hands up and down as if weighing two points. "Reconquest... invasion. Invasion... reconquest. Depends on who is telling the story. A good reminder that there's usually more than one version to history."

Ben trapped the last crumb on his plate between fork and one finger, sucked it in, smacked his lips, and patted his belly. "You get Kenny started and he'll tell you more about the Pueblo Revolt of 1680 than you could fit into a dozen books. That's when Po'pay and other Pueblo leaders organized to push Spanish settlers out of their villages. A couple decades later, the Spanish came back with a vengeance. Many people left their villages for safety. Kenny says the rock art and artifacts found in *Dinétah* show some Pueblo people lived there for a while, mixing customs and culture with the Navajos. He's already published a paper on Pueblo presence in Lejos Canyon. I'll get in touch with him."

The afternoon began to cool. The children were getting cranky after a day of tearing around chasing Tio Tony's goats and eating too many desserts. The Gaspars stood on the veranda, receiving lots of hugs and thank yous. Folks drifted to their cars and pickups.

Bailee strolled over, tapped the table for attention, and announced, "I've decided to volunteer to help you guys at the Peralta Ranch. Tia Della said I can stay here for a few days. I can get away with missing a few classes next week and maybe I can get credit for historical research experience."

"Wait a minute, you'll need to get volunteer authorization from BLM to work at the site," Millie said.

"Not a problem. My Tio Tony knows the area manager. We'll go see Mister Hernshaw tomorrow. Come on, Gavin, I need to know when your Californians get that ancient experience."

Bailee and Gavin started toward his van. "I'll see you out at the homestead," Bailee tossed over her shoulder to Millie and Lydia.

"She could at least ask if we wanted help," Millie said.

"It'll be fun to have her, Millie. In fact, just what I need," Lydia said, giving a contented grunt as she pushed herself up from the table. "I'm about to take dimensions of the cabin and outbuildings, she can hold the measuring tape while you're off counting plants."

They watched Bailee and Gavin nodding in agreement about something by his van. He drove off and Bailee got a rolling suitcase out of her MINI Cooper and walked toward the house.

Lydia gathered as many paper plates, cups, and utensils that she could carry and headed toward the veranda. "I'm going to go help Mrs. Gaspar clean up."

Millie rose and motioned Ben to follow. "Come on, I'll show you the casita I'm renting this summer."

After a brief tour of the adobe house, Millie and Ben sat on the porch steps. She described how serendipitous it was to have found the place and learn the connection of the Gaspars to the Peralta site.

Ragged Ear poked his head out of the lilac bushes, stretched, sauntered over, and sat down between their feet. His ears swiveled back and forth between Millie and Ben as they caught up on the last several months, neither touching on feelings of missing each other. The cat's stare became increasingly intent on Millie, with an occasional fast blink toward Ben.

"I think Ragged Ear is telling me it's time for his supper. And we've both got work tomorrow."

Ben patted his stomach and stood up. "For once, I don't even want to think about food. What 'cha doing next weekend?"

"Not a thing that I know of." Millie's smile matched Ben's. Without so many words, they knew they'd be seeing each other the next weekend.

He waved and limped toward his bright red Mazda.

15. Bailee Volunteers

During the winter of 1829–1830, Antonio Armijo led a caravan of 60 men and 100 pack mules from New Mexico to Mission San Gabriel in California, east of Los Angeles. The caravan carried woolen rugs and blankets produced in New Mexico to trade for horses and mules.

—National Park Service/Bureau of Land Management, "Old Spanish Trail Official Map and Guide"

The Monday after the birthday party, Millie and Lydia broke for lunch a few minutes before noon. Millie wound the 100-foot measuring tape back into its shell as Lydia added the last measurement of the old corral to the diagram on her clipboard. They walked back to the cabin, left the tape and clipboard by the side door, and went to get their lunches from the Suburban.

Lydia pulled out two ratty-looking lawn chairs that

she had acquired at a rummage sale and set them under the shade of the back lift-gate.

Millie poked at the sagging seat webbing before she sat down. "Do you always shop at rummage sales?"

"Not always. Sometimes I find what I need at thrift stores," Lydia said with a perfectly straight face, then broke into a grin. "Only time I ever saw my mama buy a new dress was for my brother's wedding. She wore that same dress for every other important occasion that I can remember."

"Did she save string, too? My mother did."

"Mama had a ball of string as big as a basketball. She caught me once, rolling it like a bowling ball. I never tried that again, let me tell you. Bless her soul." Lydia sighed. "I still carry a ball of twine in my backpack. You just never know when a piece of string will come in handy."

"My mother never spent a penny if she didn't have to either. Maybe we're related."

Lydia choked on the granola bar she was munching, laughed, swallowed, and laughed some more. "Sure, anybody'd think we were sisters, if it wasn't for your being a foot taller than me, white, slim, just about everything I'm not."

Millie enjoyed kibbitzing with Lydia during their breaks. Her companionship helped dispel the feeling that the homestead was cut off from the rest of the world.

"I don't know about you, Millie, but I've had enough measuring for today. I'll fill in the outbuildings diagram this afternoon based on the readings we got this morning. Tomorrow we'll do the cabin." Neither mentioned that all the outbuilding dimensions were already recorded—except for the root cellar.

"I'm okay with that. I'll start clearing what I can find of the vegetable garden. From what Mister Gaspar said about José and Rosalinda, they weren't here long enough to get much started."

"Now I know why I feel a sadness inside that cabin," Lydia said. "That's something, isn't it, how Antonio Gaspar's grandmother kept the spirit of that young couple so real for him? He talks about Rosalinda as if he knew her, even loved her as much as his grandmother did. And now he passes the story on to Bailee."

"Bailee did seem more taken with this place than the other students on the field trip, didn't she? Wonder if she'll show up and help, like she said she would."

"Speak of the devil," Lydia said, "look who's coming up the road."

Few vehicles passed along the Lejos Canyon road, so the chile-red MINI Cooper was unmistakable.

Bailee parked next to the dusty Suburban and bounced out holding a supersized cup of soda. She reached back into the car with her other hand and came out with a brown cap, snapped it on her head, and said, "Look what that nice area manager gave me this morning." The triangular patch on the front of the cap matched the BLM logo on the Suburban's door, except the word Volunteer was stitched under the patch. "What do you want me to do?" Bailee looked from Millie to Lydia.

Millie greeted the eager helper, "So you're now an official BLM volunteer. I'm sure we can find some jobs for you."

"Whatever you want me to do, just say the word. This will look great on my resume."

After a morning's work, the two women's energy level was no match for Bailee's. Lydia sent a quick wink to Millie and said, "The first thing I do, Bailee, when I start work on a new site, is spend a couple hours just getting acquainted, like with a new friend. I walk every part of it, sometimes

I talk to it. Like the cabin over there. I might say, 'I do not plan to do you any harm. I will not yank boards off your wall, I will not laugh at your lopsided fireplace. I just ask that you reveal to me your story. You were loved once, built with great expectations of joy and long-life. Please let me write your history, so your story lives on.' That's what I do, make peace with my new friend."

"Wow, you do that? Does it work?" Bailee's wide eyes fixed on Lydia. "It's like you really care about these old places." She took a couple of steps toward the cabin, put one hand on her hip and jiggled ice in the cup with the other. After a long pause, Bailee said, "I'll do it. I want to know the Peralta story, too. After all, José was my great-great-great something or other."

Millie picked up on Lydia's plan. "Start with the widest circle you can make and still keep the cabin in sight. That way, you can get a feel for what the homesteaders first experienced coming here."

Millie shared a look with Lydia and smiled. This was more than a ploy to get the eager volunteer to work off a little energy. It was a ritual they each did on any site where they worked. First, become acquainted.

An hour later, Millie watched Bailee walk past the scraggly rose bushes by the cabin's kitchen window and caught a few mumbled words: "mother's rose bush... miss her... go see Margarita next week..." It sounded like Bailee was making Rosalinda's lonely life become real.

When Millie next saw Bailee, beads of sweat showed under her turquoise bangs, the big cup was replaced by a quart-sized aluminum water bottle, and her hiking shoes were covered with dust.

"The vibes on this place are awesome," Bailee puffed out. "Now what do you want me to do?"

For the moment, Millie was enjoying Bailee's excitement. "It's nearly quitting time. Let's head back to Wellstown."

"I want to look in the root cellar, too. Gavin told me all about how he found that dead man," Bailee said.

"What? Gavin said *he* found the body!" Millie's jaw dropped.

"Yeah, it was that professor Lydia talked about at the party. What do you think happened to the rosary with a silver cross he was looking for? Maybe we can find it."

"Lydia was talking about some old notes that Robby Ramirez—that's the BLM law enforcement officer—showed us. We don't know for certain what the professor was looking for."

"I'm still going to look for the cross," Bailee said.

Millie took a deep breath, searching for the best words to squelch any rumors that Lydia might have started. "You heard what Carlos Lucero said about that legend of a precious silver cross. He called it a fairy tale. Your Uncle Antonio said the same thing."

"Not really. Tio Tony said there's no need to look anymore. He said people got buried with things like that. Just think, buried Spanish treasure. The ghost story of a young bride looking for her husband. This place could be a tourist attraction. Maybe even charge admission to look into the cabin."

"Oh, Bailee, you've got some imagination. There's no buried treasure and no ghost. There's no Bigfoot, either."

Millie's scientific training didn't include ghosts and speculation. She worked with facts, the only way to maintain credibility. The reality was that there had been two murders here, one long ago and one in the recent past. She considered telling Bailee about Robby's warning—whoever killed the professor could still be around—but that would put a shadow over Bailee's enthusiasm about the

Peralta Homestead. Unlike Bailee who looked for angles to exploit the site, Millie's goal was to protect it.

"Come on, time to go. Tomorrow morning, you can ride here with Lydia and me. You can help Lydia take measurements on the cabin. Later, I'll show you what I'm doing to catalog the garden area."

***

When Lydia stopped to pick up Millie the next morning, Bailee came flying out of the Gaspars' house, carrying a small pack with lunch and water bottles. By the time they arrived at the site, Bailee had them talked into opening the root cellar.

"Let's work on that first thing," Millie said. "We need to document that feature of the homestead sooner or later."

Lydia equipped herself with camera, clipboard, and measuring tape. Millie got the flashlight out of the dash compartment.

The path to the root cellar and area around it had been tromped down by the medical investigator and law enforcement personnel during and after removal of the body. Bailee flipped open the double doors with ease, prompting Lydia to command, "Careful! The wood on these doors can't take banging around."

Bailee said, "Sorry, I forgot. Even the doors are part of the historical structures. I need your help to learn what to do." She stepped back and moved behind Lydia. "You go in first."

Lydia didn't move.

Millie had the flashlight; she had to go first. She stretched taller and looked up and down the road. Only the Suburban by the road. No one else around. She moved down the steps into the root cellar.

Morning sunlight penetrated what Millie remembered as a gloomy interior draped in cobwebs; the shelves and floor were now fully visible. She hardly needed the flashlight to make a cautious scan of the interior. The earthy smell was the same, but trails of dust on the wooden shelves showed that the washtub, bushel basket, and broken crock had been picked up, inspected, and moved aside. Every inch of the dirt floor showed impressions of boot soles. Millie relaxed.

Lydia followed and moved around Millie, allowing room for Bailee to enter.

Millie pointed to triangular markers that outlined where the body had laid. "That's where the body was, Bailee. The crime scene folks put markers there when taking photos."

Bailee stared, "Huh, so here's where that professor bit the dust."

The blasé comment shifted the atmosphere from dark memoires to the here and now, with work to be done.

Lydia tapped one of the markers. "Do you think it's okay to remove these? I don't want to have crime scene tags in my report images."

"Let's ask Robby. Remember she said she'd be coming by. She wanted to look over by the sheep pen, see if she missed anything there. I'll call her when we get back tonight." Millie handed the flashlight to Bailee and eased back up the stone steps. "You can help Lydia while she shows you how to describe a historical feature."

Lydia made a *gee, thanks* face at Millie and said, "Here, Bailee, take the clipboard, write down my comments while I take photos of the interior."

By noon, Lydia and Bailee had finished notes and measurements on the root cellar. Millie joined them at the Suburban. The three got their lunches and climbed the nearby hill to let Bailee in on one of the perks of field work.

At the top of the hill, Millie and Lydia settled into their usual spots beneath the piñon pine. Bailee slowly turned in a complete circle, taking in the view across the canyon beyond the cabin to the tall red cliffs to the west. Bailee declared, "This beats any lunch place back in Fresno." She found a sandstone outcrop to perch on and proceeded to lay out plastic containers that appeared to contain leftovers from the birthday party. "Tia Della packed bizcochitos for all of us." She handed the largest container to Millie, who lifted out three of the anise-flavored cookies and passed them on to Lydia.

Bailee said, "Wish my high school buds could see me now. Orchards, orchards, and orchards all around is what I grew up with. Nothing like this view. People think just because I'm from California, that I'm a rich surfer-girl. I've hardly ever seen the ocean."

Conversation tapered off as they ate their lunches. When Millie finished savoring the bizcochitos, she said, "Tell Mrs. Gaspar thanks."

"Sure," Bailee nodded, and looked down on the cabin. "One side of my family moved away to pursue paradise in California. The Peralta side moved here to tragedy."

"Wow, this is getting philosophical," Millie said as she stood up, ready to get back to work. "Bailee, you can help me survey the garden."

"Sure thing, Millie," Bailee said, but she didn't stir. Her gaze traveled from the cabin to the wash, which had standing water in a few places left from spring rains, then beyond to the other side of Lejos Canyon. "Sometime this week, would you walk with me across the canyon? I want to look for traces of the Spanish Trail."

Millie paused and looked across the canyon. "Good idea. I remember you told us about your summer internship at the Palace of the Governors archives, studying the Old Spanish Trail."

"I'll come, too," Lydia said. "This site has so many layers of history, don't know how we'll get a handle on it all."

***

Millie and Bailee detoured to the orchard to pick up tools while Lydia put their lunch remains in the vehicle and resumed work at the cabin.

The old garden had occupied a spot on the opposite side of the cabin from the shed and corral. Millie pointed out to Bailee what she had worked on so far. "I've done some brush clearing and found a few stones marking what I figure is a border around the garden."

Millie wielded a spade and Bailee scraped with a trowel, steadily uncovering blocks of sandstone from three to five inches thick. They were a reddish color and had probably been collected from along the red cliffs across the road.

"Wonder what they grew in the garden?"

"Most likely vegetables like sweet corn, chile peppers, cabbage, a kind of wild spinach called lamb's quarters. They'd have staples like pinto beans, onions, and garlic, those could keep for several months in the root cellar. I've been researching heirloom fruits and vegetables. The varieties of vegetables planted back then were different from what we get now at a grocery store. There were pumpkins, for example, called Cow and Yellow Pie pumpkins."

"Yeah, I remember what you told Gavin and me at the orchard the other day. People really want these heirloom types, better adapted to this climate and all."

Millie shook her head. Sometimes Bailee seemed hard-edged, center of her own world. Yet, she absorbed everything around her.

"Fruit trees, like the ones in the orchard, they had wonderful names. There were apples called Fall Queen, Maiden's Blush, Cedar Hill Black, and Summer Rose. The cherry trees might be Montmorency, Queen Anne, or Black Pie. Kinds of peaches were Champion, Crawford, Alberta, Hale, and Snow Cling. Apples could be stored for a few months, but the rest of the fruit would be dried or made into fruit leather, jellies, and jams. I figure José must have brought a few saplings to plant every summer he came to work on the place."

"What about chile, like Tio Tony grows? He said his is special, because the seeds came from Taos and are handed down by his relatives. Tia Della says they don't taste as good as the chile you get from southern New Mexico. It's one of their favorite things to argue about."

Millie laughed, "I've heard those arguments, too. Mister Gaspar really got into it with that friend of his that stops by sometimes to visit. Mister Lucero insisted the best chile comes from Española. They were like fanatic baseball fans arguing about their favorite teams. What they were talking about was landrace varieties. The Hispanic farmers would save chile seeds from the best producing or best tasting plants to grow the next year. Families that did that year after year developed what horticulturalists call a landrace, a variety that over time becomes particularly suited to local growing conditions."

Bailee stood up, stretched, squatted back down, and continued gently cleaning off stones, bringing them into sunlight for the first time in decades. "Tio Tony loves to grow things. Funny how he keeps that ugly, old rose bush he dug up here."

"I guess it's his way of keeping a connection with this place and his grandmother, Margarita."

"Sad what happened to Rosalinda," Bailee said.

"Do you think José made this garden before he brought Rosalinda here?"

"Hard to say. Your Uncle Tony said José worked here for two summers to build the cabin and get the place ready before they got married."

"Know what I think? I think it was Rosalinda. I know just what happened. They were strolling around one evening and walked over to see the rock art on the cliff that José had told her about. She saw how pretty these red stones were and wanted them around her garden. That's what happened."

Millie laughed, "Bailee, I think you are trying to channel Rosalinda."

Bailee jiggled the last stone into place, stood up, and exclaimed, "Look, Millie, we did it. We uncovered the whole garden."

"That's a good day's work," Millie said. "Tomorrow, let's hike across the canyon to look for the Spanish Trail. Who knows what we might find?"

16. A Bronco In The Canyon

Dust Devil: A small, rapidly rotating wind that is made visible by the dust, dirt or debris it picks up. Also called a whirlwind, it develops best on clear, dry, hot afternoons.
— National Weather Service

Upon arriving at the homestead the next morning, Millie, Lydia, and Bailee got busy pulling supplies out of the Suburban and gearing up for the hike across the canyon to look for evidence of the Old Spanish Trail.

The smell of sunscreen floated around the vehicle. All three had bottles of water and lunch stowed in their packs, but Millie and Lydia also carried field gear including cameras, notepads, and first aid kit.

Lydia pulled out a hiking pole and adjusted it to the height of her hand while holding her arm at a right angle. Millie flashed back to the previous summer when the tick, tick, tick of a nearby rattlesnake caused her to carry a stick for the rest of the day. "Not a bad idea to have that along," Millie said.

Once past the orchard, Millie suggested they walk a few feet apart from each other. "Look right and left watching for any differences in vegetation that seem to follow a somewhat straight line, and maybe a slight depression. Such an old trail will be hard to spot, but the desert keeps its scars for a very long time."

"Some of the mule trains had, like, three to four hundred pack mules," Bailee said, "but they didn't always follow the exact same path. It depended on where grass and water was when they passed through."

"Hmm, the more spread out they were will make it harder to spot the disturbance."

"Know what?" Bailee remarked. "Most people driving north from Albuquerque don't even know that the Old Spanish Trail exists here, even though the paved highway parallels part of this old route."

"Well I sure didn't. I hardly learned anything about Southwest history in school," Lydia said. "I'm glad you told us about it. It's another part of the history here that will add to the story of the homestead."

"Antonio Armijo was the first man to make the journey round trip. He left from Abiquiu in the fall of 1821, got to California early the next year, sold all his stuff, and got back in April." Bailee was on a roll, contributing her research to the trio's exploration.

"What stuff did those poor mules have to carry all that way?" Lydia asked.

"Stuff made from wool. Blankets, serapes—that kind of thing. By then, New Mexico had lots of sheep."

Millie again vacillated in her opinion whether Bailee was a flippant airhead or serious student.

The broad bottom of Lejos Canyon with its sparse vegetation made for fairly easy walking. They moved at a leisurely pace, occasionally calling out something of interest, a deer skull, a claret cup cactus with its flaring red flowers, a weathered leather strap that had been part of a horse harness. Bailee let out a whoop when a covey of Gambel's quail exploded into flight in front of her.

When they came to the Lejos Wash that meandered along the lowest part of the canyon, they moved back together and followed along the bank, looking for a low place to cross. Millie spotted what appeared to be a deer trail opening in the sagebrush that angled down the three-foot sandy bank. Sliding sideways and sinking into soft sand, they reached the bottom of the wash and found it firm under their feet since there was some moisture from spring runoff still close to the surface. The streambed was wide enough to accommodate a six-lane highway. Only a trickle of standing water wandered down the very center. The deer trail led to a low spot on the opposite side of the wash, making for an easy climb out.

They stopped to sip from their water bottles. Millie looked back at the homestead and then to the opposite side of the canyon. "Let's spread out again, but see that cluster of piñon pine halfway up the cliff, they're a little taller and darker green than the surrounding junipers? Let's use that as the marker to head to, which puts us directly across from the cabin."

Nearing the base of the cliff, they came back together, but said little, not having seen anything that could be interpreted as evidence of the long-ago mule trains.

Lydia looked at her watch. "Time for lunch, I'd say, even if it's only eleven o'clock."

"Suits me," Millie said, swinging her backpack to the ground. "Ouch, damn." She brushed a knuckle against her jeans to wipe off blood seeping from a small scratch. "Wolfberry, no wonder." She carefully grasped the tip of the three-foot high bush and bent the branch sideways. "These little leathery-looking leaves hide some serious, sharp thorns."

"Millie, did you say that's wolfberry?" Lydia was scrutinizing the surrounding bushes.

"Yeah, pale wolfberry, its scientific name is *Lycium pallidum*. In Latin, *pallidum* means pale. These little flowers are yellowish now, but when they first came out, they were greenish-white, pale-looking."

"Look, it's all along here." Lydia's voice was rising, her words coming faster and faster. "There's some of those tall jimsonweed plants like what we saw over by the cliff." She took a couple of steps and picked a bright green cluster from a bush no taller than her knee. "And I believe this is fourwing saltbush. I'll bet you five bucks there's an Ancestral Puebloan ruin here. Make that fifty bucks."

"So that's what jimsonweed looks like." Bailee started toward the jimson plants, but she stopped and squatted down. "No way," she shouted, "here's a row of rocks, then a corner, and another almost straight row."

She popped up, open-mouthed, looking at Lydia. "How'd you know? How did you know there'd be a ruin here? These stones—they show there's a wall beneath, right?"

"Pretty likely," Lydia said, dropping her backpack and stepping next to Bailee. "O–M–G, it *is* a ruin," Lydia spluttered, clapped her hands, and laughed.

"Let me see." Millie shouldered her way between the two explorers, dropped to one knee, swept a hand across the row of stones, and breathed a reverent, "Wow."

Forgetting about lunch, the three edged around the line of rocks that outlined two rectangles, each approximately 8 by 10 feet. It appeared that a third rectangle may have existed because two sides extended for a couple of feet, ending in scattered rubble overgrown with brush.

"Looks like there were three rooms, from what's showing on the surface, but could be more or other features nearby that have been covered up by blowing sand and vegetation," Lydia said. "I wonder if any archeologists have surveyed this site. Probably, but who knows, maybe wind or erosion exposed this room block after the homesteaders left this canyon."

"Wouldn't it be rad if we were the very first ones to see these rooms?" Bailee pronounced.

"We wouldn't be the very, very first, Bailee," Millie chided. "Think about the people that built it hundreds of years ago." She scanned their surroundings. "There's nothing special about this spot that would attract anybody's notice. There are those smooth rocks up there on the cliff that look like hard rains would pour over making a mini waterfall. Kind of makes sense there was occupation here, what with the rock art across the canyon, and José Peralta had some kind of reason for making a homestead claim here."

Lydia had stepped to the center of the end room and was turning slowly, looking at the ground. "If this site has been recorded, there should be an LA number somewhere. Sometimes it's attached to a piece of rebar stuck into the center of a site and measurement data is figured from that point. Sometimes, on a site where there's more showing on the surface that's likely to catch the eye of a casual passer-by, the tag is placed in a more inconspicuous location."

Lydia shook her head, "I don't see any LA number here. You guys look for a small metal tag posted somewhere. I'll take a GPS reading."

Millie slowly traversed one side of the ruin. Bailee angled the opposite direction, while asking, "LA? What's that stand for?"

Lydia pulled a GPS unit and camera out of her backpack and answered Bailee's question while taking a location reading and pictures. "LA stands for the Laboratory of Anthropology. Way back in the early 1900s, a man named Harry Mera was a public health doctor and traveled around New Mexico as part of his work. He also explored archaeology sites and kept his notes on index cards. Mera later went to work for the Lab of Anthropology and they kept using his numbers. LA numbering is unique to New Mexico. It's one of the oldest state-wide recording systems. There were so many interesting sites, early archeologists did a lot of work here."

"Lydia, you'd make a great teacher," Millie called to her.

Lydia beamed a smile at Millie and resumed snapping pictures. "As far as knowing there'd be a site here, when Millie said wolfbane, I looked around for other indicator plants. Certain plants, called indicator plants, are often found where Ancestral Puebloans made settlements. Wolfberry, for example, produces edible berries. Fourwing saltbush has palatable seeds that can be ground into a meal. Jimsonweed was possibly used in ceremonies because it can cause mind-altering visions."

Bailee stopped in her tracks, seeming fascinated by Lydia's repertoire of archaeological facts. "They grew that kind of stuff on purpose?"

"Well, not like in rows in a garden the way we think of growing food. They'd collect seeds, berries, maybe parts of certain plants like the root or stem, to bring back for food, making dyes, medicines. Some of these plants especially like disturbed soil, so dropped seeds would take root. It could be that some plants got transplanted here on purpose. For sure, if one of these useful plants grew close-by, they'd let it grow, that is, they encouraged it, not walk over it or anything. So that results in these indicator plants remaining more numerous around ruins."

Bailee called out, "Yeah, you ought to be a teacher. Hey, I found a piece of pottery." She was waving a flat, irregularly shaped object the size of a quarter in the air. "Look, it's grayish-black and has indentations like it's been burnt."

"Probably from a cooking pot," Lydia called back. "Leave it where you found it."

"Yes, teach," Bailee said. She put the sherd on the ground, then bent down again and moved it a couple of inches, to place it in exactly the same spot she'd found it.

Millie noticed a pottery fragment in front of her toe and picked it up. "I found one, too. It's as big as the palm of my hand and curved and has a black wavey line painted across it. Bet it was part of a bowl." She replaced it on the ground and listened to Bailee call out, "found another, and another."

"That's a good sign that this site had not been picked over and looted," Lydia commented, as she put her equipment in her backpack. "I'll check with the state office folks whether this site has been surveyed and recorded when I get to Santa Fe to research the homestead records. But right now, I'm more interested in lunch."

"I'm with you on that, I'm ready for shade, water, and food," Millie said.

As soon as they got settled on a log or a rock, Bailee announced, "Guess what? Tia Della put bizcochitos in my lunch for you guys again."

"You don't make your own lu—" A swirling breeze sent Millie's hat sailing and tumbling toward the ruin. She sprang after it and caught it just before it flipped onto a prickly pear cactus.

Bailee didn't seem to notice and chattered on. "If we could get cell phone service here, I'd look for that LA number now. I think we discovered this site. Let's call it the B-L-M Discovery, for the Bailee, Lydia, Millie site."

Lydia shook her head, "Oh, no, no, no. The general public does not have access to that archaeology database, for obvious reasons."

Apparently not so obvious because Bailee said, "Like what reasons?"

Lydia paused from devouring her sandwich. "Pot hunters, grave robbers—people that steal artifacts and even human remains, to sell on the black market. Most every major archeology site all over the country has been impacted. People even dig up graves in old church cemeteries looking for valuables."

Millie reached into the container of cookies, grumbling, "How low can a person get?"

Bailee handed the container on to Lydia. "That's like what Tio Tony said at the party, that the silver cross the professor was looking for would have been buried with Rosalinda."

Millie's precision memory kicked in. "That's not quite what Mister Gaspar said. He said it was a custom to bury items, he didn't say that's what happened. And his friend, Carlos, said it was all a fairytale."

Optimistic Bailee countered with, "But... but ol' Manuel seemed to think the cross is still with the family."

Lydia's hat was the next target of the increasing wind. Bailee caught it and returned it to Lydia who was pulling her backpack.

The lack of any sign of the Spanish Trail mule trains and increasing wind caused them to walk at a faster pace back toward the homestead. Still spread out with eyes to the ground and pushed by the wind, they missed the place where they had crossed the wash earlier, ending up farther south along its bank.

Millie found a spot where they could drop down the soft, sandy bank without too much sliding and sinking in. They crossed the wash and looked for a good place to get over the opposite bank.

About to climb up and angle in the direction of the cabin, Millie saw a swirl of leaves rising from the ground. "Uh oh, there's a dust devil heading right toward us. Hold onto your hats and cover your eyes." Instinctively, they ran a short distance to huddle against a higher bank.

The whirlwind whooshed over them. The spinning updraft blew itself out halfway toward the cabin, releasing its rustling debris to settle back on the ground. Silence enveloped the canyon.

Bailee was the first to recover. "Awesome! What an adventure," she shrieked and danced down the wash singing out, "YOLO, YOLO."

Lydia bent her head sideways and tapped her ear. "Gawd, I've got enough dirt in my ears to grow a garden."

"Guess that gives me the full southwest experience," Millie laughed. "I've been threatened by a rattlesnake and now hit by a dust devil."

Bailee had disappeared beyond a curve in the wash, but her voice was clear, loud. "Come here, you guys. I found something." She sounded unsettled, mystified by her second discovery of the day. "An old car."

Millie trotted to her and Lydia soon caught up. They stood without speaking, staring at the half-buried vehicle. The front half was nosed into the bank, the entire engine compartment and all but the very top rim of the windshield covered by sand. It was dark red, the color of dried blood. The frame rested directly on the ground. The tires, if it had any, were buried.

"What's it doing here?" Lydia whispered.

"Looks like somebody crashed it here," Millie said. "But how'd they ever ram through all that sagebrush and get it here?"

"So what happened to them?" Lydia's eyes slowly widened. She put her hand on Millie's arm. "Are you thinking what I'm thinking?"

"Uh, uh, I'm not thinking that. Finding one dead body is enough." Millie took a deep breath and stepped closer. "I guess there's only one way to find out."

Millie used her sleeve to clear a spot on the driver's side window and peered inside. "Nobody in there."

Lydia let out a ragged sigh.

"Let me see." Bailee cupped her eyes and pressed her nose against the window. "There's stuff on the back seat, maybe a duffle bag or something." She yanked on the door handle, but couldn't pull it open. She tried the back seat door handle with no better luck.

In unison, they stepped around to the back of the vehicle.

"It's a Ford Bronco, not that old," Lydia said. "I can tell because I drove one of those the summer I was on a dig in Kansas."

Millie reached down and brushed dirt off the license plate. The sand-scoured plate was barely legible except for TEXAS in big letters at the top. The letters might have been red when new but now were a faded pink. Millie opened her water bottle and splashed water over the plate. She crouched down on one side of the plate so the others could watch as she ran her fingertips back and forth over the raised lettering. She read slowly as she made out the shapes. "There are three letters, what looks like a flag, then numbers. Ha, at the bottom, it says '150

Years of Statehood'. I can hardly read what year is on the registration sticker."

Bailee was taking selfies with her cell phone with the Bronco in the background, but stopped next to Lydia to listen. She snapped a photo of Lydia's hat pushed askew by the wind and of Millie beside the license plate.

Millie handed the water bottle up to Lydia. She pushed her hair aside, brushing her hand over the scar on her forehead, and licked her thumb. She touched the moisture to the small sticker on the upper right corner of the plate. "Okay, I can read it now. Ninety-six."

"That would be 1996... why does that date sound familiar?" Lydia muttered.

"Because," Millie drew a deep breath as she stood up, "that's the last date in the professor's notebook... the year he went missing... when he was killed."

17. Junk Car—So What

We know, too, that men who want to further both the beauty and bounty of America must constantly search for the right balance between development and preservation of resources.

— Stewart L. Udall, Secretary of the Interior, 1961–1969

Neither the afternoon heat nor erratic breezes slowed the trio as they scrambled out of the wash and hustled toward the homestead. Millie led the way back, outpacing the other two with her longer legs. Finding the abandoned SUV gave a new dimension to the desiccated corpse found in the root cellar. She tried not to picture the professor driving up to the site, parking the Bronco in the same spot as the Suburban was now, poking around the premises, scribbling in his notebook. His quest for the silver cross got abruptly terminated. *Would her and Lydia's survey come to a similar end?*

It took only a few minutes at the Suburban for them to throw packs into the back compartment and hop in, slamming doors shut almost simultaneously.

Millie drove while Lydia in the front seat and Bailee in the back seat tested their cell phones until Lydia called out, "Okay, I got bars. Do you have Robby's number?"

Millie braked at the next wide-spot in the road, woke up her phone, and spun through contacts until she found Robby Ramirez's number.

Before the BLM Law Enforcement Office could get through her usual formal greeting, Millie, trying to keep her voice even, said, "Robby, there's a car buried in the wash."

"So what. There's a junk car in every other wash in this county."

"It's not that old, Robby."

"Big deal, an abandoned vehicle in a wash, nothing new about that."

"Robby, listen, it's got a Texas license plate. The registration sticker shows 1996."

No response. Millie held her phone out and stared at it, as if peering at Robby through a wireless connection could somehow make her understand.

"Come on, Robby," Millie shouted at the phone, "that's the year in the professor's notes."

"Are you saying..."

Now Millie had Robby's attention. The law officer's questions came faster than Millie could answer them. "Bronco. Yes—a duffle bag or something on the back seat. The license plate? I... I don't remember what the number was. Guess I should have written it down."

"Don't tell me you didn't get the license plate number."

Robby sounded a bit peeved.

"Wait a minute, Bailee got some pictures on her phone." Millie ignored Robby's "who's Bailee?"

Bailee was already maneuvering one of her selfies to show a close-up of the license plate. She held her phone out to Millie.

The greatly enlarged image was badly pixelated but readable. "Okay, Robby, I'm going to read the numbers off to you. Are you ready?"

Millie could picture Robby flipping open her ever-present stenographer's notebook.

"I found it first," Bailee spoke into Millie's phone.

"Huh? Who's that? Never mind. Tell me what you saw."

Millie read off, "J-R-M four-seven... that's all I could make-out."

"That's a start," Robby said. "I'll look up the missing persons report. It's likely to have info on what the professor was driving and if we're lucky, the license plate number. Where are you guys now? How far is the Bronco from the cabin? What direction?"

Millie answered Robby's rapid-fire questions, but couldn't ignore Lydia and Bailee making exaggerated panting and swooning gestures. Millie pushed her hair off her sweaty forehead and felt grit left by the whirlwind. "Look, Robby, I know it's only three o'clock, but it would be dark before you could get here and hike back to the wash. That Bronco isn't going anywhere. We're heading back into town. I'll tell you all the details when we get to the office."

"Okay, come on back to the office. I'll get onto that license plate number. Meet me in Wirt's office." Robby clicked off.

Bailee asked to be dropped off at her aunt and uncle's place, saying she had to pack-up and get ready to go back to NAU by Monday. "I can't miss anymore classes. Besides, I'm helping Gavin with the tour group he's bringing through this weekend. I need to get the dress he wants."

Millie glanced at Lydia, whose arched eyebrows showed she was equally as baffled. "A dress?" Lydia mouthed silently to Millie.

Bailee just chattered on. "I'm going to ask my advisor about getting extra credit if I draw up a tourism proposal for the Peralta Ranch. I've got a lot more ideas about what to do at the homestead now. I can picture a big attraction sign, a parking lot for busses, port-a-potties, paved paths to all outbuildings, interpretive brochure with great graphics. Legends, ghosts, mystery car, can't get any better draw than that. Got to move that wrecked car up by the sign. What do you think?"

Millie clutched the steering wheel, looking straight ahead. "First, I think ninety-nine percent of tourists would have to be lost or crazy if they'd drive that far on rough roads to get to the Peralta Ranch. Second, dozens of people tromping around that property will destroy vegetation and make shortcut paths that'll erode in no time. Third, the more people that know about a place, the more graffiti and vandalism that's likely to happen."

Bailee's head and shoulders now appeared between Millie and Lydia. She was kneeling on her seat. "Come on, that's selfish. You just want to keep it all to yourself. What do you think, Lydia?"

"Ah, don't go putting me in the middle of this. What you're saying, Bailee, and what Millie is saying, well, I've heard that argument all my career as a historical archaeologist. How can you get people to support historic sites if they never experience them? Preservation versus visitation, can you have both?"

Bailee flopped back on her seat and didn't say another word until Millie pulled into her own driveway. Bailee hopped out and headed toward the Gaspars' house. She waved and called over her shoulder, "It's been a blast, you guys. See ya."

They sat for a moment, both staring out the windshield, letting Bailee's whirlwind energy subside.

"Do you think she's mad at what I said?" Lydia was the first to speak.

"No telling what goes on in Bailee's brain. Seems like sometimes she's keen on continuing her family narrative, sometimes it's only dollar signs floating in front of her eyes. Why is it that me and Bailee are always butting heads?"

"That's because you two are close in age but worlds apart in the way you were raised. Bailee's got that California culture of sun and fun. You were helping your parents with cleaning offices when you were twelve."

"Yeah, if there was a world record for emptying waste baskets, I'd hold it. How come you're so smart about people, Lydia?"

"True, grasshopper, I am older and wiser." Lydia lifted her head and looked down her nose, imitating the look of a wizened mentor. "But there's another factor. Look at the professions you and I chose. You were attracted to a career in botany. There's a reason that botany became your thing—you think like a dichotomous plant taxonomy key—it's either this or it's that."

"Well, how else can you figure things out?"

"Archeologists, on the other hand, interpret, reconstruct how people lived by considering all aspects of human behavior. You've got to have a penchant for a human-centered view of the world."

Millie envied Lydia's broad view of their work. She decided Lydia's confidence in her field came with age and experience.

Lydia moved around to the driver's seat, backed down the driveway, and pulled to the side of the road to wait for Millie. They'd agreed that Millie would follow in her Honda so she could make the drive back home after meeting at the office, allowing Lydia to remain in Wellstown.

The commotion in his driveway woke Ragged Ear. He sauntered over to the porch steps, expecting an early supper. His tail dropped when Millie started her car. "Sorry buddy, I can't stay. I hate being stuck in the middle of this murder mess, but I want to hear what Robby finds out." Ragged Ear turned his back to her.

***

It was nearly quitting time when Millie and Lydia came through the back door of the BLM building from the vehicle yard. Robby was leaning her elbows on Momma Agnes' desk, waiting for them. Robby's greeting was, "Good, you're here."

Momma Agnes caught Robby's sleeve as she turned to go into Wirt's office and whispered, "When you're done, you come tell me everything they saw."

As they settled into chairs in the area manager's office, he closed a folder on his desk and leaned back in his chair. Wirt held up a hand and said, "Okay, one at a time, tell me what happened. First, Lydia, why were you wandering around Lejos Wash way beyond the Peralta site? Millie, how was it that you two just happened to come across what you think was the professor's car? Kind of a coincidence after your discovery in the root cellar. Then Robby, you can fill us in on what you found out on that vehicle."

"It's the Old Spanish Trail, Wirt," Lydia said. "We know the Peralta Homestead goes back to the early 1900s. We know the nearby rock art dates all the way back to the six or seven hundreds. The Spanish colonial period fills in the gap of human presence. It's all part of the fascinating history of that area, don't you think?"

"What I think is that archaeologists see the world upside down, going backwards in time," Wirt said. "Did you find it, where the trail went through?"

"Well, not exactly. But we did find a small ruin, more evidence of centuries of occupation."

Lydia's cogent view of the past was not lost on the area manager. "Guess all that strengthens the case for protecting the area." He shifted his attention to Millie. "So no mule tracks, but you found a prehistoric ruin and the vehicle."

"It was the dust devil that hit us on the way back," Millie said. "We took cover. When it was over, we were farther south than I expected. Bailee saw the car first. You know Bailee, you gave her that volunteer cap."

"It's a wonder the whirlwind didn't send that cap into the heavens. I'm pretty sure it scoured one or two layers of skin off my face," Lydia said.

This made Wirt smile. A good sign that he didn't mind this disruption to the office routine. In fact, he seemed eager to hear every detail. Perhaps he was curious about the professor's fate, perhaps he missed being out in the field rather than being immersed in paperwork, administrative duties, and meetings.

Robby had her notebook ready. "It's the professor's vehicle all right. What Millie got off the license plate matches the missing persons report. We just might have a break-through about what happened at the homestead."

Wirt nodded and said, "Check it out, Robby. Keep me apprised of what you find."

"I've already called the sheriff's office for their forensics folks to meet us at the homestead first thing in the morning."

As they left the office, Momma Agnes was signaling Robby over.

On the drive home after the meeting, Millie's head swirled with thoughts, questions, and nagging worries coming and going as fast as the dust devil had blown past. *We didn't really look inside the Bronco. What if... there was blood on the floor, or something worse? How will they move it? Will this put an end to the case, so we can get back to normal routine, without wondering if whoever murdered the professor might target our fieldwork?*

18. Thanks Lizard

I believe that there is a subtle magnetism in Nature, which, if we unconsciously yield to it, will direct us aright.
— Henry David Thoreau, American Naturalist, 1817–1862

For once, Lydia was on time to pick up Millie the next morning. When Millie climbed in the passenger's seat, Lydia pointed with her thumb to the back of the Suburban. "I packed a few snacks and drinks. I figure a little hospitality always makes things go better."

"I hope so. This has got to be the end of this murder craziness," Millie replied.

"I don't know. They say trouble comes in threes."

"There's no science to back that up."

"Ah, don't be so sure, Miss Millie, there's always some truth to these old sayings. Mark my words, you'll see."

There wasn't much more to discuss, except for wondering why Bailee needed to get a dress for Gavin and commenting on how green the irrigated hay fields along the San Juan River were looking.

Shortly after they arrived at the homestead, Robby pulled in and parked next to the Suburban. The BLM badge on her tan shirt gleamed in the early morning sunlight. She adjusted her wide leather belt crowded with the tools of law enforcement, swung a pack onto her shoulder, and said, "Let's go."

"Don't you want to wait for the sheriff's people?" Millie asked, but Robby was already heading toward the wash.

"I'll wait here and direct them to the Bronco," Lydia offered.

Millie caught up with Robby. They walked straight out from the homestead until reaching the wash, then found their tracks from yesterday, and followed them to the half-buried vehicle.

Robby gawked at the wreck. "How the hell did it get this far from the road? Whoever did it must have been batshit crazy."

Millie crossed her arms and waited for Robby to get through the same reactions that their discovery had engendered the day before.

Robby inspected both sides and the back of the vehicle. "Looks like the driver kept going as far as he or she could until the engine and tires gave out. This has got to be a quarter mile from the cabin, plowing through brush and over rocks."

For once, Robby was without her notebook, but she pulled a folded-up note out of her pocket and held it next to the license plate. "Perfect match, this is the professor's vehicle, no question."

Robby gave the door handle a good yank, but had no better success than Bailee the day prior. She cupped her hands around her eyes and looked in the small circle cleared on the window. "There's the duffle bag. I hope there's more in it than the man's underwear. Something that'll give us a clue why he never left this place alive." She stepped back and lowered her pack to the ground. "Did you find anything else, maybe a part broke off, something like that?"

"We, uh, didn't really look, once we realized it was the professor's car. Finding the body was creepy enough. Finding this hulk, well, it just brought it all back."

"I'll get photos while it's just our tracks here. How about taking a walk around, see if there's anything got dropped or thrown out."

Millie followed the depressions in the sand they'd made the day before up the side of the wash. This time, she walked purposefully, scanning the ground for anything man-made. She stopped and stood motionless at movement beneath a rabbitbrush. A collared lizard dashed out into the open. Its turquoise-colored back, spotted with small black dots, contrasted with its flashy yellow feet. "Oh, just a lizard," Millie whispered. An unexpected gem in the desert. The creature's body was more than a foot long, its tail, narrowing to a skinny point, making up more than half its length. "What a handsome dude you are. I assume you're a male, so bright and show-offy."

"Find something, Millie?" Robby called up to her.

She waved back, wagging her head side-to-side in an exaggerated *no* motion. The lizard lifted one foot, put it down, lifted another, and another, until all four had a relief from the hot sand. The last hind foot put down teetered on the edge of something round extending out of the sand. It's rusty-brown color barely contrasted with the ground, but it's shape definitely was not natural. The lizard looked in her direction, ducked his head two times, and scooted under a fourwing saltbush. Millie took a few steps closer and nudged the object with the toe of her boot, dislodging a key ring. She poked an index finger through the ring and lifted it to eye-level. Two keys and a small metal ornament dangled from it.

Millie hurried back to where Robby was waiting. "See anything?" Robby asked.

"Sure did," Millie said and dropped the keys in Robby's hand.

"Where'd you find this?"

"About twenty feet beyond the wash."

"Anything else? Footprints, broken brush?"

"No, the cryptobiotic crust would still be crushed if someone had walked around there even that long ago. But there's a couple purple penstemon flowers still in bloom."

Robby rolled her eyes. "Not what I meant. My guess is whoever drove it here threw the keys as far away as they could. Hey, maybe I can unlock a door." She tried inserting the key but a grinding sound made it clear that the key-hole was packed with sand.

Hearing voices striding toward them ended Robby's futile attempt to force the key into the lock. Robby greeted Detective St. Claire with a friendly fist bump, indicating a long-time working relationship. St. Claire was tall, brawny, and had frizzy fair hair, just the opposite of Robby who was short, wiry, and had black hair controlled in a bun. The detective introduced her companion as Deputy Bub Begay. His bright smile reminded Millie of Ben's, but his narrow face and eyeglasses made him look like a studious type. He was carrying a hard-plastic case the size of a briefcase.

While the team from the sheriff's office took their

turn ogling the derelict Bronco, Millie silently kicked herself for not getting a picture of the collared lizard with her cell phone. Then she looked over the officers' uniforms of tan shirts and olive-green pants made of what looked like substantial material and wondered how they managed in the summer heat. Her thoughts snapped back to the task on hand when Detective St. Claire began asking her questions about finding the car.

"Who were you with? Who touched the vehicle?" St. Claire went on with questions. "Since finding the body in the root cellar, have you noticed anything unusual, like vehicles slowing down as they drive past? Has anybody stopped, asking a lot of questions about what you are doing?"

"We had a ton of questions when Gavin McIntyre brought a bunch of NAU students to learn about the site."

"Hmm, Gavin McIntyre. That's the guy you said was here when you opened up the root cellar. And he was back, huh? Anybody else poking around?"

"One of the students, Bailee Fernandez, came back the next week as a volunteer. If it wasn't for her, we wouldn't have found the Bronco."

St. Claire added Gavin's name to her list. No wonder Robby had said the detective was bulldog persistent with a reputation for picking at cold cases and never letting up. It seemed the detective wanted every detail.

Deputy Begay stood with his hands in his pockets, chewing on a toothpick, occasionally rocking back and forth heel to toe. A junk car abandoned in a wash appeared to be all too routine to him.

He shifted into motion when St. Claire told him to set up photo markers. He balanced the box on one knee, snapped it open, and got out yellow plastic markers with large black numbers and a measuring tape.

While they documented the scene, Robby filled them in on what she had gleaned from newspaper accounts. "I've dug up a little more about Doctor Bernnard. His hometown newspaper did a few stories on him at the time. Of course, they glommed onto the disappeared-without-a-trace angle. It seems he was well-known in the community, giving lectures, active in civic clubs, that kind of thing. There were quotes from his wife and from the university department head. His wife said he bought this Bronco new, just for his trip to New Mexico. He called it a reward to himself for making tenure the year before."

Millie bit her lip. This faded wreck had been someone's pride and joy. She knew the happy feeling of buying the car you really wanted for yourself.

"And here's something that didn't show up in the missing persons report." Robby paused until the detective looked at her. "The department head said, 'he'll be missed, a good teacher and a good researcher. He was never without his leather satchel overflowing with papers,' or words close to that."

St. Claire absorbed the meaning of that. "So you're saying we should be on the lookout for something like a leather briefcase. We've found Doctor Bernnard and we've found the Bronco; what's still missing is the satchel."

An image of a rumpled professor with a leather bag slung on his shoulder took shape in Millie's mind. *Maybe there are ghosts here. The professor was an academic looking for a lost artifact. What was he trying to find that would cause him to be brutally murdered? He devoted a lot of research time and energy looking for something at the homestead. Had he discovered a secret, and someone wanted him dead because of it? Would that same someone want to keep her and Lydia from finding what the professor had discovered?*

"Oh, and here's something else we found, well, Millie found it." Robby handed the key ring to Sylvia. "I figure it's keys for the Bronco."

"Hmm, Bub, what do you think?" St. Claire passed the key ring to her assistant.

He held the metal tag by the projections on each side and said, "It sure fits with the license plate. See, it's a Texas longhorn. You know, the Longhorns, the University of Texas football team."

"Hook 'em Horns!" Robby shot her fist in the air with index and little finger extended.

The gesture was lost on Millie, but she gave a silent thanks to the lizard for helping to find the key ring.

"I suppose you already tried unlocking the Bronco," St. Claire said. "Go ahead and bag it, Bub. And pack up your kit. There's no use trying for fingerprints, not with wind sandblasting it for nearly thirty years."

Sandblasted is right. Millie patted her face, still raw from being hit by the dust devil.

St. Claire said, "I have a tow truck coming but it's going to take more than the usual transport to get this car out so we can examine the interior. You say there's no phone coverage here?"

Begay snapped his case closed and said, "Then let's get out of here and go where we can get cell service. The towing service needs to know what they're dealing with."

Collard Lizard

19. A Second Pearl

Property conflicts, religious differences, racial struggles, cattle and sheep disputes, robberies and hangings. ... It was a rough country and we must admire the pioneers who risked everything to come and settle in this land.

— Marilu Waybourn, *Crimes of the County. Northwest New Mexico 1876–1928*

"Incredible," Millie declared, "Lydia, you are just incredible." The archeologist turned hostess had a jug of lemonade, a container of pita bread sandwiches, a platter of cut-up vegetables, and a bowl with granola bars laid out on the back of the Suburban. Her two ratty lunch chairs were now placed next to two more threadbare folding chairs.

"Help yourself, folks. I figured we'd be here most of the day, so here's a little something I put together last night."

Help themselves they did, among comments of "never expected this," "thanks," and "so field work isn't all sweat and toil, huh?"

While eating their lunch, St. Claire and Begay conferred about getting the Bronco out of the wash. It was decided that Bub would drive back out on the Lejos Canyon road until he could get radio coverage and tell the towing service to send their big Mack truck with its side winch.

"I know what to ask for because I saw it in action this spring," Bub said, took a gulp of lemonade, and squeezed his eyes closed. "Geez, did you forget to put sugar in this? Anyway, the driver of a fully-loaded water tanker lost control, slid the rig off a gawd-awful muddy back road, and mowed down a couple of juniper trees before hitting a boulder. Me and a couple other guys had to use the jaws-of-life to extricate the driver. He wasn't hurt much. That guy, he scrambled back up on the road, took out his wallet, and crumpled his commercial driver's license in half. He said, 'I ain't never gonna drive one of those again.' He got in the back of my squad car and didn't say another word." Leaving the others chuckling, Bub went to call the towing company.

Robby saluted Lydia with her lemonade cup and plopped in a chair. "One thing about police work, you gotta be good at waiting and take advantage of a break when you get one."

St. Claire picked up another handful of celery sticks and settled in a chair. "Something's been bothering me. We know the professor went missing in 1996, but why was he here?"

"The silver cross," Lydia said and glanced at Robby, as

if checking whether to continue.

Robby responded, "Go ahead, tell Sylvia the whole legend, ghosts and all." Then she closed her eyes and went so slack that Millie wondered if she had gone to sleep. Millie wasn't as good at waiting; she leaned on the shady side of the Suburban, drumming fingers silently on her jeans-clad leg.

"Millie's the one that figured it out. Millie, you tell her. I've got to get these leftovers back in the cooler." Lydia picked up the vegetable tray and fussed around the big cooler in the back of the Suburban.

"I'm all ears," St. Claire said, sprawling out, getting comfortable in her chair. "I know he was looking for a rare antique silver cross. I figured that out from his pocket notebook. There was a sketch of a baroque-looking cross, with the curved, lobbed ends. But those pages and pages of names, Spanish words he'd copied, just went on and on. I skimmed over all that scratchy little handwriting. I couldn't make heads nor tails of it. So why here, why this abandoned homestead?"

Millie moved over to a chair next to the detective. "Here's what I gleaned from the copies of the notebook that you gave Robby. I can read a little Spanish, had a whole year of it in high school. Doctor Bernnard and apparently other historians have searched for years for a cross they traced back to a church in Spain. What Doctor Bernnard figured out is that somewhere, somehow over time, the cross was attached to a rosary. Maybe it was to disguise its true value, making it seem part of what at that time was a fairly common possession."

"How'd he come up with that?" St. Claire shuffled her chair around to face Millie, seeming to be re-appraising her as more than just a by-stander in the case.

"The notations he made on the dates he was in Santa

Fe, along with the sign-in sheets Robby obtained from the Palace of the Governors archives showed Doctor Bernnard was researching family documents, journals, letters, and diaries. He could read Spanish well enough to follow the cross to the New World, and he concluded the pearl rosary with the cross attached was being handed down to the oldest daughter when she got married, from one generation to the next. Which took him to Rosalinda's family. That oldest daughter was Rosalinda who married José Peralta. They are the ones that built this homestead, the Peralta Ranch."

Lydia snapped the lid on the last container and went to the remaining folding chair. "So sad, what happened to that young couple."

"What happened?" asked the detective.

Millie answered St. Claire's question with a question. "Did you know the professor was the second murder on this homestead?"

"What? Second?" St. Claire's voice was so loud that Robby opened one eye and winked at Millie.

"Who else got killed here?" St. Claire asked.

Lydia answered, "The wife, Rosalinda. She and José were married just two months when it happened."

Millie took up the story. "Uh-huh, there was an unsolved murder here in 1913. My landlord happens to be a third generation descendant. Mister Gaspar said the husband, José, was out working one day, probably taking care of sheep or something, and when he got back to the cabin, he found Rosalinda raped and murdered. Well, Mister Gaspar called it 'taken advantage of.' José rode after whoever did it and never came back. José's sister and her husband buried the woman and took over the ranch. This sister was Mister Gaspar's grandmother, he gets the story directly from her. That's why people say the place is haunted."

"Jeez, that's the basis of the ghost story?"

"It's not clear where she was buried—on the property or in a local cemetery."

"Sounds like the professor thought the cross is still here somewhere," St. Claire said.

"Sure does," Millie agreed. "According to the notebook dates, he talked to the Gaspars and looked at property records in the county building. Then he spent days here looking around. He even made a map of the place, from the orchard all the way over to the sheep pen by the cliff. Like a treasure map."

"That's all a good story," St. Claire said, "but right now, all we've got is that the dude's wallet and briefcase are missing. Could be just a robbery."

Robby roused up enough to say, "But why would a run-of-the-mill robber go to so much trouble to hide the body and the Bronco?"

St. Claire shrugged and relaxed back in her chair.

No one spoke for a while. There seemed to be nothing more to add about the two tragic events.

Except why here? Millie's thoughts kept gnawing on the question. *Could these two murders be related? No, how could they be, a century apart. Only link is the rosary and family tree. Not quite legal, taking over the claim by the Gaspar family. The rosary was hers, Rosalinda's. It goes to the oldest daughter, sad she never got to pass the rosary on to a daughter of her own.*

The sound of a diesel engine coming along the road roused them. Deputy Begay arrived, jumped out of his vehicle, and waved at the tow truck driver to stop about a tenth of a mile down the road. "I saw a break in the trees back there where the truck can go cross-lots directly to the Bronco. I figured you wouldn't want him driving

173

through that old orchard." He trotted back down the road and started motioning the driver to follow him toward the wash.

Even over the grinding of gears, Millie could hear brush being crushed and mangled as the wrecker moved across the canyon. She put her hands over her ears and wavered back and forth about staying with Lydia or following Robby and St. Claire who were hurrying toward the Bronco.

"I'm staying here," Lydia pronounced. "I don't want anything more to do with this."

A raspy voice calling her name made Millie spin around. "*Señorita* Millie, what is happening here?" Antonio Gaspar was approaching with Carlos Lucero close behind.

For a moment, Millie was so surprised she could not form words. Mr. Gaspar's pickup was parked along the road where the path to the cliff began. The wrecker's noise and her absorption with the ruts it must be making on the fragile desert crust had masked their arrival.

"Oh, Mister Gaspar, how are you today?" It was the best Millie could come up with. "Mister Lucero, it's nice to see you again. You remember Lydia."

Without looking in Lydia's direction, Mr. Gaspar said, "Of course. Della says you should come to make bizcochitos with her." It sounded as if he'd rehearsed the line, perhaps as an excuse for dropping by. His dark eyes darted from Millie to the cabin to the tow truck now parked parallel with the wash. The big truck overshadowed the three uniformed figures next to it. Begay had his arm raised, signaling the driver.

Mr. Gaspar stepped around Millie and stretched as tall as he could. "What are those people doing?" Mr. Lucero moved to his side.

"We found the professor's car. They're pulling it out,"

Lydia said and began pouring cups of lemonade for the visitors.

"Yes, yes, Bailee told Della and me when you dropped her off yesterday that she found an old car." Mr. Gaspar grasped his companion's forearm. "Carlos, do you see what they are doing? They look like policemen, lady policemen."

"That's Detective St. Claire from the sheriff's office and Officer Ramirez, our BLM law enforcement officer," Millie offered.

"Why would they do that?" His voice was insistent, trailing off in a whine, reminding Millie of the way Ragged Ear demanded his supper.

"They want to check it for evidence, maybe there's something inside that might help uncover what happened to the professor," Millie said.

Mr. Lucero puffed out a dismissive whistle. "Bah, won't be nothin' in there. Why not just leave it there?"

They stood staring as a mechanical revving sound started up.

Lydia held out a cup, but Mr. Gaspar waved her away. "Let's go, Carlos. I don't want to be here when they bring that car up." Then he added, as if for Millie's sake, "That big truck's ripping up our land."

Millie and Lydia hardly heard the pickup leave. They watched the winch and cable working as the back of the Bronco slowly came into view. The passenger side door must have sprung open. It was flapping like a bird with a broken wing.

Lydia nudged Millie and handed her the cup of lemon-ade. "Let's go meet them when they get back to the road and say good riddance to anything and everything dealing with that poor man."

Millie took a sip and sucked in her lips. Bub Begay was right about a lack of sugar. "Good idea. Once that car's

175

gone, we can get back to work."

They strolled down the road to wait for the truck. Begay was the first to step onto the road. He looked both ways and motioned the driver to pull onto the road and stop. The Bronco was centered on the truck's flatbed. Millie's jaw dropped when she walked to the front and saw one headlight still intact. The corner of the other side was smashed in, but not as much as she had expected. When she first saw the vehicle, it looked like it had been rammed deep into the sandy bank. Instead, the desert had been reclaiming the eyesore, leaving only part of it visible.

The tow truck driver climbed up on the bed of the truck and tightened the front and back straps tying the vehicle down.

"Be sure those doors don't spring open again," St. Claire called to the driver. There was duct tape slapped across the passenger door as a temporary fix.

"Sorry ma'am, I didn't mean for that to happen," the driver said. He began wrapping a nylon strap over the top of the Bronco and back around the bottom of the front doors to ensure they remained closed.

"I don't think anything dropped out before we got that door taped shut, do you Robby?" St. Claire asked.

"Nope. I took a good look in there before he lifted it. Wasn't anything except a Saint Christopher's medal pinned to the visor. The ash tray was slid part way out. I scraped the contents into an evidence bag. A few coins, a toothpick, and some kind of a bead."

"A bead?" Lydia said, reaching for the bag. "Mind if I take it out and look at it?" She didn't wait for a response but began coaxing the small object out of the bag. She got hold of it between her thumb and index finger and held it up to eye level, turning this way and that. "It's another pearl, Millie. It's just like the one I found in the cabin. Here, look."

Millie accepted the pearl in the palm of her hand and cupped her other hand underneath to steady it. She gazed in the direction of the cabin, but was more aware of images, penciled notes, and an old man's voice reciting the story about a young bride's murder.

When she felt Lydia's tug on her arm, Millie came back to the present. "It's from the rosary. Doctor Bernnard found the rosary."

20. A Raven's Call

Time among the ancients invites us to better understand the entire landscape, and our relationship to it. Any archaeological site, whether petroglyph or pueblo, lithic scatter or lone object, invites us to stop and consider the surrounding environment.
— Bruce Hucko, *Time Among the Ancients*

Detective St. Claire and Deputy Begay drove off, following the Bronco strapped to the big transport back to Wellstown. Robby lingered by the remaining vehicles. She looked toward the cabin and the tumbled-down shed, then up and down the road. "This is one isolated place. I can't imagine living here without a neighbor in sight. Keep in mind that finding the Bronco is going to resurrect all the speculation about why the professor went missing. Be on the lookout for anybody driving by, going slow, watching what you are doing." With that she got in her patrol pickup and headed back to the office.

Lydia dragged a folding chair over to the shady side of the Suburban and plopped down. "I'm glad that's over, but it kind of scares me the way Robby keeps telling us to be careful."

Millie shuffled another chair adjacent to Lydia's and sat down, giving a sigh of relief. "Yeah, I know what you mean. Until whoever killed the professor is found, we can't assume we are safe working here. That's Robby's job, anticipating the worst."

"I suppose," Lydia said, "but we can't stand by the road watching vehicles go by. There are a few oil and gas field hands and ranchers on this road every day. And every once in a while people come to look at the petroglyphs on cliff.

Millie laughed, "That's what I was thinking. We can't wait at the road for the one vehicle to go by in an hour, maybe two an hour if it's a busy day. But that could change, I'm afraid. If word gets around that Doctor Bernnard found part of the rosary, which means he was on the right track to finding the cross, it'll stir up the treasure-hunters, and I'm including Doctor Bernnard's fellow historians in that category."

"Maybe not, Millie, maybe Professor Bernnard didn't find the rosary. It was just one pearl in the Bronco. Maybe he had been rooting around in that same pack rat nest where I found that other pearl. As far as we know, he was the only one that figured out the cross was attached to a rosary. He could have found that one bead anywhere around here."

"I hope you're right, Lyd. But what if he talked to somebody in town? His notes said he met with descen-

The Pearl Plot

dants of the homesteaders. That has to be Antonio and Della Gaspar. Or he could have called his history department about making progress on his research by finding the rosary. All those articles he wrote in professional journals makes it sound like finding the silver cross is the holy grail for Spanish colonization researchers."

Lydia shifted in her seat. "Then careful we'd better be. What Professor Bernnard was doing here is not that much different from what we're doing. And he got killed doing it."

They sat for a few more minutes, taking a break to let the morning's events settle.

Millie looked at her watch, "It's a couple of hours before quitting time. Let's take a walk around the cabin and plan what needs doing for next week. Another week, and we should be able to wrap up this field work."

Lydia began picking up the chairs and stacking them on top of the coolers in the back of the Suburban. "Yup, then the write-up begins. The job isn't finished until the paperwork is done—that's kind of the archaeologist's lament because nobody likes that part."

They were halfway to the cabin when someone drove up and parked next to the Suburban. The driver stepped out and gave a hearty wave.

Lydia poked Millie, "Hey, that looks like your boyfriend, Ben."

"Ben's not my boyfriend and that's not him," Millie countered, turning to meet the visitor.

"Seems like open-house day. We've been getting visitors all day. Glad I made sandwiches."

Millie anticipated this would be Lydia's first thought, get out the food. "Hold on, Lydia. Let's see what he wants."

The man was about Ben's age, but with a stouter build. A slight paunch pressing against his button-down cotton shirt and gray twill pants put him in the office-worker category.

As the visitor approached, he called out, "Ben Benallee told me to show up here. He said to go to the place where that man died. That could be any one of a dozen homesteads out here, but I knew just where he meant. I'm Kenneth Conroy."

Lydia grabbed his outstretched hand, shook it, and said, "You must be Ben's roommate from college that he told us about at the Gaspars' party. Now you're a professor researching Pueblo migrations."

"That's me. And you are Millie, the tall one, Ben told me," he said, shaking hands with Millie. She felt the man's charm woosh over her and saw that Lydia seemed about to hug him.

"Call me Kenny. Let's go look at the petroglyph cliff. It's one of my favorites."

Millie glanced at her watch again. This would be a good way to use the rest of a chaotic day. "Ben said you could give us more background on this site. Thanks for coming."

Lydia offered to get out the sandwiches left over from lunch, but Kenny declined the offer with a "maybe later" and headed toward the road.

When they passed Kenny's SUV, Millie stopped and pointed to the bumper. Lydia read out loud, "My life is in Ruins." She laughed and said, "I want one of those."

As they made their way along the path that led to the sheep pen, Kenny explained that he and Ben had met their first day at Northern Arizona University. Even though Ben was Navajo and Kenny a member of the Hopi tribe, they'd hit it off and palled around together for the next four years. "Ben will claim this place is *Dinétah*, Navajo homeland. That's true, but ancestral Puebloans lived here hundreds, perhaps thousands of years before the Navajo arrived around the 1300s. After that, it was mainly Navajos residing here. But my research shows considerable Pueblo influence in Lejos Canyon after the Spanish reconquest in 1692. I believe some of the people from the Rio Grande pueblos escaped and took refuge in Lejos Canyon. I'll show you Pueblo images here in the middle of *Dinétah*."

Kenny's assured stride along the path indicated he was familiar with the way. Even Millie had to lengthen her steps to keep up. Kenny was at the sheep pen resting his hand on the gate post by the time Lydia came puffing along.

Nothing had changed since Millie and Lydia's earlier visit, except the Russian thistle inside the old corral was much taller. The fast-growing cheat grass already had drooping seed heads that, in another month, would be dried out and scattering seeds.

Kenny pointed at the round shape just to the right of the pen that Millie had thought was a sun.

"See, up there, that is a Puebloan sun symbol with the four rays. It had to have been made by a Puebloan. Navajo suns have multiple rays extending in all directions."

He moved 30-feet along the cliff and pointed to a figure higher than even Millie could reach. "Now here's something I'm sure you will recognize."

Millie frowned. "It's a swastika. Why would that be here?"

Lydia took on a thinker pose, propping chin on her hand, elbow planted against her chest. "That's a trick question, Millie. Remember these petroglyphs were made before Europeans reached this far west."

Kenny chuckled, "It's easy to want to interpret rock art based on something familiar in our backgrounds. Humans have formed this symbol for thousands of years. Different cultures have given it different interpretations. For Hopis, it represents migration. Navajos call this whirling log. It can mean well-being or motion."

"Figured it would be something like that," Lydia said, "but what I wonder is how did who ever put it there reach up that high?"

"They might have used a log with stubs of branches or notches chipped out to make a kind of ladder. But you always have to remember that the ground where we stand today may have been lower or higher back then, due to wind or water eroding the ground away or depositing sand and debris against the rock." Kenny skirted around a sprawling prickly-pear cactus and continued pointing out panels. "What do these remind you of?"

"Crosses, but these are kind of angled sideways," Millie offered.

"Ah, that's the thing with rock art. From your Christian background, you see a cross. These are Navajo symbols for stars."

Lydia, still in her thinker pose, turned to Kenny. "There are different meanings to different viewers, but it all reveals human occupation in Lejos Canyon."

"Right. It is human to say, 'I was here, I exist. Here are representations of what is important to me.' Rock art, that term includes petroglyphs—which are chiseled, scraped, or pecked into stone—and pictographs which are painted on stone, exists all over the world. The human hand is the most common symbol found world-wide. Second most common are depictions of game animals and hunt scenes."

Kenny grinned, seeming to enjoy their interest. "Only the maker knows for sure what was intended. I turn around to see what the maker was seeing, what did the environment look like then." He turned his back to the cliff, crossed his arms, and took a wide-leg stance. "No doubt there was more grass and forbs covering the canyon floor before sheep and cattle grazing changed the vegetation make-up. But why was this particular site chosen, over the course of hundreds of years, to record messages in stone?"

Carvings in stone, messages meant to outlast the maker, to record what was important, for remembering, Millie thought to herself. She placed her hand flat against the enduring sandstone cliff and looked at the marks left by those who had passed through here. She felt the awe of knowing her life's span was just a short dash on the long line of individuals who walked on this ground.

Lydia mused, "We can find material evidence of past residents, like we've found pieces of glass, cutlery, and leather harness around the homestead, but only art and symbols tell us what people believed and valued. There are different meanings to different viewers, but it all reveals human occupation in Lejos Canyon."

"There's another way of knowing, not from things," Kenny said.

Millie shifted her attention back and forth between the cliff face and Kenny. "A better way?"

"Listening—listening to my elders. They tell of how our people originated, how to hunt for food, how to honor the kachinas for our welfare."

Kenny continued along the cliff where it curved somewhat inward, making a shallow alcove. When he stopped, he pointed out the human form etched into the rock with the long hair streaming to one side that Millie and Lydia had encountered earlier. "A child of the sixties might recognize this as an interpretation of someone experiencing visions. And there's the source, right over there."

Kenny angled away from the cliff and went to a massive cluster of dark green leaves with a half dozen white trumpet-shaped flowers, wilting in the daylight.

"Jimsonweed."

"*Datura wrightii*," Millie said.

Lydia joined them. "Is that the plant, Millie, that we saw before? The one you said is hallucinogenic. The flowers are beautiful. They'd make a nice bouquet, if they weren't so droopy."

"It's the same. We saw a smaller one by the sheep pen. The flowers open only at night because they're pollinated by moths."

Kenny stepped between Lydia and the bush. "Jimsonweed is not something you want to take chances with. All parts—leaves, roots, and seeds—can cause mind-altering reactions. The shamans, spiritual leaders, medicine men, call them what you will, they practiced inducing visions under carefully controlled conditions, coinciding with appropriate ceremonies. If not handled properly, users can be in serious trouble, maybe even die."

Millie's attention went from the plant, to the streaming thoughts figure on the wall, to Kenny. "You believe that picture represents someone that ingested jimsonweed?"

"Yes, possibly as a tea or ground up seeds. It allows the taker to experience visons not attainable in actual reality, sometimes telling the future."

Millie studied the figure. "There's more at work in human nature than five senses and replicable scientific experiments can reveal. The mind's imaginations and inspirations need to be considered."

Kenny pointed up. "I hope that raven doesn't let loose on this rock art. Their poop is acidic, really corrodes the stone surface."

The raven perched on the cliff top just above them. It let out a mighty caw that seemed to drop like a blanket over them.

Lydia clamped her hands over her ears. Millie gave

a knowing smile to the bird, thinking of the raven as a caretaker.

Kenny chuckled. "That bird just told me something very interesting. The Ancestral Puebloans may have chosen this particular place because of its acoustics. Did you notice how loud that raven's call was?"

Lydia agreed, "Really loud. It sounded like it was right next to my ear, not way up there."

Kenny looked up at the raven and said, "Thank you, raven friend. There is a recent trend among rock art enthusiasts called archaeoacoustics, to check whether a site may have especially good acoustics. Let's try it. On the count of three, clap your hands."

Each of them clapped, at slightly different times at first, but soon in synchrony. Sharp beats reverberated off the alcove walls.

The raven ruffled its feathers, then flapping hard, swooped away from the canyon wall and glided just above their heads.

Millie ducked and Lydia threw her arms over her head.

Kenny seemed frozen in place. "I've never seen a raven come so close. Some peoples consider the raven a messenger. It doesn't want this sacred place disturbed."

Lydia un-wrapped her arms but held them out as if to ward off another attack. "It makes sense that people who use oral tradition to pass down knowledge would choose a site like this for ceremonies with singing and chanting."

Millie kept her eye on the raven which was circling high above them. It dropped out of sight, between their location and the road. It must have landed on the big boulder with the nude rock art carving.

"I know what you're looking at, Millie," Kenny said and laughed. "That's an example of what we call sheepherder art, but I have a little trouble calling that particular one 'art.' Let's go take a look."

Millie tried hard not to look at Lydia when they arrived at the big boulder. She wanted to avoid falling into a giggling fit like the first time they encountered the life-size figure portraying a nude woman in a relaxed pose, one arm dangling over a bent knee, fingers holding what appeared to be a cigarette. Millie concentrated on the way two large juniper trees on each side of the boulder seemed to frame the figure. This would be a pleasant place to rest in the shade. Lydia managed to let out only a muffled chuckle.

Kenny stood back and looked the boulder up and down. Finally, he shrugged and said, "I have a question for you. Is this graffiti? I mean, the petroglyphs on the cliff face indicate this is a sacred place. This, on the other hand, is more like doodlings of a bored person."

"If it happened today, it would be considered graffiti, destruction of a cultural site even," Lydia declared. "But this is more than fifty years old, so it falls under protection of the 1966 National Historic Preservation Act. Besides there's nothing against a lonely sheepherder making himself some pretty company."

Millie pointed to the letters next to the 1924 date. "This name looks like Gaspar. That's the family that owned the homestead before it went to the BLM. And I ended up renting a house from their descendants before I even laid eyes on the homestead."

"I want to talk to you more about that. But wait, see up there?" Kenny was pointing to a hole less than a foot from the top edge of the boulder. The two-inch round cavity was chipped around its edges. "It wasn't there the last time I was here. That's what we call a bubba-glyph."

"Huh?" said Lydia.

"A what?" added Millie.

"A bubba-glyph occurs when some Bubba with a rifle feels the need to make his or her mark on the rock, as well. Kind of monkey-see, monkey-do behavior. Now let's go find those sandwiches that Lydia mentioned when I first got here." Kenny's laugh was echoed by Millie and Lydia.

"But first, I've got to get that darn cheat grass out of my sock." Kenny sat down in the shade of one of the junipers, pulled his left boot off, and worked the offending sharp seed out of his sock. "I hate cheat grass." He got his boot back on, stood up, and ground the oat-sized nemesis into the sand. "That won't kill the damn thing, but it won't get me again. Hey, want to hear my cheat grass song? Me and Ben made it up once when we were out hiking. Here goes:

Oh how I hate cheat grass,
let me count the ways.
I hate it in my socks,
It plugs up gate locks,
It gets in my lunch box,
I've even seen it on a fox."

***

Back by the parked vehicles and sitting in one of the not-quite-trusty camp chairs, Millie watched Kenny devour the remaining three sandwiches and take the last celery stick from the veggie tray that Lydia pushed toward him, saying, "I can see why you and Ben were friends in college. You both like to eat!"

"We've been known to make a couple all-you-can-eat lunch places change their signs," Kenny mumbled and kept chewing.

When he finished eating and waved away Lydia's offer of a second cup of lemonade, Millie said, "Thanks for coming today. You've given us a deeper understanding for interpreting this landscape."

"There is something I want you both to know." Kenny's voice had changed, becoming solemn. "It is a good thing that the Bureau of Land Management made this land exchange with the homestead's private owners. It is a good thing that you study what is here, make a written record of human occupation of this location. What you must not do is make this a public site. It must not appear on the BLM website for recreation places. No signs. There must be no disturbance to the sacred rock art."

Stunned silence followed his almost chant-like words, as if the man were channeling spirits that resided here. The profound silence returned that Millie had experienced the day she put herself in the new bride's shoes. The silence that Rosalinda had lived with each day until her José came home.

Millie followed Kenny's gaze toward the red cliffs across the road, looming above the piñon and juniper, soon to hide the sun and put the sheep pen in shadow.

The sound of ripping canvas yanked them back to the present. Kenny struggled out of the lawn chair that was slowly dropping his behind toward the earth.

"What the hell?" Kenny yelped, struggled to stand up, and kicked the disintegrating chair. He turned at the outburst of giggles from Lydia and Millie.

Kenny shrugged and began laughing too. Perhaps to cover his embarrassment, he addressed Millie with, "You ever been to a pow wow? I bet you'll like the one tomorrow."

"What pow wow?" Millie asked.

"Ben's taking you to the pow wow at the fairgrounds. When he called about coming here, he told me about you."

"That figures," Millie mumbled. She expected to see Ben this weekend, but this was news to her. "Want to come, Lydia?"

Kenny gave a slight shake of his head. Lydia took the hint.

"Nope, three's a crowd. Plus, my date is in Della Gaspar's kitchen. We're going to make bizcochitos." Lydia smacked her lips and made a mmm sound.

"It's not a date. Ben's just a friend." Millie ignored the smirk that Lydia exchanged with Kenny. But she looked at her watch and started planning what to wear for tomorrow.

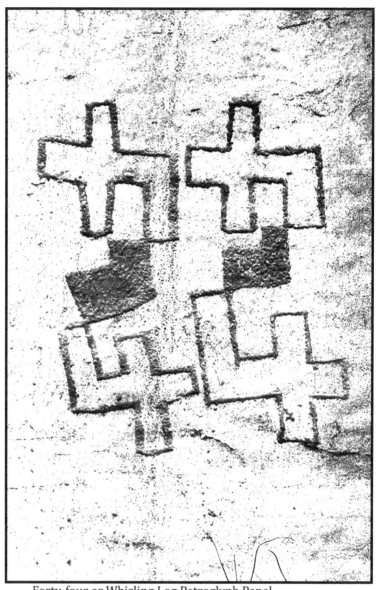

Forty-four or Whirling Log Petroglyph Panel

21. Pow Wow

It is not length of life, but depth of life.
— Ralph Waldo Emerson, American Philosopher, 1803–1882

Millie slipped on the silver bracelet with the yucca designs, looked in the mirror, debated a moment, then undid the top button on her turquoise blouse. "Don't look at me like that, Ragged Ear. I can dress up every once in a while. And promise, I'll be back in time for your supper." She picked up the cat and pushed him out the front door.

Ben pulled into her driveway and responded to Millie's "good morning" with a high-spirited "*yá'át'ééh.*" Ben's red Miata looked like it had just been washed and waxed. "Ready for your first pow wow, New Jersey girl?"

"So are you going to tell me where we're going, and why I should want to go to a pow wow?" Millie teased.

He sent a dazzling grin in her direction. "You'll like it. This is Spring's first time dancing at a pow wow. Spring's mom is my Auntie Elaine. You met her last summer at Sheep Camp."

"Your little niece? She's just a little tyke."

"She's in the Tiny Tots division. It's for four- and five-year-olds. She's so excited. This is a contest pow wow, more for entertainment, not like a real traditional cere-mony on the reservation. This one is at the fairgrounds, inside the big coliseum where they have horse shows and stuff."

"Um, doesn't that make it a little messy for dancing?"

"Don't worry. The arena gets cleaned up and the dirt packed down. And there'll be lots of booths set up outside selling jewelry and food and supplies for pow wow outfits. We can get a smoked turkey leg for lunch."

"I was hoping for fry bread."

"Oh, they'll have that too. Theirs will be round, not like the one you made last summer at Sheep Camp."

"Yeah well, you ate it all, didn't you?" Millie was start-ing to get used to the Navajo way of friendly teasing that she'd experienced at that pot luck up in the mountains. Her first attempt at patting fry bread into shape landed on the ground. Her second fry bread came out lopsided, but Ben had pretended to admire it anyway.

A half hour later, Ben pulled into a parking lot big enough to serve a major league baseball stadium. He passed by the area marked off for large vehicles. It was crowded with campers ranging from tiny to deluxe. A few pickups with horse trailers were parked among the campers.

Millie said, "I'm seeing license plates from Oklahoma, Wyoming, and Arizona."

"Sure, this is one of the big events, with big prizes. Some of those with the big rigs follow the pow wow circuit all season. They need a place to change between events. Their outfits are expensive and sometimes passed down from one generation to the next. A lot of the time you can tell which tribe the dancers are from by the regalia they are wearing."

Ben parked in the area designated for non-contestants and ushered Millie toward the large coliseum building. They passed tents and tables displaying items for sale. Millie stopped at one offering materials for making dance outfits. She was dazzled by the array of beads, sequins, feathers, porcupine quills, and soft leather hides.

Ben tapped her shoulder, "Come on. We need to find Grandfather Sageman. He hasn't done very much since Grandmother passed last winter."

"Oh, that dear lady is gone? I'm so sorry, Ben." Millie touched her fingers together remembering the feel of the willow basket Emma Sageman gave her. It must have been one of the last baskets the woman made, making it even more treasured.

"Yeah," Ben's voice quavered, "she loved her sheep and knew all about which plants are used for what. Spring's mother and her brothers are in the Grand Entry, so you and me are going to keep Grandfather company."

It took a few moments for her eyes to adjust inside the large building, but Millie liked the earthy smell of the dirt arena and expectant buzz coming from the gathering crowd. They made their way along the bleachers raised above the arena and found Mr. Sageman sitting on a bottom row, holding his walking stick between his knees to avoid tripping passersby. Upon spotting Ben, the elder's face broke into the same fetching grin as his grandson's. Millie stepped forward and Mr. Sageman stood up to shake her hand, holding it for a moment, letting fondness flow between them. "Ben tells me you are working next to the Lejos Canyon petroglyphs. This is an important place to us Navajos."

"Yes, sir. Kenny Conroy told us about some of the meanings." Millie made her voice cheerful, trying to cover up the shock she felt at the difference in this bent and desolate man compared to his appearance last summer. He looked as if he had lost half his heart.

At the rattle and screech of a microphone, Ben sat down next to his grandfather and patted the spot next to him for Millie. "The Grand Entry is about to start."

A thunderous drumming came from the arena floor below their seats. The sudden roar made Millie sit back, but then she leaned forward to see six men clustered around a broad-surfaced drum. Four more drum circles were spaced around the arena. A tall man wearing a black cowboy hat, pearl button shirt, jeans, and pointy-toe boots strode to the arena's center. "*Yá'át'ééh*, wel—," screech from the microphone.

The drummers softened their sound, tapping gently with their leather covered drumsticks making a tremulous sound. The Head Man started again and the drummers paused. "Welcome ladies and gentlemen, please stand. Host drum, bring in the dancers!" The nearby drums rumbled again. A young man dressed in buckskins stepped into the arena. Feathers and fur pelts dangled from the staff he carried, which was twice as tall as himself. Men, women, and children of all ages followed, stepping in time with the drums.

Millie had never seen such colorful costumes and pageantry. Three, four, or five abreast, families and singles followed the head dancer. "There's Spring." Ben pointed to the pair moving toward them. Spring's shiny yellow silk dress reached to her ankles, allowing just her moccasins and a few inches of white buckskin leg wrappings to show. She stepped in unison with her mother until she spotted Mr. Sageman, Ben, and Millie. She stopped, tugged her mother's arm, pointed, and waved. The dancers behind her skirted around and moved on. Her mom nudged her along. Ben whispered, "My auntie isn't dancing this year. She used to. Now she's helping little Spring learn. That's why she just threw on a shawl to be part of the Grand Entry."

The dancers progressed solemnly. All the while, the drummers kept a steady beat, a rhythm that has stirred mankind to movement and ceremony since the beginning of time. Older women moved with great dignity, holding a silk or woolen shawl folded over one arm. A few senior men were dressed to perform, but others walked in regular jeans and western-style shirts just to be part of the celebration of their tribal history and culture.

Millie felt a poke from Ben when two men in their fifties passed by. They seemed to be making unsuccessful attempts to pull in pot bellies that rolled over their belt buckles. Millie ignored him, giving her full attention to the spectacle proceeding around the arena.

Lithe young men and teenagers pranced and twirled, full of energy and eager to show off their prowess to protect their tribe, just like their ancestors. Young women and teens glimmered and shone with internal pride, wearing exquisitely crafted costumes. The little tykes, dressed like the grown-ups at their side, tried their best to replicate their steps.

By the time the last group entered, the flow of colors nearly encircled the arena. The drumming stopped as the

Head Man walked back to the center. "Please stand. The Shiprock High School R-O-T-C cadets will now present the colors." Ben helped his grandfather up. Two teenage girls bearing an American flag and the New Mexico yellow flag with red Zia symbol marched into the arena, followed by pairs of boys or girls carrying parade rifles. The color bearers held their flags at attention while the team marched in place, spun their rifles, and clicked their heels together in an intricate precision drill. Millie watched with awe at how confidently the young people carried themselves in their trim uniforms.

The drill team finished and the Head Man spoke again. "We are privileged to have Miss Navajo Nation here today. She will now lead us in the Pledge of Allegiance."

Millie ogled the college-age woman's crown and wide, beaded sash. Miss Navajo took the microphone and began reciting, "I pledge..." The crowd joined in, hands over their hearts. Mr. Sageman straightened and snapped his hand to his forehead in a salute to the flag. Ben whispered, "Grandfather was a Marine in the Korean War."

The crowd's earnest recital ended, the flag bearers led the way out of the arena, and the Head Man began to introduce the drum circles. "Take it away Northern Navajo drummers from Shiprock." The drummers pounded out thunder accompanied by an ear-splitting yell. Millie flinched. Ben laughed, "They're just getting warmed up." A similar zealous rumble erupted from each of the other drum groups as they were introduced, one from Gallup, one from Utah, and two from Arizona.

"Thank you, thank you." The Head Man took over. "Let's have the Teen Traditional Dancers into the arena. Teen Traditional, get ready. Meanwhile, folks, remember to support the vendors outside that bring us eats and treats." As the teen boys shuffled in, pretending to be nonchalant about the whole business, the Head Man entertained the crowd. "Ever notice when geese fly in a V formation, one side is always longer than the other?"

Millie, along with those around her nodded yes, that's a familiar sight. He continued, "That's because there are more geese on that side." Millie joined the crowd with a groan.

Ben laughed, "Nobody has worse jokes than a pow wow announcer."

At a call to the drum circle, the pounding beat started up again. The dancers burst into action. Decorated in feathers, furs, and beads, the dancers whirled, leaped, dropped to one knee, sprang up, and continued in feverish movement.

Sageman grumbled just loud enough for Ben and Millie to hear, "Pfft, those young 'uns just showing off in all those fancy outfits. Act like they got ants in their pants jumping around like that."

Millie soaked up the pageantry, shifting her attention from dancers in the arena to observing the other, mostly Native American, watchers sitting in the bleachers. Youngsters squirming and escaping from relatives' arms, grandmothers adjusting cushions on their seats, a steady flow of people sidling out of their row and coming back carrying drinks and tantalizing-smelling food.

When Ben asked if she was ready for lunch, Millie said, "You bet."

Ben helped his grandfather up and they made their way out into bright sunshine. The vendors were doing brisk business, especially the food booths. Ben led the way to his aunt's camper. "This is Spring's mom, Elaine. She's my Auntie Louise's sister." After this quick introduction, Ben asked Millie and his grandfather what they wanted to drink, and trotted off to get lunch.

Millie shook Elaine's hand. "I remember meeting you at Sheep Camp last summer." Spring came around the camper and presented herself in front of Millie. Taking the hint, Millie said, "Spring, you were the prettiest dancer out there." The little girl's giggle made Mr. Sageman laugh.

They settled into lawn chairs and chatted about the weather and Millie's work at the homestead. When Ben returned, Kenny Conroy was at his side. Kenny shook hands with Mr. Sageman and offered his condolences on the loss of his wife. He greeted Elaine and admired Spring's shiny dress. When he got to Millie, Kenny said, "Watch out for Ben here, he's been known to steal food right off your plate." He winked at Ben.

Ben laughed and waved to his long-time friend as Kenny moved off in the direction of the coliseum. Ben passed around paper plates, napkins, and bundles of plastic utensils. Then he distributed the hugest drumsticks and pickles that Millie had ever seen. Elaine pulled a strip of meat from her turkey leg and put it on a plate for Spring.

Millie eyed the little girl who was weaving in and out around their chairs and sporadically practicing a hop on one foot. But she managed to carry the plate and munch on the turkey without smudging her treasured outfit.

"What was your favorite dance?" Elaine asked.

With a nod to Spring, Millie said, "Well, the tiny tots did the best job, but after that, I thought the shawl dance was amazing. The way those girls combined such fancy steps and swirled those beautiful fringed shawls at the same time looked like a field of wildflowers twirling in the wind."

Elaine smiled, "That was my favorite, too, when I used to perform. I'm saving my best shawl for when Spring is older."

Millie settled in her chair, crossed her legs, and

watched her toe dip in rhythm with the drum beats that still sounded in her head. She felt in harmony with the sun, delicious food, and present company. If she were back home at a family backyard get-together, it would probably be raining and relatives would be asking whether she had acquired a suitable marriage prospect yet.

Mr. Sageman cleared his throat. "These pow wows, Millie, they are nothing like a real ceremony. Those fellows hoot and holler like they think they're real warriors. Ha, they're wearing plastic beads and waving around feathers that somebody picked up in a chicken pen."

"I don't know, Grandfather," Ben said, "I'd rather see them using poultry feathers than eagle feathers."

Mr. Sageman countered with, "It used to be that capturing an eagle for its feathers, taking only a few and releasing it, was a sign of bravery."

"That's when there used to be more eagles—and more game—and a lot fewer people. Our wildlife department fines people for poaching game out of season. Molesting eagles is even more of an offense. It's sad to see such magnificent birds shot at just for their feathers."

"I know, I know, Grandson. It's a good thing these dancers don't use the genuine article. Everything's changed." Mr. Sageman sighed and set his plate aside.

Ben grabbed his grandfather's half-eaten turkey leg and added it to his plate. "I'm glad I didn't have to catch an eagle with my bare hand to prove myself in the old days. We got a call just last week about a big Golden eagle hit by a car. When we got there, it was flopping around on the side of the road. It took two of us to capture that dude. My partner threw a blanket over it and I used leather gloves to grab it by the legs. It still got me on the wrist." Ben turned his wrist upward, showing a red welt.

Spring went over to Ben and patted his hand.

"I'm okay, kiddo, it didn't hurt, much," Ben assured her.

Millie's eyes were wide. "What did you do with it?"

"We wrestled it into a big dog carrier and took it to the raptor rehabilitation center. If it can heal enough to fly, it'll be released back into its former territory. If it's too badly mangled and can't be saved, the feathers will be sent to the Fish and Wildlife Service. Tribal members can request them for religious ceremonies."

Millie admired Ben's gentle words to his niece and his dedication to protecting wildlife. But now he was leaning over and checking out her plate. To Millie's amazement, she had already eaten the monstrous turkey leg down to the bone.

Elaine stood up and folded her chair, causing the others to stir. Ben helped her move items back into the camper while Millie gathered empty plates and took them to a trash bin. They strolled back to the coliseum, where the drumming and dancing were as energetic as ever.

For part of the afternoon, Elaine and Spring sat on one side of Millie, with Ben and his grandfather on the other. When Spring's wriggling turned into pestering, Elaine picked up the tired girl and took their leave. Another family took their place, giving Millie a reason to shift close to Ben. Not long after, Mr. Sageman was ready to leave, so Ben and Millie walked with him to the parking lot. With a nod to them both, the elder climbed into his pickup and made his lonely way home.

Ben yawned and Millie rubbed her back, a mutual agreement to call it quits after enough hours sitting on bleachers. On the way back to Millie's place, Ben talked more about problems with poaching wildlife, from wounding trophy elk to collectors that snuck onto the reservation to catch lizards and snakes for the black-market reptile trade. As Ben pulled into Millie's driveway, he pronounced, "It'll rain tomorrow, you know."

Millie laughed, "There's not a cloud in the sky."

"You'll see," Ben said. "When you get all those Indians dancing like that, it's sure to rain."

"Gawd, Ben. Only you would say something like that." Millie liked that they could joke with each other. "What adventure do you have in mind for next weekend."

Ben reached for her hand. "I'll think of something."

She thread her fingers through his. "It'll be hard to top the pow wow, Ben. But I'm game for whatever you come up with."

They sat in companiable silence until Ragged Ear leaped onto the Miata's hood and looked through the windshield. He settled directly in front of Ben and stared at him with piercing golden eyes. And stared.

Ben let loose of her hand and said, "All right, all right, go feed that damn cat."

Millie gave his hand a quick squeeze and got out. She used both arms to lift the big cat off the car. At the porch, she turned and watched Ben back down the driveway. He gave a wave and was off. Ragged Ear pushed his face against her chin, reclaiming her attention. His rumbling purr felt like the tremulous drumbeats at the pow wow. Or maybe it was her pounding heart she was feeling.

22. Rain, It Did

New Mexico's average rainfall is 13.9 inches.
— New Mexico State University Climate

Millie was surprised to wake up in the morning to see raindrops splattering the driveway. By afternoon, she was staring out the window at a steady rain. Her phone rang; it was Mrs. Gaspar inviting her over for snacks. She had expected a few people to come by after church, but so far it seemed the rain had discouraged any visitors. It didn't matter to Millie whether Mrs. Gaspar had prepared too much food or just thought she may be lonely, she welcomed the invitation to break up the dreary day. Millie put on a raincoat and headed next door.

When Millie stepped up on the veranda, she saw a

table with much more than snacks. It was loaded with a crock pot, a stack of tortillas covered with plastic wrap, a few casserole dishes, and a big tray of bizcochitos. Mrs. Gaspar said, "Help yourself to a plate, dear. Don't mind me not getting up. I got all this food ready and now you're the only one who's come to eat it. Guess no one wants to get out in this rain."

Her husband responded with, "Don't complain, Della. This rain makes the chile grow."

Millie laid her wet raincoat behind one of the wicker chairs, filled a bowl out of the crock pot, got a tortilla, and added a heap of salad to her plate.

"Thanks. This posole is just the thing for a day like this." A few weeks ago, Millie would have felt the need to make conversation. Now she just let the posole's green chile warm her insides and took comfort in sitting quietly with her neighbors, friends, and landlords all rolled into one.

Millie expected Mr. Gaspar's usual question to come anytime—how are things at the Peralta Ranch? But no, the first to speak was Mrs. Gaspar. "That was a handsome young man who brought you home yesterday, Millie."

Whatever she said next, Millie knew, would get passed on to Momma Agnes. "That was Ben Benallee, he took me to the pow wow at the fairgrounds. That's the neatest thing I've ever seen. We—"

She was interrupted by a loud screech of brakes from a vehicle arriving in the driveway, then spasmodic revving of an out-of-tune engine before it was shut off.

"Carlos is here," Mrs. Gaspar said. "That's his old turquoise rattletrap of a truck."

A minute later, Mr. Gaspar called out, "Come in out of the rain, *mi amigo.*"

The tall man ducked into the veranda, taking two

steps at a time.

Millie hoped she'd be as spry as Mr. Lucero when she was in her eighties. When she first met Carlos Lucero, she thought he could pass for one of the *Zorro* movie characters, with his trim goatee and iron gray hair. She could picture him with a red sash around his waist bowing to a beautiful lady dressed with lace and emeralds.

Now he was bowing to her. "How are you, *Señorita* Millie?"

"I'm just fine, Mister Lucero," Millie declared.

He stepped back and with an exaggerated frown said, "Now how many times have I told you to call me Carlos? Or am I going to have to address you as Madam Whitehall all the time?"

Millie giggled. "I can't help it, ah... Carlos. It's just hard for us easterners to get used to being so informal with our elders."

"Ha, elder, she calls me. What do you think of that, Antonio? Are we elders?"

Her landlord laughed. "Well, she can call me Mister if she wants to. I am older than you, Carlos."

Mrs. Gaspar took up the teasing. "I'm surprised you made it, Carlos. It's a miracle that old truck of yours would even start in this wet weather."

Her husband chimed in with, "Why don't you get rid of that pile of rust. Maybe get something with all the conveniences of this century, like air conditioning?"

Mrs. Gaspar followed with, "Ah, he won't sell that old junker. It's a classic."

Millie watched the back and forth among old friends. She figured this conversation had occurred about as often as the red versus green chile dispute.

Carlos stretched his long legs across the veranda. "Now how could I impress the girls with some ordinary, run-of-the-mill BMW? They stopped making the F100 in 1960. Let me tell you, that turquoise beauty turns the ladies' heads when I drive through town. I bought that Ford truck the same day I proposed to Viola. I think it was that pretty turquoise color that won her over. I paid it off two years later."

Mention of his deceased wife curbed the conversation for a while. They watched the rain sheet off the roof and splatter on the edge of the veranda's tile floor. Millie had adopted the New Mexican pastime of just enjoying gazing at precious rain nourishing the earth.

In time, the question came that Millie knew would— how are things at the Peralta Ranch?

"Mmph," Millie swallowed her third cookie, "you were there when they pulled that SUV out of the wash. It was Bailee who saw it first, an old Ford Bronco. We found a little prehistoric ruin across Lejos Wash from the cabin, too."

"What were you doing so far from the cabin?" Mr. Gaspar jerked around to face Millie.

Mrs. Gaspar laughed, "Tony hears better when he sees a person's lips."

"Looking for the Old Spanish Trail. Bailee told Lydia and me about the Armijo mule train that went through Lejos Canyon back in the mid-eighteen hundreds. It took goods from Santa Fe to California."

Carlos pulled his legs back, leaned forward, and asked, "That SUV in the wash, was there anything special about it?"

Millie shrugged, "Looked like something on the back seat, that's all." She didn't want to admit the way they'd skedaddled out of there after finding it.

"Still don't think you should be traipsing around and not doing your work at the cabin."

"But Mister Gaspar, we were." Millie felt a little annoyed at being told what she should be doing. "It's important to investigate all aspects of the site, how it ties into the history of the state and local communities. We want to make the strongest case possible to get it on the National Register."

Carlos came to Millie's defense. "Never mind, Antonio. It's nothing to worry about. I mean, that's pretty common around here. Used to be how people would get rid of junk, just dump it in a wash."

The rain let up to a slight mist. Millie stood and said, "I'd better check on Ragged Ear. He wouldn't go outside this morning in the rain." As she left, Mrs. Gaspar was taking food back inside and the two old friends were huddled together in earnest discussion.

Millie figured they were probably back to the best chile debate. But she wondered why they weren't more interested in the Old Spanish Trail since they seemed so keen on history of the area.

23. Stay Away

The New Mexico Legislature adopted the biscochito (bizcochito) as the official state cookie in 1989. This act made New Mexico the first state to have an official state cookie.

— New Mexico Secretary of State, About New Mexico

A couple of puddles remained on the porch from the previous day's rainstorm, causing Ragged Ear to refuse to go out. He dodged around the living room then under the bed. Millie gave up, grabbed her lunch and coffee cup, and started down the driveway, relieved for once that Lydia was her usual late self. The sky was especially blue after the rain and the air felt fresh but chilly. She went back inside to get a flannel outer shirt and pulled it on as she trotted toward the Suburban just pulling up.

Before Millie even got the seatbelt fastened, Lydia held out two bizcochito cookies. "You spent Saturday in the Gaspars' kitchen? How many dozens did you make?"

"Enough so I had two big packages to send off to my boys. Della let me have the Blue Bird flour sack. She said people like to make aprons and things with them. I even kept the string." Lydia seemed more buoyant than ever after her weekend devoted to her favorite pursuits, cooking and mothering.

"You've got a thing for string, Lyd. Mmmm, these are, ah, interesting."

"I added my own secret twist and I'm not going to tell anybody what it is." Lydia steered around a branch blown onto the road during the rainstorm. "Now, tell me all about your weekend."

Millie pretended not to hear. Whatever she told Lydia would get to Momma Agnes in no time, then throughout the office.

"Come on, spill the beans, how'd it go with Ben?" Lydia pried, then added, "Do you like the sour cream I put in the cookie dough, that's what makes them soft. Don't tell Della, she wouldn't like anybody upstaging her cooking. She wants me to show her how to make hush puppies."

"Sour cream, huh, that's what makes these so different." Millie couldn't hold in her excitement any longer. "The pow wow was the most awesome thing I've ever seen. It went on all day. Dances for men, women, and kids of all ages. Costumes, colors, and the drums! The drums, I can still feel them pounding in my heart."

The sloppy, wet Lejos Canyon road made for slow going, but Millie was still talking about the pow wow when they arrived at the homestead, mostly because Lydia persisted on extracting every detail, especially regarding the food and Ben's every move.

As Lydia opened her door, she said, "And you ate a whole turkey leg, a whole turkey leg. Smoked turkey. I want to go to a pow wow."

Millie got out and drew a deep breath, taking in the petrichor, the incomparable scent of wet earth mixed with the fragrance of sagebrush pelted by yesterday's rain. She felt good, positive, ready to finish recording the homestead and moving on to the next step of making it an officially designated historical site. Last week's upheaval of finding the professor's car, watching it pulled out of the sand bank, and Robby's warnings seemed washed away.

Still, she sensed a whisper of concern about Kenny Conroy's admonition that the sacred rock art not become a public spectacle. Would making the homestead a national historical point of interest result in sightseers tromping all over the grounds? What if it became something like Bailee Fernandez's crazy idea to "monetize" history by recreating Old Spanish Trail mule-train tours. Or worse, the location goes viral on Instagram for adventure seekers showing off for selfies inside the cabin. *No, no way could Bailee's vision of big signs, paved paths, and playing up tales of ghosts and murder ever come to pass.*

"What's that?" Lydia was pointing to something white on the ground next to the path to the cabin. "That wasn't there last week."

They walked over to see a pile of soggy cloth. Millie lifted the edge with the toe of her boot. A beetle staggered out from underneath the cloth and scurried off to freedom. Sequins sparkled as Millie gabbed a handful of silky-looking fabric and lifted it to shoulder height.

"What in the world?" Lydia exclaimed.

Millie shook and spread the cloth until she could grasp the dress by the shoulder seams, facing her. "It looks like a wedding dress."

"A wedding dress," Lydia repeated. "What's it doing here?"

"Good question. It's wet and muddy, but looks like it was pretty at one time."

Millie turned the gown to face Lydia. She gave it a once-over with a practiced eye and said, "Style looks a little old, like maybe ten or twenty years out-of-date."

Still holding it up, Millie ran her fingers along the neckline. "Look, here's a tag. Ha, it says Animal Rescue Thrift Store, fifteen dollars. It's from a second-hand store."

Lifting the skirt, Lydia remarked, "The hem is really muddy. Oops, here's a safety pin tucking in the waist a couple of inches." She felt the other side. "It was pinned here, too. Whoever wore it last was a lot smaller than whoever it was made for."

Millie draped the gown over a sagebrush, lifting and spreading the skirt to dry out. "Kind of sad to see a once very special dress thrown aside like this."

"You're not thinking about wedding dresses are you now, Miss Millie, after your weekend with that cute boyfriend?" Lydia teased.

"That's crazy, Lydia. And this is crazy," Millie said, pointing to the white dress.

Lydia chuckled, then remarked, "Robby said to be on the lookout for anything unusual. Bet she didn't have a wedding dress in mind. Wait till she hears somebody left a wedding dress here."

Millie scrutinized the path. "It's more like somebodies, not somebody, were here," she said. Slight impressions of human tracks still showed after the hard rain. At least three or four people had been on the path. She looked around, to see if there was anything else amiss. The door to the outhouse hung open, it didn't look right.

"That door on the outhouse wasn't open when we left last week, was it?" Millie whispered.

"I don't think so," Lydia said, "but the wind with that

rainstorm was pretty strong."

They walked toward the small outbuilding that stood halfway between the cabin and the fallen-down barn. They stopped. Lydia gasped. She read the words scrawled on the outside of the unsecured door.

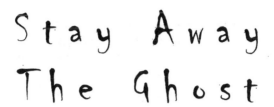

Stay Away
The Ghost

"What happened? Who did that!"

Millie looked at Lydia's anguished face. "Somebody put spray paint on that old door. That's vandalism, just plain mean vandalism."

The outhouse door silently swung partially closed.

"Um, how come the door closed like that?" Lydia whispered.

"I don't know." Millie kept her voice low, trying to sound calm. "You stay here. I'm going to go around and try to get a look inside."

Millie stepped off the path and angled into sagebrush until she could look into the narrow opening between the defaced door and frame of the outhouse. She could see enough, due to shafts of sunlight between the weathered boards, to determine that no one was inside. She motioned to Lydia, then walked over and pushed the door open. They glanced around the inside. Lydia walked around the outside. Nothing else was disturbed. Millie hooked the door closed and motioned toward the cabin. Leery of what they might find inside, they moved in silence.

Shoulder to shoulder, they leaned into the doorway.

"I don't see anybody," Lydia whispered, then in a normal voice, "I'll check the other rooms."

"Wait, don't step in there." Millie grabbed her arm. "Look." Footprints marked the floor in all directions. Protected from the rain inside the cabin, the prints were well defined, showing deep treads like hiking shoes have.

Lydia groaned when she saw a three-foot gaping hole in the outer wall. Two of the wall boards were broken, leaving a splintered ends. The missing pieces lay on the floor near the pack rat nest in the corner, along with the clothesline that someone had yanked out, breaking the board it had been attached to for decades.

Millie said, "Let's go around and look in the kitchen window."

"Look, they tried to mess with the stove," Lydia said. "There're muddy tracks all around it. Probably tried to tip it over. But that old cast iron stove didn't budge. Ha, it's set there for more than a hundred years. Nobody's going to disturb that old relic."

Millie patted Lydia's arm, reassuring herself as much as Lydia, that they could handle this incursion. "At least, they didn't use their spray paint cans in here. And the clowns probably left finger prints all over that stove. Footprints and fingerprints, Robby's going to love this."

"And a wedding dress, don't forget the wet wedding dress," Lydia added, lifting their mood a bit. Then her face clouded over, "We haven't looked in the root cellar yet."

It was Millie's turn to groan. "Um, we're not going to until Robby gets here, right?"

"Right," Lydia seconded.

"I want to look around to see if there's other damage or tracks the rain didn't wash out before calling Robby." They headed toward the orchard. She stepped over a spray paint can dropped on the path to the orchard. "Looks like they ran out of paint. That's probably why the cabin escaped their ugly messages." She reached down to pick it up, but then thought better of it. "Better leave this until Robby gets here." Instead, she toed it a couple of inches until its garish front-side label rolled into view. "Day-Glo Neon Red—can't get any uglier than that."

Continuing on, they passed a crumpled bottle of mineral water tossed next to the path and stepped over what looked like the remains of a hand-rolled cigarette.

Lydia followed Millie, a little closer than usual. "I've got the keys, Millie. Anytime you're ready to go, let's get down the road to where there's cell ser—"

A wail from Millie drowned Lydia's words.

"Damn it, damn it, damn it." Millie stood with hands on her hips, surveying broken limbs and splintered stumps that had been kicked repeatedly to knock them over. "Those assholes, look what they've done." She walked so fast into the orchard that Lydia had to trot to keep up.

"Here," she pointed to scrape marks on the trunk of one of the healthiest-looking apple trees, "somebody climbed up here." She walked around the tree, peering up into the leafy branches. "These branches have been cut, ten or twelve inches cut off each of them, leaves and all."

"That's weird. Why would anybody do that?" Lydia stretched up to look where Millie was pointing.

Millie walked farther into the orchard. "Ha, that's what I was afraid of, look at this, Lyd. This peach tree, same thing." Standing on tiptoes, Millie reached for a branch and angled it down so Lydia could see.

Lydia looked at the amputated branch, which oozed a drop of sap. "Uh-huh, looks the same, the end is cut off."

"Those vandals weren't satisfied just to deface historical structures; they clipped these branches like they planned to graft them on other fruit trees. Let me check the other trees."

Millie wove in and out among the last three rows, ignoring trees with mostly dead branches and looking closely at the more vigorous looking ones. "I spot three trees that have been clipped. All these had set some fruit, not real productive, but still, I really wanted to see what these tasted like when they ripened."

Lydia said, "Yeah, I was planning to make fruit pies this fall. You always said these heirloom trees were valuable. You think that's what happened, somebody or somebodies cut these for grafting onto other trees?"

"Looks that way to me. At least one of them knew enough about these old trees to take cuttings, while some of the clowns were kicking over stumps just to be destructive. Let's keep looking."

At the far corner of the orchard Millie stopped, breathless. She was next to the stump that marked the end of the last row of the orchard. She turned and again surveyed the venerable old trees. "Look, they rampaged all the way down here. This is the farthest you can get away from the cabin and still be on cultivated ground." The mangled stump was laying on its side, mud clinging to its fillagree of exposed roots.

"What's that?" For the second time that morning, Lydia pointed to an anomalous sight. Speckles of small white objects decorated the dirt loosened by the upturned roots. They stepped closer. A lot of wet sand had clung to the roots when they pulled out of the ground, which left a hole as big as a queen-size mattress and eight inches deep at its lowest point.

Millie knelt on one knee next to the hole left by the stump. She scooped with both hands under the white objects and brought up a layer of the small orbs mixed with dirt. "Here, hold these." Millie gingerly pulled her hands apart, letting the contents slip into Lydia's cupped hands.

"O-M-G!" Lydia squealed with delight. "These white things—they're pearls. Like the one I dug out of that pack rat nest in at the cabin."

Millie stood up, rubbed her hands on her jeans to clean off the mud, took off her flannel shirt, and laid it on the ground.

Lydia tipped the pearls onto the cloth. She squatted next to the shirt and gently tapped a bit of dirt off one and rolled it upright to see whether it was drilled as a bead. "They match, Millie," she declared, "they match the one I found in the cabin and the one that was in the professor's car."

She teased out a length of twisted, gray-black cord, and very gently straightened it. The five-inch cord passed through four pearls, spaced at half-inch intervals, held in place by knots at both ends of each bead. After the fourth bead, the cord was badly frayed. Yet, it extended to another tight knot, passed through a bead much larger than the others, then ended in a rotted lump.

Millie reached back into the hole and eased out a similar, shorter, section of cord; this one connecting three evenly spaced pearls. She laid it next to the other fragment.

Lydia placed a hand on Millie's arm. "Don't touch anything else down there. This cording is too fragile. It needs to be retrieved with specialized excavation techniques." Lydia's voice was subdued, reverent. "I know what this is. The way the beads are spaced, the larger one would be placed after every ten smaller ones. There would be five sets of ten all together, if all of its pieces are here." She swept her hand over the cavity and whispered. "Millie, we've found the rosary."

Lydia stood up and rubbed her hands together to knock off the mud. "There's likely more in there. I need to get screens, fairly fine mesh ones, to sift the dirt in order to find all of them. And my brushes, smallest trowels, and..." Her voice was rising, jubilant, then trailed off as she made a mental inventory.

"That's in your department, Lydia. Maybe there's a silver lining to everything, we never would have found these pearls if that stump hadn't been knocked over. But I still hate what happened here."

Lydia took off her pink chamois cloth shirt and laid it over the pearls on Millie's shirt. "Now can we go call Robby?" asked Lydia.

***

Lydia gunned the old Suburban around the Lejos Canyon road's curves like a race driver. "Tell me as soon as you get bars."

"If I'm still alive by then," Millie said, holding her cell phone in one hand and clutching the passenger's side armrest with her other.

Lydia ignored the comment. "How do you think those pearls got under that tree stump? Hope no one sees my shirt on top of yours and goes to see what they're covering up."

"We'll get back there as soon as I can reach Robby. When that orchard was planted more than a hundred years ago, that tree would have been a spindly little sapling. To be incorporated in the roots like that, the rosary pieces must have been put next to the sapling. As it grew, the pearls just got pulled into the dirt around it, hidden there for decades."

"I wonder who left something as beautiful as that rosary in the orchard," Lydia mused.

"Maybe they were praying for something. Maybe it just dropped out of somebody's pocket when they were working," Millie offered. "Maybe even, the string broke and the pearls dropped here. That could explain why they were so scattered among the roots."

"But wouldn't somebody go back after them? Nobody in their right mind would just leave them behind." Lydia wrenched the steering wheel back after taking a curve a little too fast, making the tires spin out loose gravel.

"Okay, stop," Millie said.

Lydia did, in the middle of the road.

Millie let go of the armrest and stepped out of the vehicle for better cell reception.

Robby answered on the first ring.

"We've been hit," Millie said.

Lydia's eyes flickered between her side mirror, rear-view mirror, and windshield, watching for any on-coming traffic. She'd pull to one side of the road if she needed to.

Millie slipped back into the passenger's seat. "Robby was in the office. She's on her way. Should be here in less than an hour."

Lydia put the Suburban in gear, crept to a wide spot in the road, got turned around, and headed back to the cabin, taking her own sweet time.

Millie didn't question why Lydia was driving at a speed that a butterfly could beat. She didn't want to do any more investigating around the homestead's outbuildings until accompanied by somebody carrying a gun.

24. Damage to Federal Property

On all public lands, unless otherwise authorized, no person shall; (1) Willfully deface, disturb, remove or destroy any personal property, or structures, or any scientific, cultural, archaeological or historic resource, natural object or area; (2) Willfully deface, remove or destroy plants or their parts, soil, rocks or minerals, or cave resources, except as permitted...

— 43 Code of Federal Regulations § 8365.1-5

Robby stepped back from the cabin door and made a whistling sound. "Looks like random vandalism to me."

"Not quite," Millie said. "Some of it was deliberate. Take a look in the kitchen window, then I'll show you what I think happened in the orchard." She led Robby around to the outside of the cabin to the kitchen window opening and pointed to the cast iron stove surrounded by footsteps.

Robby chuckled, shaking her head. "Ha, the clowns couldn't move it an inch. But it was good of them to leave fingerprints on it."

When they came to the trash along the path to the orchard, Robby stopped a couple of times to scribble in her notebook.

Millie went directly to the apple tree with scrape marks showing someone had scrambled up it. "This is what I noticed first."

She waited while Robby scrutinized the splintered bark. Then Millie stood on tiptoes to reach one of the branches and bent it down enough so Robby could see the severed end. "Here's what they were after."

"Those little twigs? Valuable? Why?" Robby's tone was dubious.

Millie led Robby to the damaged pear trees, then to the peach trees, while she explained how botanists and gardeners make use of grafted stock from heirloom plants, especially ones as old and tough as these. "But only a doofus would take cuttings to graft this time of year."

"And why wouldn't they want these twigs to stick on other twigs at this time of year?"

Millie rolled her eyes at Robby's sarcastic tone. "I can tell you don't care, but I'm going to tell you anyway. Anybody who knows what they're doing, collects cuttings in the late winter or early spring when the plant is dormant. They're more likely to attach better. The worst thing though is these raw cuts can admit disease and harm our trees here."

"I'll leave that to you. Show me the pearls."

Millie frowned at Robby's cavalier attitude toward the damage to heirloom fruit trees. Robby's reactions to graffiti on the outhouse door and damage to the cabin wall had been considerably stronger. Her responses were laced with curses and bureaucratic language ranging from "destruction of federal property" to "those f-kers didn't mess up anything in there" as she emerged from the root cellar. She had a few choice words to say about the discarded wedding dress, as well.

Millie viewed Robby as a friend and admired the tough law enforcement officer's bravery in capturing a murderous cactus thief last summer. Yet Robby's expressions made Millie ponder where she'd obtained her colorful language, whether from her south Texas upbringing or from dealing with criminals or both.

Millie headed toward the far corner of the orchard, explaining, "This is where the oldest fruit trees are. They'd be the first ones the homesteaders planted."

When they reached Lydia, she was on her knees leaning over the hole left by the stump and taking photographs of a few pearls visible in the loosened dirt.

Millie pointed to her flannel shirt on the ground. "Robby, here's what I took out of the hole this morning."

"Holy-ol'-knothole," Robby said, dropping down on one knee next to Millie's shirt. She poked a couple of the pearls, causing them to shimmer in the sunlight as bits of dirt fell off. "These are beautiful."

"Be careful, Robby," Lydia sat back on her heels. "I moved your shirt back a little, Millie, but the cording on those beads is fragile as all get out. I don't want to shuffle them around any more than necessary until I can get proper stabilization under them. Give me a hand up, will you, Millie? My knees are about to give out."

Millie gave a steady pull, noticing Lydia's preoccupied expression. Elation over finding the rosary had been replaced by concern for conserving the artifacts.

Robby stood up, took a couple steps, and leaned over the hole. "I can see at least three or four more pearls in there. For sure, the clowns that knocked over this stump didn't see these."

The uprooted tree's netting of roots hung partly over the hole, putting it in shadow. "Likely they didn't show up until that rain washed off some dirt," Millie said.

"Wonder how the pearls got under this tree?" Robby reached out and waggled a finger in some threads of roots by her head.

"Don't," Lydia called out, "don't disturb those roots or any of the dirt around here. Not until I can search more thoroughly. A few pearls could be caught in these roots. And I want to sift this dirt carefully for any remaining pearls. There might be other objects buried here as well."

"Other objects," Millie repeated. "We know the silver cross was attached to the rosary."

"That's why I'm going to sift carefully, very, very carefully, for pearls or anything else that might be with them," Lydia affirmed.

They stood quietly for a few moments. Robby wrote in her notebook. Lydia stretched backward, hands on her lower back. Millie mulled over the damage to the homestead and was the first to speak. "Like you said, Robby, the spray paint, breaking the cabin wall, trash scattered around, these all seem like random vandalism. Whereas whoever cut those branches for grafting targeted only healthy trees. I wonder if it was different people at different times here over the weekend."

"Could be," Robby said, "you've got a point there." She turned to go, "No sense standing here staring at a hole in the ground. I'm going to drive out and make a call to Sylvia, see if she can get Bub Begay or someone from the sheriff's office to come out this afternoon with an evidence kit. I'll be back after I get through."

"What about these pearls?" Lydia asked.

Robby looked back at Lydia. "As far as I'm concerned, the stump being kicked over is part of the vandalism and that's what I'm investigating. The pearls were there before that happened. Unless something else comes up, I don't see any relationship to this past weekend's damage. What you dig up is your department." She strode off toward her patrol pickup.

"That's what I hoped she'd say," Lydia said. She took the couple of steps from the hole over to the shirt and back to the hole, slowly shaking her head, apparently deciding how to proceed.

Millie was about to ask if she were feeling okay, when Lydia nodded, a look of resolve on her face.

"I want to leave them right here. I'll leave them *in situ* until I have more time and screens to shift the dirt, proper containers, and the proper equipment to excavate. I think this is the safest place for now." Lydia knelt down next to the hole and nudged dirt over the few pearls showing on the surface. She carefully ruffled the surface so that no trace was left of anyone having touched the spot after the stump's roots were yanked out.

"Now for these pearls." Lydia knee-walked over to Millie's shirt and started gently folding the cloth over the pearls and the dirt still clinging to them. "I believe this is the safest place as any to store these, as well. I don't want to risk even carrying them to the vehicle without a solid tray and padding to keep the cordage intact. Besides, it's best not to be seen carrying a package around, not even in the office. I opened my big mouth at Tony Gaspar's birthday party about the professor looking for religious artifacts and that stirred up all the old rumors about this place."

"You're right. Nobody's seen these pearls yet, except for Robby and us. Any kind of artifact brought from this homestead is sure to attract attention."

Lydia pushed herself up, bent back down, and eased both hands under the small bundle she had made with the shirt. Keeping it as level as possible, she carried it several steps beyond the orchard and sat it under a thick rabbit-brush. "Millie, bring me a few sticks and stuff to put over your shirt so it blends in better."

"Wait a minute—that's my shirt," Millie huffed.

"Yeah, but it's so dull green, it blends in here. Can't very well use mine, now, can I."

Millie had to agree. Lydia's garish pink shirt was as out of place here as a life-size plastic Flamingo.

It didn't take Millie long to collect a handful of dead snakeweed, a few dried leaves, and a dried prickly pear cactus pad for good measure.

Lydia arranged the camouflaging material in a perfectly haphazard way such that only they would know where the newly unearthed treasure was hidden.

Lydia stood up and brushed her hands together, indicating a job well done. "These pearls are priceless, Millie, not just because they are perfect in a way that's hardly found in natural pearls harvested today, but for their antique value. They're hundreds of years old. We don't know when or why the Iglesia Sagrada Silver Cross was attached to the rosary, but we do know this rosary had been passed down for generations in Rosalinda's family."

They trudged back to the road to wait by the Suburban for Robby to return. Millie had the sinking feeling that they were getting pulled deeper into the convoluted story of the Peralta Homestead. She thought back to her first couple of days at the homestead when she believed it was a remote, undisturbed, quiet place to work. Then Gavin stopped by, opening the root cellar was a nightmare, bringing police all over the place, the field trip students, now vandals. The rock art site attracted archaeological tours. Now she knew her work site was not a safe outpost in a remote canyon. It was a crucible of human and geologic features that attracted people with both sacred and evil intent.

Until the professor's murderer was found, until rumors of the silver cross treasure were put to rest, any visitors could have underhanded motives for coming here.

There was no good reason to break the cabin wall, to rampage through the orchard, to chop pieces off the venerable old trees. About to step over the plastic water bottle, Millie kicked it instead, sending it flying down the path. She shook her fist at the defaced outhouse door. Finally, she blurted, "This is what would happen if Bailee got her way for making this place a backroads attraction for adventure tourists. Trash and vandalism, that's what happens."

"I can't help but agree with you there," Lydia said. "Bailee's scheme of wanting to monetize everything would be disastrous for this special site."

"And her ridiculous idea of throwing in ghost stories and murders, one of which was her own relative even." Millie's voice dripped with exasperation.

Millie and Lydia were at the Suburban getting their lunch boxes out when Robby returned. A rumble came from Robby's stomach that reminded Millie of the sound made by the towing company truck chugging back from the wash. "Guess I didn't think to grab a lunch before leaving the office when you called me this morning, Millie."

Lydia spang into action. She lifted the back of the Suburban, opened a big white cooler, pulled out a handful of granola bars, and handed them to Robby. Then she fished in her lunchbox. "I've got a honey ham and cheese sandwich I can split with you and help yourself to these pickled okra." She opened a jar of foreign-looking, gray-green—somethings.

"Okra? What is it?" Millie asked, while handing a banana and a handful of baby carrots to Robby out of her own lunch box.

"Haven't you ever had pickled okra? My people practically lived on this stuff during hard times."

"Thanks, guys. Growing up in Texas, the only way I've ever had okra is rolled in batter and fried. I'll try some," Robby said, holding the half sandwich in one hand and reaching into the jar with her other. "Say, while we're waiting for Bub, how about showing me this boulder with the nude that you all were snickering about back in the conference room when Wirt talked about the petroglyphs."

25. Cover-Up

The flowers of scared datura are the largest of any native plant in the Four Corners region. All species of Datura have long been used by native peoples because of the plant's hallucinogenic alkaloids. All parts of the plant are poisonous and those trying to imitate Native American ways have often poisoned themselves.

— Ken Heil, *Four Corners Invasive and Poisonous Plant Field Guide*

Lydia, once satisfied that Robby had eaten as much as the skinny woman could hold, took her leave saying, "I want to figure out the best way to stabilize that breach in the cabin's outside wall before another hard rainstorm. I might be able to find boards fallen off the old barn that's weatherized enough to match it."

Lydia headed for the barn and Millie led Robby a couple hundred yards back along the road. This being a more direct route to the big boulder, rather than taking the path to the sheep pen and skirting along the cliff face.

Robby stood in front of the boulder, sipping from her water bottle, looking up and down at the nude figure. "Just buying triple-size D bras for that beauty would wipe out my whole paycheck."

Millie laughed at such a comment coming from this slim woman nearly a foot shorter than herself. Pointing to the chiseled G-A-S-P letters and 1924 date, Millie said, "Kenny Conroy called this 'sheepherder art.' Goes along with the sheep pen farther up the canyon. Come on, we've got a little time before Bub gets here, I'll show you some of the other features Kenny talked about." As they hiked to the cliff, Millie explained how Doctor Conroy had come by at the request of a mutual friend and shared his interpretations based on his research and oral tradition.

"He just happened to stop by? A mutual friend?"

Robby's tone caused Millie to pause and sigh. "Okay, you probably heard it already from Momma Agnes. Ben Benallee asked him to come."

"Ben Benallee, huh. Momma Agnes told me he's kind of sweet on you."

"Well, that's Momma Agnes' opinion, not mine. And she could just keep it to herself."

They reached the foot of the rock wall, now casting a narrow shadow that would grow as the sun traveled its western arc. Millie sipped from her water bottle.

Robby held her arms out in the cooler air. "That one looks like a deer or an elk." Robby was pointing to an animal figure carved into the rock, a foot above her head. Its outline had been chipped a half inch deep, but the groove was roughened with weathering. "It looks old, like it's stood here for centuries. I can even make out hooves and horns. Yup, big, branched antlers, got to be an elk."

"Uh-huh, Kenny called it an elk. And see that hole with splintered edges in the animal's middle. That's a bubba-glyph."

"Yeah, yeah, I've heard that one before. Some Bubba was here shooting his riffle at a rock wall. Stupid is, as stupid does. The official term is 'defacement of archaeological resources' according to ARPA, which applies to all public land and tribal lands."

"ARPA, that's the law that Lydia said put real teeth into protecting archeological sites," Millie said.

"We can slap perpetrators with fines, even serious jail time." Robby frowned and kicked at the ground, "but first we have to catch them, either in the act or with items in their possession. I hope me and Bub can find something this afternoon to nail whoever was here over the weekend."

They moved along the shaded base of the cliff where it was cooler. When they reached the alcove, Millie told Robby about their experiment of clapping hands to test the acoustics.

"Ha, I can do one better than that," Robby said. She threw back her head and let out a resounding Texas-sized whoop.

Millie flinched. A raven raised up from the top of the cliff, causing a few pebbles to clatter to the ground. The sound from the whoop and tumbling rocks continued echoing back and forth in the alcove.

Millie gave Robby a look of amazement and admiration.

Robby bent double laughing. "We used to do that in an empty grain silo when I was a kid," Robby explained.

The raven flapped by over their heads. It circled with its head hanging to one side as if looking for something. It made a steep dive and landed next to a dark spot on the ground about a hundred feet out from the cliff.

"That's curious. Why would it land so close to us?"

Millie wondered and took a step in the raven's direction.

The big bird flew off, making a soft gurgling sound, the kind Millie had heard during last summer's field season. The sound ravens make when calling to each other.

Millie walked to the spot where the raven had landed, Robby keeping pace at her side.

"What the hell? That looks fresh. Somebody's been digging here," Robby said.

Millie glanced at the hole, about one foot wide and twice as deep. Wet sand excavated from the hole was tossed aside, as if the digger had no intention of replacing it in the hole.

Robby stepped around to the opposite side of the hole, bent down, and picked up a dark green, lobed leaf. "What's this. Feels kind of velvety."

Millie pushed a similar leaf aside with her boot. "I bet you've heard of it."

"So what is it? If anybody'd know, you would."

"It's *Datura wrightii*." Millie pointed toward the cliff. "See that figure with what looks like flowing hair? Kenny believes that it is a Navajo depiction of someone having visions after ingesting jimsonweed."

"Visions? Like hallucinations? Wait, you said 'Datura.' I've always heard it called jimsonweed." Robby dropped the leaf. "I had a cousin that spent three days in the hospital after some kid dared him to chew a leaf. That's one of the drugs they told us in training to watch out for, it's not just hallucinogenic but poisonous if a person doesn't know what they're dealing with."

Millie started back toward the cliff, eyes to the ground. "Jimsonweed grows here. Could be it always grew here and that's why that vision rock art is here. Maybe plants were brought here for ceremonies. Lydia says certain indicator plants found around archaeological sites were cultivated for use year after year."

She stopped and pointed to the ground. "Damnit. The plant that was right here last week had blossoms on it."

Robby joined her and looked at the much bigger hole, dug in the same slap-dash manner. "Criminy, or maybe I should say, holy hell, instead. How many holes am I going to get to look at today?"

"Hole-ly—not funny," Millie grumbled and continued along the base of the cliff toward the sheep pen. "Here's another, littler hole here."

"You keep looking in that direction, I'll circle out and around," Robby said.

Millie walked beyond the sheep pen, a direction she had never taken before. She stepped over a fence that once stretched from the cliff to the road. Now its stubby juniper posts lay on the ground and she easily stepped over the three strands of barbed wire partially buried by sand and grasses. Millie immediately noticed a difference in the vegetation with a greater density of juniper trees and thicker clumps of rabbitbrush. The fence separated the acreage grazed by the homesteader's livestock from this natural, undisturbed area.

She saw no evidence of the ground having been dug up, only a very faint trail. Millie kept close to the canyon wall. She felt a tug on her lower leg. A warp speed image flashed in her brain—a coiled rattlesnake striking. She jumped sideways, her jeans ripping. A short branch with thorns hung from a tear just below her knee. Not a rattlesnake. She held her hand over her heart until it stopped making pirouettes in her chest.

She bent over, fingered the rip, and felt the sting beneath. She lifted and tugged the prickly twig to work it out of the cloth. She pulled up the leg of her jeans and wiped away blood seeping from a shallow, ragged scratch. She let the pant leg drop back into place, patted the cloth around the rip to absorb more droplets of blood, and looked for the culprit.

She saw a plant that was very much out of place. *Why is that here?* The rose bush had scraggy branches, all but three or four of them looked dead. It had tiny, short thorns like the rose bush in Mr. Gaspar's yard and the ones by the cabin. One very faded yellowish blossom hung from its top branch. At Millie's touch, it dropped to the ground next to the rock wall. It landed right below something carved in the stone a few inches above the ground.

Millie squatted down to examine the figure. It was so deeply chiseled, so finely finished, that she forgot what Lydia said about oils from hands contaminating rock art. She drew her finger one way vertically then across, feeling the curved, lobbed ends as if scooped out with a carpenter's finest chisel. *A cross, a cross with flared ends, like a Spanish cross.*

Millie stood, stepped back, and scanned the rock wall for other markings. This flawless cross was the only rock art visible. Like the Pueblo sun above the sheep pen, the pre-historic triangular figures, the Navajo star patterns, this cross, this message in stone, was meant to record something important to the maker.

A casual whoop and a "Millie" shout told her it was time to rejoin Robby. She took long steps and soon joined Robby who was leaning against the corner post of the sheep pen. "I only found two more holes where plants were dug up. How about you?"

Millie shook her head, "None that way. Doesn't even look like anyone's walked that way in quite a while."

Robby did not stir from her relaxed pose. "I've been thinking. It's not very often anybody walks over to this side of the road, unless they are here to look at the petroglyphs. I think the damage around the homestead was intended as a distraction—a cover up."

"You know," Millie said, "that Gavin McIntyre guy brings his Ancient Ones Adventure Travel tours here to see the rock art. At Mister Gaspar's birthday party, he said he had another group coming, but he didn't say when."

Robby shook her head. "I got to looking closer at the footprints. At least three or four dudes were tramping around here based on their prints in the fresh dirt by the holes where they took turns digging. None of the footprints go over to the cliff, like somebody looking at rock art would do. I believe it was the jimsonweed they were after."

"But what about the Stay Away on the outhouse? That's a threat. Don't vandals like to put their names everywhere, swear words, things like that?"

"You mean the F-word. Yuppers, that's a real favorite. Short, easy to spell." Robby's voice seethed with contempt. "But I still think it was a cover-up. They probably figured nobody would notice anything amiss over here. Let's head back."

Millie led the way on the path from the sheep pen to the road.

As they walked, Robby said, "By the way, did this Kenny Conroy fellow say anything else? Like maybe somebody he knows collects jimsonweed for ceremonial purposes."

"No. He didn't say any such thing." Millie dismissed the suspicious comment.

Robby persisted. "I'm still curious about why this Kenny Conroy rock art expert just happened to stop by the same day we hauled the Bronco out of the wash."

"He said Ben asked him to, that's all. He just swung by on his way to the pow wow that Ben took me to on Saturday. We saw him there."

"Millie, Lejos Canyon is not exactly 'on the way' for anybody." Robby didn't let up. "Did this Conroy say anything about the cabin, root cellar, ghosts, rumors of lost treasure?"

"Professor Conroy is an expert on this area. He wanted to help us on documenting the history of this site. That's all there is to it." Millie knew she was stretching it a bit, but wanted Robby to leave off about Ben's friend.

"There's always a reason why a person does what they do." Robby had to have the last word.

Millie kept walking, while Kenny's voice echoed in her mind. *There must be no disturbance to the sacred rock* art.

When they reached the vehicles, Lydia was handing Bub a granola bar from her stash in the cooler.

Robby gave a quick run-down of their findings across the road. "I don't like this whole situation. I think the vandalism here at the homestead was a cover-up, a diversion to keep us from noticing the dug-up plants. Although the Stay Away graffiti doesn't quite fit. Millie, let's show Bub what happened in the orchard, then you guys can head home. Bub and I will inspect the rest of what they did."

"When you are at the orchard, watch out for my string," Lydia said.

Quizzical looks were the only response to this statement.

"While you were gone, I tied a piece of twine on that bush where we hid the pearls. Millie, you might recognize every bush out there, but they all look the same to me. I was afraid I wouldn't find it again. I covered up the string with sand, sticks, and stuff. Nobody'd see it unless they knew to look for it. I tied the other end down low on the trunk of a nearby fruit tree."

Millie shook her head. "Lydia, you and your string!"

It was getting on toward five o'clock when Millie returned from the orchard and found Lydia holding a gray, weathered board against the broken wall of the cabin.

"I think I can make this one work," Lydia said. "I just need to rasp a little off this edge then dab the raw edge with a gray stain. It won't hardly be noticeable." Lydia tucked the board under her arm and headed toward the Suburban. "I'm ready to go when you are."

Millie was more than ready. She was tired, not from walking most of the morning and afternoon, but tired in her mind. She massaged her forehead and the raised welt of the scar above her eyebrow. *Could it be this long-abandoned site had multiple visitors over the weekend? Some nutjobs fond of spray paint and some sneaky, amateur fruit grower clipping heirloom trees for grafting? Or neither of those, and just one person tying to distract, to cover up the jimsonweed theft? Or was STAY AWAY the real message?*

Lydia laid the board on the back seat, got in, and started the engine.

Millie settled into the passenger's seat and gave a deep sigh. "Seems like every time we're making progress on this site, something crazy happens."

"I hear you. Just when you think your beans are cooked, the stove goes out. We found the rosary, I'm sure of it. But getting that spray paint off the outhouse door, ugh, that'll take some time."

"Yeah, and when we were at the orchard, Robby told me Wirt is going to want to hear everything about the damage we found here. I'll meet you at the office in the morning and we can check in with him. That should give us a half day back here, enough to clean up the trash, and get back to normal."

"Back to normal. I hope you're right."

Carved Cross on Sandstone

26. Stop Work

Federal Land Patents offer researchers a source of information on the initial transfer of land titles from the Federal government to individuals. In addition to verifying title transfer, this information will allow the researcher to associate an individual... with a specific location...

— Bureau of Land Management General Land Office Records

"Millie, Millie, I'm going to Santa Fe." Lydia was perched at the edge of the extra chair in Millie's office. "Momma Agnes just told me."

"At least let me put my things down before you hit me with... with, whatever you've got going now," Millie mumbled and dropped her backpack on the desk. She sat down, yawned, and swiveled toward Lydia. "How come you're in so early?"

"Oh, my boy called this morning. So, I was awake and

241

figured I might as well come in to work. He forgets that I'm in a time zone two hours earlier than he is. He just had to tell me about his new girlfriend, another barista at the coffee shop where he works. He said she has the most beautiful tattoos he's ever seen on a girl. I told him beauty is only skin deep, and that—"

Millie held up her hand and said, "Wait, why are you going to Santa Fe?"

"Momma Agnes said she'd call as soon as Wirt was available, and he'd explain everything. That's all I know so far," Lydia said. "It's probably about talking with the Historic Preservation Division folks about nominating the Peralta site for national designation. And I can hit the state archaeological office to see if they have more info on that little ruin across the canyon we came across." Lydia was talking faster and faster. "Oh, and the New Mexico history archives to look at some of those family documents that Doctor Bernnard had in his notebook."

"How long are you going to be there?" Millie asked.

"Uh, I don't know. Momma Agnes didn't tell me that. Long enough to hit the plaza and art galleries and do some shopping, I hope, I hope."

The desk phone rang and Millie answered it. "Okay, Momma Agnes, we'll be right there." She turned to Lydia and said, "Wirt's in his office. We're about to find out."

Wirt sat behind his desk, holding out a paper with thumb and forefinger like he couldn't fathom what it meant. "Robby handed me these notes she typed up this morning and left on another call. We've got graffiti, trash, fruit trees clipped, a wedding dress," Wirt's eyebrows zoomed upwards when he read dress, "and hallucinogenic plants uprooted, and pearls under a tree. Perhaps you can fill me in a bit more?"

"It's awful," Millie said, "I don't know why people do

this kind of thing. We saw the wedding dress first, thrown down by the path to the cabin. Then the more we looked around, we could see that people had been all over the homestead site and even over by the petroglyph cliff."

"An outside wall of the cabin was broken out, too," Lydia said.

Wirt laid the paper down, wrote a few words on it, and looked up. "Robby said she and Bub went over the whole place yesterday afternoon. Robby will check to see if there are any similar incidents reported by federal agencies on public lands. She'll give us a complete write-up in a couple of days."

"I don't know how much Robby told you," Millie said, "but it could have happened at different times last Saturday, before the rain. They rampaged all the way through the orchard and probably the same ones dug up the jimsonweed. But it could be somebody else that took cuttings from the fruit trees."

"Robby didn't mention that. But she did say she thought the vandalism around the cabin was just a cover up to divert attention away from snatching the jimsonweed."

Millie shifted in her chair, exchanged a glance with Lydia, and said, "That doesn't explain what was on the outhouse door—Stay Away—to me, that's a warning."

"That's the part I'm getting to," Wirt said. His voice was a little muffled behind the hand he was using to massage his eyes. Then he placed both hands on his desk and partially stood. "I'm shutting down your work at the Peralta site."

Lydia gasped and laid a hand over her heart.

Millie let out an adamant, "No," then snapped her mouth shut.

"You can write up what documentation you have. You're done there for the time being." He eased back down in his chair.

"But Wirt, the Peralta site has everything—historical significance and outstanding site integrity, despite what just happened. There's Hispanic, Pueblo, Navajo cultural affiliation and... and everything needed for national designation." Lydia sounded as incredulous as Millie felt.

Millie squeezed her hands together so hard her knuckles were white. "Why? We're so close to finishing the field work." *How could this, her first assignment on her first real job, collapse like this?*

Wirt's voice was steady, unyielding. "I'm concerned about your safely. Until I hear more about what Robby finds out, it's too dangerous around the homestead. If no connections turn up about individuals doing similar activities, I'll reconsider."

Wirt let this sink in for a few moments. "Remember, it's still a BLM property, still falls under federal protection. Maybe talk of making the Peralta Ranch a historic site got the interest of some local folks, who may, or may not, be behind giving it a national label. We know that making a place a national designation can bring more attention to it."

Wirt was addressing Lydia. "I told Momma Agnes to get the paperwork ready for up to three days in Santa Fe. That includes lodging and meals."

Lydia looked down at her wrist, as if sizing it up for the bracelet she planned to buy.

"You can drive my Expedition; I won't be needing it for a few days. I'll sign the travel authorization this afternoon and you can leave tomorrow. Talk to the Historic Preservation Division about what you've got so far. Get their take on the site's eligibility for national designation. That's all you can do for now, understand?"

Lydia, for once, remained speechless.

Millie slumped in her chair. Stuck in the office for who knows how long. Then she straightened, leaned forward, and said, "Wirt, when they dug up the Datura plants, they left big holes. And I really want to finish my species list for that part of the homestead across the road. Suppose I just work a day or two along the petroglyph cliff?"

Before Wirt could get to his second head shake, Millie kept going. "I'll fill the holes, make it look like nothing near the cliff was tampered with. I don't need to go near the cabin or the orchard at all."

Wirt was rubbing his eyes again. Lydia shot a sly grin at Millie and silently mouthed, "Miss workaholic."

Wirt sighed and said, "Fill the holes, huh. Not many people go there, but we wouldn't want to leave holes to give them the idea that it's okay to go digging around an archaeological site or take plants off BLM without a permit."

Millie kept her face neutral, despite her racing pulse.

"You just don't give up on a job, do you," Wirt said. "Okay, go ahead out tomorrow, but leave the homestead side to Robby. She's going to be cruising by there once or twice every day to keep an eye on the place."

Millie and Lydia bumped into each other hustling out of Wirt's office before their boss could change his mind.

***

Millie spent the rest of the day organizing and typing up her field notes. She made a list of nearly two dozen species from memory that she had seen along the petroglyph cliff. She kept non-native, invasive species on a separate list. Nowhere did the rose bush she found fit on these lists, but then it was on the other side of the sheep pen and not within the scope of the homestead survey.

Or was it? Did the 160-acre homestead claim encom-

pass the area where she found the rose bush? She had assumed the claim began at the sheep pen and extended along the cliff that bore the petroglyphs, mainly because the path from the cabin across the road went directly to the sheep pen, then continued in the rock art direction. Yet when she and Robby discovered the dug-up jimsonweed holes, there was that faint, overgrown trail she'd followed to where she found the rosebush.

Millie pulled out the file folder she had labeled Peralta Ranch History. She found the copy of the Peralta Ranch patent that she had printed out from the BLM General Land Office Records database. The scan of the patent was of poor quality and the lengthy legal description hard to decipher. She shrugged. She would need to track down the survey that would have been done at the time the Gaspars transferred the property to BLM in exchange for the land they now farmed near their home.

She ran a finger under M. J. Peralta de Martinez typed in the space for the claimant's name on the document. Millie smiled at the way Mr. Gaspar seemed embarrassed at his birthday party when he talked about his Grandmother Margarita Joséfina Peralta "living with" Alejandro Gaspar before they were married. Although José Manuel Peralta filed the original claim, he'd left after the murder of his wife. His sister's initials on the patent must have slipped by the officials five years later, keeping the land in the Gaspar family. Luckily for Millie, it was now under BLM management and giving her and Lydia a fascinating place to work.

Millie picked up Doctor Bernnard's article, "Religious Objects Constituted Wealth and Status for Immigrants," that Robby had found. She leaned back in her chair and skimmed the pages. She paused at the only known image of the cross presumed stolen from Spain's La Iglesia

Sagrada and carried to the New World by early Spanish settlers. Her visual memory flickered to a similar shape—the cross carved into the cliff wall by the rose bush. They both had scalloped lobes on the horizontal piece, perhaps a common way to depict a cross among certain religious sects.

Amazing that treasure hunters and even professional history researchers like Doctor Bernnard spent time and money chasing the legend of a stolen silver cross. Shaking her head, Millie pushed the papers back into the folder. Legend is hearsay and speculation. That's for treasure hunters like Gavin McIntyre to waste time on and descendants of Lejos Canyon homesteaders like Manuel Garcia to gossip about.

The antique rosary strung with pearls buried long ago in the orchard, now that was real. Doctor Bernnard had copied the exact words from Rosalinda's mother. The rosary went with Rosalinda to Lejos Canyon. And that's where the story ended for the professor.

Where will the fate of the Peralta Ranch go from here? Will listing the Peralta Ranch on the National Register of Historic Places prove to bring better protection to the site, or will it bring too much attention, too much visitation?

The vandals' message—Stay Away The Ghost—was this just a prank or was it a warning to leave things alone, let the old homestead rest in peace? Bailee's scheme to monetize the Peralta Ranch contradicted Kenny Conroy's appeal to leave the petroglyphs undisturbed.

Such uncertainty made Millie's chest tighten. Her childhood had always hinged on whether her parents' janitorial business could get and keep enough customers to subsist. When her first college botany course revealed the surety and order of science, there was no looking back. Now she was in a government agency called upon to balance multiple, sometimes conflicting, demands. Success on her job would mean learning to work in gray area, dealing with human behavior, beyond just science.

27. Old Wagon Road

Recreation is no longer simply having fun. Rather, it involves the kind of America we have, and want to have, and the kind of people we are and are likely to become.
— Laurance S. Rockefeller, American Conservationist, 1910–2004

Millie put her mind in neutral on the commute home. She needed some fur and purr time before she could relax and think. After changing into shorts and T-shirt and feeding Ragged Ear, she poured a tall glass of iced tea and went out to the front porch bench. Ragged Ear jumped up next to his food-giver and settled into a meatloaf-like position, his paws neatly tucked underneath. He burped, having gobbled his evening portion of pâté too fast, then got on to his job of purring as Millie stroked his orange fur.

Millie let Wirt's words that morning float back into her thoughts. He had said, "Maybe talk of making the

Peralta Ranch a historic site got the interest of some local folks, who may, or may not, be behind giving it a national label. We know that making a place a national designation can bring more attention to it."

Preservation versus visitation—that's what Lydia called the old argument. "What do you think, Ragged Ear, can we manage both? If people never experience natural sites, historical sites, cultural sites, how can you get support and funding for protecting them?" The cat lifted a paw and massaged his left ear, turning it inside out. "Are you telling me this makes your head hurt?" She flipped the scarred and notched ear back into place.

Ragged Ear rose up at the sound of someone coming their way, someone making a loud rattling noise. When Mr. Gaspar came into sight, puffing for breath, the cat ran to the end of the porch, leaped off, and disappeared under the lilac bushes.

Her landlord stopped and steadied himself with a hand on the porch railing. "Have you seen that damn goat, Miss Millie? Elvis, the black one, he got out of the pen, and I've been chasing him all afternoon." He was carrying a rope and a coffee can which he rattled, letting anyone or any critter within ear shot know that he was offering grain.

"Are you saying that Elvis has left the building, Mister Gaspar? No, I haven't seen him." The reference seemed lost on the old man, or he was in no mood for a laugh. "Why don't you sit down for a few minutes?"

He looked up the set of steps then lowered himself on the next to lowest step. He stretched out his left leg and massaged the knee.

Millie moved down and sat on the lowest step, but her head was still a little higher than his.

He took a few more deep breaths and looked up at

her with the question Millie knew was coming but dreaded. "How are things at the Peralta Ranch that you are studying?"

"Not so good, I'm sorry to say." How could she tell him about the vandalism? His connection to the Peralta family homestead was so strong, for generations.

Remembering to speak loudly to the octogenarian, she rushed out the words. "Some people were there over the weekend. They put paint on the outhouse, made a hole in the cabin wall, and tipped over some stumps in the orchard."

A groan escaped from Mr. Gaspar as if his lungs just deflated. He looked down into the coffee can, slowly turning it around and around in his gnarled hands. "Why, why would anyone do such a thing?" His voice was shaky, barely above a whisper. Then he straightened, his hands still. "No one has bothered that place for all these years. Maybe it would have been better not to let the government have it."

Millie pulled her knees tight to her chest. She wanted to shield herself from his distrust of the BLM's ability to care for the site. Without thinking, she rolled her thumb along the scar on her forehead. Nothing like this had happened prior to her and Lydia's work there. Not for decades anyway, not since the professor was dragged into the root cellar.

She looked beyond his slumped shoulders. "I'm sorry that happened, sir. The damage will be repaired, I assure you."

"It is not for you to be sorry, Miss Millie. There is no one to blame except for the foolish people who do not respect the old ways." He swirled the grain around and around in the can. "What about the sheep pen across the road? Did they go near there?"

She was relieved that she could put off telling him the worst news for the moment, that Wirt had shut down their work at the homestead. "They went on that side of the road, too. They dug up jimsonweed plants all along the petroglyph cliff."

"The sheep pen. The sheep pen—did they do anything there?"

His troubled voice made Millie feel even worse. "They went on the path between the cabin to the pen, but probably walked past it to get to the plants. I was there with Robby, our law enforcement officer. The only disturbance we found were holes left in the ground."

"Did you look *all* around?"

"I went along the cliff beyond the sheep pen. Didn't see any other problems. Oh, I did see something unusual—a rose bush, just like the one you have here."

The grain made a different rattling sound in the can cradled in his shaking hands. "You should not go wandering around there. It is okay for people to go look at the rock art that begins by the sheep pen. They follow the path along the cliff. That is where people should go, only. They should not be around the sheep pen."

Her landlord's concern about the area around the sheep pen perplexed Millie. Then she remembered warning Lydia to watch for rusty nails in the boards fallen off the old corral. That must be why he was asking.

"Don't worry. I will be careful. I will fill in the holes along the petroglyph cliff. I know how to naturalize damaged areas by scattering brush and a few stones over it. It'll look like nothing happened." Lydia had done just that in hiding the rosary beads. Something prevented Millie from mentioning finding the pearls. Perhaps because Lydia wanted them hidden in the orchard until she was able to properly excavate the find.

"But the orchard. You said some stumps got pushed over. How can anyone put them back? The cabin is old. A hole in the wall. That must be fixed right away."

No more skirting around what would upset him the most. She tightened her hands on each knee and said, "The area manager has stopped our work at the cabin."

He turned and looked up at her. "No more work? You said what you are doing will help protect the ranch. What will I tell Della?"

"It's temporary. Just until our law enforcement officer finishes investigating the vandalism and says it's safe to continue our work. In fact, he's sending Lydia to Santa Fe to talk to the state historical preservation department about putting the homestead on the National Register."

She loosened her hands and let them dangle over her knees. "We are too close to completing the documentation not to finish." She wished she could be more sure of that, but wanted to reassure him, and herself. "After I fill in the holes tomorrow, I'll continue inventorying the plant species on the cliff side. Wirt told us not to work around the cabin, but okayed my working on the petroglyph side of the road. Robby will be checking on the homestead buildings pretty often."

"You'll be going there tomorrow, by yourself?" Mr. Gaspar sat the coffee can down, and tapped a finger on Millie's sneaker. "If your boss, Mister Wirt, does not want you near the cabin, I will tell you a place to put your vehicle. It is a safe place to park a vehicle off the road and away from the cabin. There is an old wagon road that the sheepherders used. My grandmother's common-law husband, Alejandro, showed me this a long time ago. It goes by the boulder where he carved his name. There's some, um, other carvings, too."

Millie giggled. "I know what you're talking about. It's

down the road a ways from the cabin."

Her landlord's face took on a shade of red, but he chuckled too. "Alejandro, he said he carved his name there. That's his name you see by the 1924 date. But his son thought it needed a little more decoration. The young man did it when he came back from Europe after World War Two. They put him to herding sheep out there until he got right in the head again. It gave him something to do while watching the sheep. He made it just like the Lucky Strike girl."

"What's the Lucky Strike girl?" Millie guessed it was something from way before her time.

"You know, Lucky Strike cigarettes. They used to give Luckies to the soldiers during World War Two. Part of their C-rations. Every tent camp had its share of Lucky Strike posters with fancy girls."

"Hmm, I suppose pictures of partially clad females were pretty risqué back then."

He picked up the can and shook it hard. Still no animal in sight. "The old wagon road is just, maybe, thirty yards back down the road from the boulder. It's grown over, but you'll see it if you're watching for it. Pull in. Better place to leave a vehicle off the road." He shook the can again.

Elvis came poking along the row of bushes that lined the driveway. He had a ruby red rose hanging out the side of his mouth.

Mr. Gaspar grunted and pushed himself upright, mumbling, "Damn goat, that's off my prize-winning bush." Then he switched his tone to friendly cajoling. "Come here, Elvis. I've got something for you."

The goat trotted to the man, dropped the rose, and stuck his nose into the coffee can. "Come and get this rose, Millie. This *tonto* is going back to his pen."

Millie watched her landlord limp off toward the back

yard. The goat following him, alternating between sticking his head in the can and butting against his owner's unsteady legs.

She picked up the rose, drew in its elegant aroma, and went back to the porch. She twirled the flower beneath her nose, matching her spinning thoughts. She'd do what Wirt said, stay away from the cabin. For the time being.

Their thorough documentation would surely qualify the homestead for the National Register, giving it stronger protection. For the Gaspars, it would mean recognition of the stalwart Hispanic settlers in the northwestern corner of the state; a concrete reminder of the Hispanic history of the region, often overshadowed by the better-known Santa Fe history.

Ragged Ear leaped onto the bench, climbed on Millie's lap, and nudged her face for attention. She spoke into the cat's soft ear. "I'm not going to let the Gaspars down. Lydia and I have put too much heart and soul into that place to just have our work shoved in a drawer somewhere."

The Gaspars had made her feel part of the community. They looked out for her, like Mr. Gaspar telling her about the old wagon road. He said it was a safe place to park by getting the vehicle off the road. He seemed more concerned about her safety than the damage around the cabin.

He was as protective as Robby, with her warnings to be careful. But then the words on the outhouse appeared in her mind's eye—STAY AWAY THE GHOST

And there was Lydia's axiom, trouble always comes in threes. Hogwash. Just because there had been two murders at the homestead, separated by nearly a century, another one was a mighty slim probability.

She rolled the big cat onto his back, stroked his belly, and murmured, "I won't let warnings and sayings keep me from doing my job. Tomorrow, I'm back to the field. I'm used to working alone."

Raven

28. The Best Part of Being a Botanist

Most young people find botany a dull study. So it is, as taught from the text-books in the schools; but study it yourself in the fields and woods, and you will find it a source of perennial delight.
— John Burroughs, American Naturalist, 1837–1921

The next morning, Millie left her Honda in the BLM employee parking area, stopped by Momma Agnes' desk to sign out for the day, and went to the vehicle yard.

"Hey, Millie, you're on your own for today." Millie turned toward the cheery voice calling her name and greeted Lydia with a broad smile.

"I'm on my way to Santa Fe." Lydia sang the words to the tune of the "Do You Know the Way to San José" song. She gave the briefcase she was carrying a little lift. "I've got my notes on all the structures at the Peralta Ranch and pulled together some of the history pieces surrounding the place. That should get the Historic Pres folks interested in the site. I'll get a sense of whether they're likely to push it forward for national designation."

Lydia held up a key ring and jingled the keys. "I looked at the boss's car, Millie. It's huge, it'll be like driving a tank. I've read Santa Fe streets are narrow, left over from mule trails. Wait till they see me coming in that Expedition."

"Having ridden with you, Lydia, all I can say is, look out Santa Fe."

Millie watched Lydia take two tries climbing up into the driver's seat. The seat clunked forward, and Lydia's forehead appeared over the steering wheel. Millie waved to Lydia and went to the beat-up Suburban. She tapped a gob of mud off the triangular BLM logo on the door and dropped into the driver's seat. "I'm your driver today, ol' buddy. Lydia is off to Santa Fe."

The drive to Lejos Canyon was a familiar routine. Millie joined the pack of oil and gas field hands driving their white pickup trucks to service the numerous wells that crowded the energy-rich San Juan Basin.

The shovel and rake in the back clanked together when she swung off the highway onto the dirt Lejos Canyon road. Most of the oil and gas trucks had already pulled off onto side roads, with only the orange flag attached to their cabs visible over the sagebrush.

Millie ignored the tools rattling on the bumpy road as she worked out her plan for the day. First, in the morning's coolness, she would fill the holes where the jimsonweed had been dug up, smoothing and naturalizing the disturbances to make them inconspicuous. Then she would return the tools to the vehicle, get her pack with clipboard, forms, and plant identification guides, and begin inventorying vegetation. That was what she loved to do, the best part of being a botanist in New Mexico's wide-open spaces. A quiet, uneventful day of peace to enjoy being out in the high desert, so very different from the closed-in deciduous forests she'd explored as a child.

About a quarter mile before the cabin, she slowed to a creeping pace. If she missed spotting the old wagon road, not a problem. She could park next to the road where the occasional archaeology group stopped to visit the petroglyphs. The road was a little wider there due to vehicles and feet trampling the vegetation where the path led directly to the cliff with the most interesting rock art figures. The path also led past the boulder with the sheepherder art, always a popular stop for visitors.

"Ah ha, there's the old wagon road, just like Mister Gaspar said it would be." The path started about thirty yards farther down the road.

Millie pulled to the side of the road, put the Suburban in park, and got out to look at the opening, a wider space between the juniper trees than would occur naturally. She walked the almost completely overgrown wagon road for two vehicle lengths, looking for ruts, stones, or brush that could damage the undercarriage. The grasses and a couple very small sagebrush would not present any problem. There was a small prickly pear cactus with three pads that she could straddle between the tires without harming it.

Not a bad idea to get the vehicle off the road so passersby are not likely to notice it. Here by myself, with no cell service, best not to draw attention. During the back-country orientation Wirt had taken her on the previous spring, he said always park facing out so you can leave in a hurry if you need to. The area manager's words echoed in her mind. Pointing to the BLM logo on his vehicle door, he'd said, "Some yahoos might think it's a target. If you ever see anything unusual, get the heck out of there." Millie backed the Suburban into the wagon road.

She took out the rake and shovel, walked the short distance along the road, and took the path. She stopped at the boulder and considered the carvings.

Ever since her landlord told her about the wagon road that passed by the boulder, about Alejandro carving the 1924 date and later, his son carving the nude, Millie had thought of this house-sized rock as "the Gaspar boulder." Three generations of the Gaspar family had stood in this spot, making this place, this land, their story.

Millie moved on to the first hole where the raven had landed, bringing her and Robby's attention to the stolen plants. Filling the hole with its loosened sand was easy. Circling out and around to collect dead brush and a few stones to scatter over the spot took longer. She stepped away and looked over her handiwork. The spot blended in with surrounding sagebrush and grasses. Satisfied, she moved on to the next hole.

She finished naturalizing the next to last hole and began walking toward the last one, but stopped. Someone was standing by the sheep pen, leaning against the gate post. Tilting her head to listen, she could hear a familiar out-of-breath puffing. "Mister Gaspar, what are you doing here?" She beamed a broad smile in his direction.

He raised the hand holding his walking stick in a wave, but continued steadying himself against the post with his other.

She laid the rake and shovel over the last hole. As she walked toward him, Millie wondered how sensible his coming here was, considering his difficulty walking. And why had he come to the sheep pen on this side of the road when the cabin should be his main concern?

"You didn't tell me you'd be coming today. I thought

I'd be working all day by myself. It's good to see you."

He took a couple more deep breaths before saying, "I had to come and see for myself what those vandals did." His hands clenched and relaxed around the walking stick.

"It'll be okay, Mister Gaspar. It can all be restored." Millie stooped down a little to look directly into his eyes. "Lydia knows how to repair the cabin and remove the spray paint so the damage won't be noticeable. Come and see if you can even tell where I've covered the places they dug up the jimsonweed."

Her landlord looked away from Millie, as if he wanted to go in the opposite direction, but sighed and said, "All right, you can show me what you are doing."

Taking what seemed like baby steps, she walked beside Mr. Gaspar to where she'd left the tools and stopped. She swept a hand in the general direction of the holes she had covered up and naturalized. "There, can you see anything different here?"

He stacked both hands over the top of his walking stick and studied the area. "No, Miss Millie, I can't see anything different. You did a good job."

Millie beamed. For some reason, hearing those words made her feel warm inside. Perhaps it was because, through her high school and college years helping with her parents' janitorial business on nights and weekends, she'd never heard those words. Whenever she finished cleaning one office, her mother would just tell her to get started on the next one.

Pointing to the tools, Millie said, "It won't take me long to fill this last hole, then I'll walk you back to your car."

"Don't bother. You've got work to do." He gave a dismissive wave and turned to go.

"No wait, let me walk you back."

"You think I might lose my way, miss, when my family

has walked this land for generations?"

"I just figured you could use some company." Millie didn't like to think of his unsteady legs along the path with its stones and thick brush.

"Hmph, I'll go where I want to." He looked beyond the sheep pen, then back to Millie. He hesitated, as if deciding what to do next. "I'll go myself. I don't need babysitting."

"I didn't mean to..." Millie called after him. He didn't turn back, just continued hobbling toward the path back to the cabin.

She watched him a little longer, shrugged, and started filling the last hole. Millie hoped she would not be that erratic when she got to be his age. He'd always made her feel part of the family, then suddenly he made her feel like she'd said something wrong.

On the way back to the Suburban, Millie stopped often along the cliff, admiring a few more petroglyphs that she hadn't noticed before, perhaps because more detail was discernable in the late morning sun. One, somewhat higher than her head, drew her attention for several minutes. "I do believe that is a yucca blossom," she said out loud. A vertical three-foot-long stem was the center of teardrop-shaped, four-inch petals extending out from both sides. It looked just like the yucca image on the silver bracelet a Navajo woman had picked out for her at the Shiprock flea market last summer.

She opened the back of the Suburban, pushed the tools inside, slung her backpack over her shoulder, and headed to the Gaspar boulder.

Millie figured the boulder would make a good place for lunch. She nodded to the nude figure and brushed off a beetle that had landed on the A in the G-A-S-P letters. After scanning the boulder's base and glancing under the junipers to make sure no snakes rested in their shade, Millie sat down, her back against the boulder beneath the nude's dangling cigarette. She opened her lunch and stretched her legs out. Much as she enjoyed Lydia's company and looked forward to telling her about finding the old wagon road, Millie craved time for herself.

Not many decades earlier, sheepherders whiled away their time here, making their mark on the boulder and probably taking a good many siestas in its shade. She fought off drowsiness, helped by the increasing chill in the boulder's shadow and the steady breeze that had come up while she ate lunch. She stood up, gathered her gear, and got back to work.

An hour's slow pacing and an occasional check of the ID guide produced seven more species to add to her plant list. After squatting next to a ground-hugging *Astragalus* for several minutes to tease out its species name from among the several milkvetches extant in the Four Corners area, Millie stood and stretched backwards until she faced the blue sky. As she lowered her head, she looked in the direction of the road and noted the gathering clouds, dark and threatening rain. *I need to keep an eye on those. I'd just as soon not have to spend a night here due to washed out roads. Then again, maybe I'd have company with Gavin's pretend ghost in the homestead cabin.*

Movement caught her eye. A hairy, canine tail waved steadily above the sagebrush. Millie stood motionless, watching to see what the coyote was after. The animal plunged into a wolfberry bush, out of sight for a moment, then came up with a lizard's tail wiggling from its jaws. It began trotting toward Millie. She tried to stay still. The animal looked like Ragged Ear when he caught the lizard under the lilacs. But instead of disappearing under bushes, the coyote tossed its prey into the air and caught it with a frightening snap of its jaws. Millie gasped. She clamped a hand over her mouth, but too late. The coyote dropped down, belly almost on the ground, and slunk away, jostling the sagebrush that made a slight clattering sound.

"Ugh, too bad, lizard," Millie said. "There are always predators around, aren't there? Kill or be killed seems to be the norm around here." It sounded louder, as if another person had said the words. She'd been so focused looking down at plants that she hadn't noticed she was in the alcove that amplified sound. She wiped dust and moisture off her forehead, and pressed lightly along the raised scar. She pulled a water bottle out of her pack's side pocket for a drink, but froze, listening. There were other voices, men's voices.

She shouldered her backpack, moved to the shadow of the cliff wall, and walked in their direction. Before rounding the curve of the alcove, she halted. The voices came from the trees beyond the sheep pen. She could not hear what words the men were throwing at each other, but their tone made her heart quicken. One voice was loud, angry. The other was gruff and shaky. Mr. Gaspar's. *But he went back to his pickup—didn't he?*

29. I Know You Know

The ignorant mind, with its infinite afflictions, passions, and evils, is rooted in the three poisons. Greed, anger, and delusion.

— Bodhidharma, 6th Century Buddhist Monk

"I know you know where it is, old man." Millie had heard that voice before but could not place whose or when. The words vibrated with anger.

"I don't know what you are talking about." Mr. Gaspar's voice was dismissive.

Millie eased her backpack down by the corral post. Heart racing, she moved toward them. Someone was threatening Mr. Gaspar. She stepped carefully, avoiding crunching on sticks. She spotted her landlord's white shirt through the trees. All she could make out of the other man were glimpses of blue.

"That cross is going to be mine. You're going to show

me where it is." Gavin McIntyre's voice. The tone of his voice. It was the same as when he talked about the New Agey types who had a lot of money to spend; the same as when he said he needed the upcoming California tour group in order to make his van's insurance payment. A lusting for money.

"I talked to your *Señora*. She told me you were here. You wouldn't want Della to worry about you not coming back now, would you?"

"You don't deserve anything that our beautiful Rosalinda touched. Stop pushing me."

At a thudding sound of something hitting the ground, Millie moved closer. Gavin's blue shirt clung to his back with sweat stains. He was breathing hard. And pointing a gun at Mr. Gaspar, who lay face down on the ground.

The octogenarian rolled over and struggled to get up. Halfway onto his feet, he fell again, one foot caught in a strand of barbed wire. Millie recalled stepping over the old fence the day she found the rose bush. The strands were partly embedded in the ground, but still easy to trip over.

Millie reached out, wanting to help Mr. Gaspar. Neither man knew she was there. She should back away, run to her vehicle, and drive out to call for help. But she was held frozen in the sphere of Gavin's malevolence, and she could not leave her frail landlord in danger.

"Stop stalling, old man. Get up." Gavin held his foot on the wire so that Mr. Gaspar could free himself.

Slowly, Mr. Gaspar got on his knees. Gavin kicked the walking stick toward him. It hit against Mr. Gaspar's leg.

Too proud or too stubborn to ask for a hand up, Mr. Gaspar, using the walking stick hand-over-hand, pulled himself upright. All the while glaring at his antagonist.

Gavin waved the gun enough to draw Mr. Gaspar's

attention to it, then held it steady, pointed directly at his victim's chest. "Now show me where that silver cross is buried. I heard you say at your big birthday bash that it is custom to bury the dead with a treasured piece of jewelry. Don't deny it. I got no plans to mess with that woman's corpse. Show me where the silver cross is and you can go home."

Gavin eased back a couple steps, giving his prey more space. "Now, come on, old man. We both know that professor what-ever-his-name-was didn't come here for nothing. He knew the cross was here. I'm half a mind to think it might've been you who killed him."

Gaspar spat and hissed a contemptuous snarl. His face was flushed. He puffed out uneven breaths.

Millie's hand shot to her mouth. He looked bad, barely able to breathe.

"No, you bastard. I won't help you. You can kill me first."

"You don't mean that. We wouldn't want to make Della a widow, would we? You understand?"

Gavin took another step back, thrust out his chin, and lowered the gun. "But I mean this." The shot hit the ground between the two men, peppering them both with sand.

Millie clasped her hands over her ears. The sound ricocheted off the cliff wall and around her skull. A whiff of gunpowder floated to her nose.

Mr. Gaspar collapsed into a sitting position, shaking the noise out of his head.

Millie's shoulders tensed. She had to help her friend. She shouted, "Gavin, leave him alone."

The pistol and Gavin whirled toward Millie. "Wha..." he began, "oh, it's you, the plant girl." His glare, even diffused by the branches between them, made Millie's throat tighten.

The gunshot's echo faded away. The rising wind stirred juniper branches. The cry of a raven landing on the cliff top gave a moment's interlude, enough for Millie to formulate words that she knew would lure Gavin's attention.

"That silver cross is a legend, Gavin. Who knows if it even exists? But I know where there's a stash of pearls, antique pearls. They're worth a lot of money."

Gavin took a step toward Millie, tilting his head to see her better. "What are you talking about?"

"We found pearls. Real pearls, old ones. Lydia and me. In the orchard."

"How'd you find anything like that?" He stepped back over the old fence, moving closer to her.

Mr. Gaspar had rolled onto his knees, positioning his walking stick to get up. Millie's heart slowed a beat. *Maybe he's not hurt; he's getting up.* Yet the red flush on his face sent her heart back into racing mode.

"Somebody put them next to a peach tree. A long time ago. The tree grew over them, but it's been dead for a long time. Just a stump. But it got knocked over last weekend, along with other wreckage that went on."

He did not blink an eye, did not ask what happened, just fixed his full attention on Millie.

"You know about that, don't you," Millie accused. "You brought a tour here didn't you? The California group, that you said liked to detour for drugs."

Her words made no dent in the intensity of his stare. He hesitated, then said, "Ha, pearls. If there'd been any pearls lying around, I'd of seen them."

"Nobody would have seen them before that rain the next day washed them off." Millie chattered on, keeping his attention. "Lydia said they were part of a rosary. That's what Doctor Bernnard was looking for, I swear."

"No rosary," Mr. Gaspar said in a weak voice, "never found the rosary." He sank back down until he was sitting on the ground.

Gavin turned to the collapsed man. "What'd you say, old man?"

"N... nothing. Why don't you get out of here? Leave us alone."

Her landlord's words were defiant but his voice weak. He could not endure more of Gavin's menacing. "Listen to *me*, Gavin," Millie yelled, "I can take you to the real thing. Handfuls of pearls. Lydia said old ones like that are worth a lot. Better than what people can get now. So they'd be valuable. Real valuable."

Gavin's head swayed from Millie to Gaspar and back to her. He licked his lips. "Show me."

30. The Ghost Appeared

We may stumble and fall but shall rise again; it should be enough if we did not run away from the battle.
— Mahatma Gandhi, Indian Political Leader, 1869–1948

Millie could smell sweat from Gavin's body. He followed close behind her. She glanced back once. Mr. Gaspar was laying on his side on the ground. No longer was her landlord's face red, now it was ashen. This alarmed Millie even more. It meant heat stroke or possibly going into shock.

She had to get help for this man who provided her a place to live, who made her part of the family.

At the sheep pen, she bent to pick up her backpack.

"Leave it." The command stopped her in mid-reach. "No telling what you have in there."

Perhaps she could at least keep Gavin distracted.

271

Perhaps Mr. Gaspar could regain enough strength to get himself to a place to hide from Gavin's harassment.

"Geez, Gavin, just a clip board and plant books, what do you think? I never figured I'd need to defend myself against rabbits and juniper trees."

He shoved her, hard. "Don't get smart with me, plant girl."

Millie stumbled backward, almost tripping on the fallen down boards that once made up the gate. She recovered, but not before colliding with the broken wire that used to latch the gate closed. Millie straightened up. Pain blasted throughout her shoulder and upper arm. She grabbed her left shoulder with her other arm. Gavin twitched at the sudden movement. Millie hesitated, then began slowly rubbing her arm. Blood seeped through a rip in her sleeve. The point of the rusty wire wrapped around the top of the post gleamed red.

Gavin shifted from foot to foot, his nostrils flaring, spittle at the corners of his mouth. Gone was the friendly tour guide. The man in front of her was a creature of desperation. Yes, he needed money, as he'd said himself, to pay insurance on his van, to protect his livelihood. Still, there was more here. There was a fanaticism for silver, for treasure.

No longer was she dealing with a logical person. She feared for Mr. Gaspar's survival, and for her own.

"I'll show you right where we left the pearls. They're covered up at the end of the orchard. You wouldn't find them without me." Millie kept her voice even, reassuring.

She put one foot in front of the other. The road came into view. *If there's a vehicle coming by, I'll step right out in front of it. Somebody's got to help Mister Gaspar.* At best, a half dozen pickups might travel the Lejos Canyon road in a day, a busy day at that. This thought made her feel like a drowning person reaching for straws.

Still holding her shoulder with one hand, Millie stepped onto the road. The only vehicles in sight were parked across the road from her, the Ancient Ones Adventure Travel van and Mr. Gaspar's dusty pickup. Gavin's heavy footsteps crunched on the gravel directly behind her.

Advice from a campus safety awareness workshop surfaced in her mind—appeal to the male upbringing to be a protector. Put the harasser in the role of helper, let them see you are not a threat, that they don't really want to hurt you. "I'm thirsty, Gavin. You carry extra water bottles in your van, don't you?"

"Too bad. Keep going," he growled.

It didn't work.

She had no weapon, no phone, no one around for miles. Except for Mr. Gaspar. And no telling what condition he may be in; they'd left him lying on the ground.

"Take me to the pearls."

The last time she walked the path from the road to the cabin with Gavin, they had walked side-by-side in strained conversation about why he left when they opened the root cellar. Now he walked a few paces behind her, his footsteps hitting the ground hard.

Instead of veering toward the door where Lydia had stood that day talking to the students, Millie kept to the path that ran between the cabin and the corral.

His footsteps stopped. "Hey, what happed here?" He indicated the gap in the cabin's wall with the revolver's barrel.

"As if you don't know." Millie turned to face him. "Your tour creeps hit this place."

He continued looking at the jagged edge of the broken boards. "I never told them to tear things up. That damn

California bunch. I could tell right off, in Albuquerque when I picked them up at the Sunport, this was going to be a wild party to deal with. I even cut the day at Mesa Verde short because they wanted to cruise Durango for anything and everything to get high with. The best I could do to herd them along was to promise this stop for jimson-weed. It was you that clued me in that it grew over by the cliff. When I told them about the jimsonweed, that there was even early native rock art showing someone having visions, they thought it would be cool to take some en-chanted weed back to California."

Millie bit her lip. It hurt that something she said could be so perversely construed by this man. She turned her back to him and walked another fifteen yards. She stopped kneading her arm long enough to point at the glaring red STAY AWAY THE GHOST scrawled on the outhouse door.

Gavin stopped a few feet behind her. He rubbed his chin with his free hand, not saying anything for a moment. "I didn't mean for that to happen either. They must have done it after Bailee did her thing."

"Bailee? Bailee Fernandez? She was here, too?"

Gavin's next words sounded normal, back to the guide entertaining tour participants. "I'd been priming those dudes all along, see, about the murdered bride's ghost here at the homestead. She played it just like I wanted her to."

"So that's what the wedding dress was all about." Millie shook her head, trying to dislodge the image of Bailee's face and turquoise bangs hovering over the soggy, muddy, once-treasured wedding dress.

"You should've seen Bailee floating out the cabin door." His laugh was loud enough to attract the attention of anyone on the whole homestead site. Except there was no one else to hear.

"She freaked them out. Two of the girls ran all the way back to the van. Then, when she tried to get out of that wedding dress, two sizes too big for her it was, her pants dropped to her knees. Oh, those dudes got a good kick out of that." He used the knuckle of his gun hand to wipe laugh tears from his eyes.

Whatever mixed feelings Millie had about Bailee evaporated in the increasing wind, strong enough to rattle the outhouse door. Gone was any credibility about Bailee's pretense of interest in the Hispanic settlements of Lejos Canyon. Making a mockery of a long-ago murdered ancestor by pretending to be her ghost, that was no way to honor the family heritage.

"And it was Bailee, wasn't it, that wanted the cuttings from the orchard? She said her brother owns an orchard near Fresno."

"She remembered your saying farmers like to get pieces of heirloom varieties to graft onto their own fruit trees.

Millie shifted her eyes beyond his shoulder for a moment. The BLM law enforcement vehicle was coming along the road at a snail's pace. *Robby! She's here. She's making her drive-by patrol. I'm not alone.*

"What's the big deal. Just a few twigs. Don't look so antsy." Gavin continued standing in the same spot, relaxing both arms such that the pistol now pointed toward the ground.

Robby's got to see what's happening. She'll stop to look over a pickup unfamiliar to her. The pickup that wouldn't be here if Mr. Gaspar had gone home like he said he was going to, and she wouldn't be talking to this madman.

Her eyes riveted to the slow moving vehicle, Millie took a step sideways.

So did Gavin, blocking her view of the road. "I hear it.

Don't think I'd fall for that old trick. It's just some rancher or oil and gas hand driving by. Let's not wave or do anything stupid to draw attention. You understand?"

That's what he'd said to Mr. Gaspar just before firing a shot next to his feet. Millie nodded and dropped both arms to her sides.

Act like it was just some passerby. Keep him talking. "Why? Why did you let them rampage through the orchard, knocking over stumps?"

"Must have happened when me and Bailee were getting the fruit tree grafts. I didn't figure on them messing up the homestead. Those dudes were wound up, needed to work off their crazy energy. I feel kinda bad about the damage."

"Sure you do," Millie's voice dripped with scorn. "That's why Bailee was so interested in jimsonweed. She wanted that to take with her, too."

"No, no. She left right off with the twigs. Said she had a bucket of water in her car all ready to put them in for the drive to Fresno." Gavin flailed an arm backwards, toward the road and the cliff beyond. "Bailee was gone before the rest of us went over to get the jimsonweed."

Millie glanced in that direction. The BLM vehicle was still moving slowly but going away! She reached out, as if to make it stop. Mouth gaping, her eyes followed it until it disappeared from sight.

Gavin must have thought Millie's anxious face was triggered by Bailee's involvement. "You two never hit it off, did you? She's not a bad kid, just out for some fun and to earn a few bucks that I said I'd pay her."

He fingered the wallet in his jeans back pocket. "That cut into my tour income, but was worth it. Those goofballs handed over some pre-t-t-y nice tips when I dropped them off at the Sunport. God knows, I needed it. A guy can hardly make a living driving dudes around and scouring this godforsaken land for antiques and artifacts." The mention of money seemed to tug Gavin back to his greedy self. He waved the gun once toward the orchard then held it steady, pointed at her chest. "Get moving. I want to see those pearls."

Millie thought her knees might buckle, but she started walking. Nothing to see now toward the road. *Robby was gone.*

Gavin pushed her with his free hand. "Go on. Old Antonio walks faster than that."

She wasn't sure if Mr. Gaspar could even walk now. He looked so weak when he fell, possibly seriously hurt.

Gavin's manhandling made the pain in her arm flare. Millie wrapped her other hand over it. She felt a trickle of blood drop from her elbow. She knew the wire had ripped a serious gash along her upper arm.

"I'm taking you there," she said through clenched teeth.

But then what? What happens once he gets his hands on the pearls?

31. Never Say Girlie

You gain strength, courage, and confidence by every experience in which you really stop to look fear in the face. You are able to say to yourself, 'I lived through this horror. I can take the next thing that comes along.'
— Eleanor Roosevelt, United States First Lady, 1933–1945

Millie hesitated at the corner of the orchard by the blue tarp that she used for her gear. *Could it be only a few weeks ago that she and Lydia started work at the homestead?* The place was so quiet then, undisturbed. The valuable heirloom fruit trees seemed a treasure then. Now she saw only the spaces among gnarled trunks that offered no protection, no place to hide.

She stopped at the first apple tree where she'd found branches had been cut. "You did this. I just hope it survives any insect infestation because of it." She led Gavin to the next tree with damaged branches, paused without looking at him, and let out an aggrieved sigh. She did the same thing at the next attacked tree.

"Come on. You're just fooling with me. I'm starting to wonder if these pearls even exist."

Millie's mind darted, grasping for a way to deal with this man, a way to escape and get help for Mr. Gaspar.

"Of course they exist. Remember when you brought the university students here and Lydia talked to them by the cabin?"

"Yeah, she held up some dinky white thing, said she found it here. The students ate up every word she said. They liked exploring this old homestead as much as the big archeological parks I took them to."

"We didn't know it then, but that bead was part of the rosary that Doctor Bernnard traced all the way from Spain."

"How do you know that?" He passed the revolver to his left hand, letting his right arm dangle downward to rest. Gavin seemed to like gathering tidbits of history to tell his tour participants.

Millie turned a little toward him. "Remember when you had Lydia open the root cellar? All we could see was the back of a corpse?"

"What the hell does that matter. What about these so-called pearls?"

"That was Doctor Bernnard and the pearls are why he came here. He traced a pearl rosary to this homestead and had the idea that there was a stolen cross attached to it."

Millie shuffled around a few inches more, not quite facing the man, but enough to see him make a go-on motion with his gun hand.

"In the front pocket of his shirt, Doctor Bernnard had a notebook. His research, jotted down in that notebook, is what you heard Lydia talking about at Mister Gaspar's birthday party. He was a history professor tracking religious objects from Spain brought by early Hispanic settlers. A silver cross got stolen from a Spanish church about the time people were emigrating to Mexico. The professor had a theory that the cross might be with a rosary, a rosary made with pearls, that was given to the couple that built this homestead. But the wife got murdered and the place was abandoned."

Gavin put the gun back in his right hand and held it steady, pointing at Millie. "So the cross is not just a legend. It's here somewhere. I'm going back to that old man. I'll get where it's buried out of him one way or another."

"No, wait." Millie's mind spun fast as a whirlwind. "You saw the pearl that Lydia found in the cabin. Proof there was a pearl rosary. There was a cross stolen, yes, but that was a couple of centuries ago. It was just a hunch on Doctor Bernnard's part that it was attached to this rosary. There's no real evidence that the cross even got to Mexico. Then brought here? What's the chance of that? The silver cross is all a legend, as far as we know. The professor's notes said there *was* a rosary. The pearls are for real. They could make you a rich man. I know where they are." Millie let go of her injured arm long enough to point to the far corner of the orchard.

Gavin took a step sideways to look where she pointed. He swayed from one foot to the other, the gun swaying with him.

Millie's pointing hand flew to her throat. Beyond Gavin's shoulder, there was another gun pointed in her direction. A gun held just below a badge. A badge on a tan shirt. Worn by the BLM law enforcement officer.

Robby was sneaking through the orchard. *Robby, she did see us! I can't let Gavin know she's here.*

Robby gave a quick nod and motioned Millie to keep moving.

Millie waved her good arm to grab Gavin's attention. "Follow me, Gavin. We're going to the far corner of the orchard, where the stump was knocked over."

Millie turned her back to Gavin and started walking. "Are you coming or not? You'll see the roots sticking up. The rosary was buried underneath them."

He followed close behind her. Even without eyes in the back of her head, Millie perceived Robby matching their steps, slipping closer.

"Wait a minute." Gavin stopped.

Millie swung around to face him. With a racing heart, she forced her eyes to stay on Gavin's face.

"How come Lydia had that one pearl up at the cabin, if they were buried here?" As Gavin spoke, Robby worked her way closer, slinking cat-like from tree to tree.

"Um, yeah, I can see why you'd ask that." Millie made digging motions with her good arm, keeping Gavin's attention. "She dug it out of a pack rat nest. Some rodent must have carried it up there. Come on."

Millie started walking again, talking in a loud voice, suppressing a dread that Gavin might spot Robby. "Lydia could tell it was the antique rosary, even though the cording was mostly rotted apart so the beads got separated."

Millie took two quick steps, stopped next to the hollow left by the uprooted stump, and vigorously pointed downward. "Right there, Gavin, that's where the rain washed off a few pearls so we saw them on top of the dirt."

He dropped down on his knees, in the same spot Lydia had knelt while picking out the bits of cord still knotted around beads. He leaned over the hole and ruffled his left hand through the loose dirt. "There's nothing here. You think if you keep stringing me along, you're going to save old Gaspar. I'm going after him."

Keep him talking. "You can't hurt Mister Gaspar. He needs medical help. He could die back there. I guess that wouldn't matter to you. You've already killed one man."

Gavin sat back on his heels, raising his face and his gun hand toward Millie. "If you're saying I killed that professor, you're crazy. I was barely twenty years old when that happened. Shoot, I never heard of Lejos Canyon until I was thirty and got hired on a couple of archeological digs up this way."

Just a few inches of Robby's skinny form now showed behind a trunk twenty yards away.

"Why should I believe that? You told me and Lydia you'd been all over Lejos Canyon, nosing around in abandoned homesteads. Did you steal artifacts, too, from the archeological digs you worked on when nobody was looking?"

"Maybe I did, maybe I didn't. But I know enough about the black market for old stuff to know those pearls would fetch a pretty penny. But not nearly as much as what a solid silver cross would go for. You've been lying to me all along. There's nothing here. I'm going back to where we left that old man."

"Wait. I told you Lydia took them out and hid them so only me and her would know where they are." Millie's eyes shifted to the nearby rabbitbrush where the pearls were sequestered in her green shirt. She couldn't let her eyes move in Robby's direction. She backed up several steps and plopped down on her butt.

"Jeez, girlie, you are a pain in the ass," Gavin growled. He stood up and moved toward her, eyes blazing with anger. "I'm tired of you jerking me around." He raised his arm, ready to strike.

He took a step toward Millie and crashed to the

ground, face first. His gun hand landed next to her boot.

She raised her leg and smashed the heel of her boot down on his hand, making a satisfying crunching sound.

"I hate being called 'girlie.'"

32. That's A Lie

The object of the superior man is truth.
— Confucius, Chinese Philosopher, 551–479 BC

Millie kicked the gun away with her other foot. It spun across the ground and landed near the rabbitbrush that sheltered the hidden pearls.

Robby darted forward. She stopped just behind Millie, teetered a bit from her sprint, and took a wide stance with her gun pointed at Gavin. Without taking her eyes off Gavin, she tossed a "Good job" comment to Millie.

Gavin raised up and steadied himself on his knees.

"Hold it right there. Put your hands over your head." Detaching handcuffs from her belt, Robby stepped around behind him. She snapped on one, pulled the arm behind his back, grabbed his other arm, and clamped it in the other cuff. The startled man looked over his shoulder and muttered, "What the hell?"

"You are under arrest. You have the right to remain silent." Robby continued reading him his rights.

Millie crab-walked backwards on her fanny until she bumped against the next peach tree. She put her uninjured hand on the ground to push herself up. Her fingers slid through a loop of twine knotted around the trunk. The string—the string that Lydia said to watch out for, that she had laid out so she could relocate the pearls—that's what caused Gavin to trip and fall on his face. Millie sent a silent *thank you* to Lydia.

Gavin growled, his face twisted into a vicious scowl. "You've got nothing on me."

Robby took a few steps, placing herself between Millie and the enraged man. "I already saw enough, you asshole, to come up with a half dozen charges."

Millie stood and held onto the trunk until she stopped shaking. "So, you did see me, Robby, when you drove by— see what he was doing."

"Uh-huh. You were out in the open. No cover. I knew if he heard the vehicle stop, well, I don't know what he would have done. I pulled over just down the road. I ran back as fast as I could."

Gavin, fighting the handcuffs, bent into contortions getting onto his feet.

"Get going, Gavin. Walk behind us, Millie. Leave that gun where it is. Somebody will retrieve it later and bag it as evidence."

Gavin kicked a clump of loose dirt into the hole, almost throwing himself off balance. "I can't walk with my hands behind my back like this."

Robby gripped his upper arm and motioned with pursed lips toward the cabin.

Gavin began walking, at first taking short steps. As they left the orchard, he blurted out, "I didn't hurt anybody. All I came here for was to get the silver cross."

Millie sucked in her breath. "That's a lie." She lifted her hand from the rip in her shirt and saw that the wound had started oozing drops of blood again. "You pushed Mister Gaspar. He was lying on the ground when we left him over there. He's old. He might be really hurt."

"Gaspar is here too?" Robby asked. "That's his truck next to the van?"

"I was across the road, restoring where those jerks dug up jimsonweed like I told Wirt I was going to. I saw Mister Gaspar by the sheep pen."

Robby glanced back at Millie. "Why would he show up over there?"

"Last night, I told him about the vandalism to the cabin. I knew he was angry about it, but I never expected him to come out here, much less follow the path over to the rock art cliff. I showed him what I was doing and offered to help him back to his truck. He brushed me off and started walking in that direction, so I got back to work. Later, I heard voices arguing and realized he didn't leave."

"If you'd minded your own business, I'd have that cross by now," Gavin growled.

"That's what he kept saying to Mister Gaspar, demanding that he tell where the cross is. Gavin pushed him down, scared us both with a shot to the ground, threatened to kill him. All I could think of was to make Gavin leave Mister Gaspar alone. I told him about the pearls, how valuable they are."

"So that's how you came to be over here, after you promised Wirt to not go near the cabin."

"I didn't have much choice at the time, you know. I had to think of something to get him away from Mister Gaspar," Millie snapped. Bucking authority wasn't something she was accustomed to doing.

"That cut on your arm, how'd you get that? How bad is it?"

Before Millie could answer, the screech of worn brakes and rumble of a bad exhaust system caused them all to look toward the road and watch a vehicle slide to a stop. The driver whipped an old turquoise truck in next to the Adventure van.

A tall man unfolded himself from the driver's seat, took a few steps in their direction, and paused to look at them. He went to the passenger's side and lifted out a shotgun.

Gavin stopped and half turned toward Robby. Drops of sweat tricked down his face. He seemed unsure whether her gun or the stranger's shotgun posed the greater threat.

Robby tensed.

"It's Carlos Lucero. I know him." Millie rushed out the words. "He must be looking for Mister Gaspar. I've seen him at the Gaspars' house lots of times."

"You know him? Trust him? Then keep moving, Gavin." Robby motioned toward the vehicles.

Mr. Lucero stood in front of his truck, dangling the shotgun in one hand. He backed away as the small group reached the road. "Hello, *Señorita* Millie. It looks like you've been having some trouble here."

His voice was calm, gentlemanly, but Millie saw his tense stance, ready to react with lightning speed to any threat to herself or Robby. "Della called me. She told me this man here showed up at their house, wanting to talk to Antonio. She told him to come back later, that Antonio wasn't home. He got so pushy and demanding that she told him where Antonio was. She got worried about the mean way this guy was acting. She asked me to go look for her husband."

Robby circled Gavin to stand next to the tall man. She motioned for Millie to move behind them and glanced down the road.

Millie followed her eyes and saw the BLM pickup parked in the distance.

"I've got to call in, get back-up from the sheriff's office."

Robby's eyes swiveled from a defeated-looking Gavin slumped against the Adventure van, to her truck, then to Mr. Lucero. "Can you keep an eye on this dude? I'll tell them to send for an ambulance, too. Gaspar hasn't shown up yet; he might need medical assistance. Check that wound on your arm, too."

"Did something happen to Antonio? Where is he?" Mr. Lucero's voice trembled with concern. He shifted the shotgun, rested it in the crook of his arm, casually pointing it at Gavin. "I will make sure he is here when you return, Officer. If there has been any harm to my friend Antonio, I'd like an excuse to blast this bastard."

"You can't leave me with this old coot," Gavin sniveled.

"Sit down, Gavin," Robby commanded. "I'll be back in five minutes."

The empty-handed treasure hunter eased down the side of his van, leaving a clean streak where his shirt brushed against the door.

Millie started walking across the road to the path to the sheep pen.

"Where are you going?" Robby, half turned toward her vehicle, called to her.

"I'm going to where we left Mister Gaspar. I've got to find him."

"That arm needs medical attention."

Millie kept walking.

Robby's last words were lost in a clap of thunder.

289

33. Something I Must Say

The generations of living things pass in swift succession, and like runners in a race they hand on the torch of life.
— Lucretius, Roman Poet, 99–55 BC

Millie hit the path at a trot, lengthened her stride, and kept that pace over the uneven ground until she reached the sheep pen. Slowing to a walk, she called out, "Mister Gaspar, it's me, Millie."

There was no answer, at least not one that she could hear over a second roll of thunder. She picked up the backpack that Gavin made her drop and stepped away from the post with the wire that had pierced her arm. Positioning the pack across her back was something she had done so many times she usually didn't even think about it. But now she gently maneuvered one strap under her left arm, hoping not to start the wound bleeding again, and settled the pack on her shoulders.

A minute later, she was on the path and working her way through junipers to where she last saw Mr. Gaspar. Spotting the barbed wire on the ground, Millie stopped and put the toe of her boot on it.

Millie stretched tall to see the rose bush, then walked over to it. Mr. Gaspar was gone. He had gotten away, somewhere.

She glanced at the cross carved into the rock, then studied the ground where Gavin had pushed her landlord down. Small indentations in the sand showed where he had jammed his walking stick down. Millie assessed the scene and figured he had made two or three attempts to stand based on the boot scrapes around the deepest walking stick pit. Being careful to step back over the wire on the ground, she saw where the poke marks followed the path toward the sheep pen.

She could have seen the marks as she hurried along this path minutes ago, but she wasn't focused on anything other than finding her landlord.

At the sheep pen, Millie stopped for a moment and watched the shadow made by the encroaching dark clouds flow across the ground and up the petroglyph cliff. Fat drops of rain dotting the ground drew her attention. *Where is he going? How far could the elderly man go in his condition?*

The walking stick marks continued along the base of the cliff, alongside hobbling footprints. Suddenly, she knew. *Of course, the Gaspar Boulder. Where his family has rested for generations.*

She followed her landlord's trail, moving rapidly along the path. So sure was she that she covered several yards between stopping to check for poke marks. At the last petroglyph she paused to confirm that Gaspar had turned in the direction of the boulder. She hoped that he had managed to continue walking out to the road but was almost certain she would find him by the boulder because of his weak state and fear of Gavin.

As soon as she came in sight of the boulder, she again called, "Mister Gaspar, it's me, Millie. You're safe, Gavin has been arrested."

The sound of a low groan spurred Millie on. Mr. Gaspar sat slumped against the boulder, his arms crossed and chin resting on his chest. He was in the same spot where Millie had sat for lunch a few hours earlier.

The dark, erratic clouds no longer dripped rain, but the chill breeze stirred juniper branches on both sides of the boulder.

She kneeled on the ground and leaned close. "It's me, Mister Gaspar. Are you okay? Can you walk?"

One hand twitched and his head jerked upright. "Just taking a nap, Miss Millie. I'm fine. Just give me a minute or two." His thickened voice and ashen face belied the words.

"The BLM Officer, Robby Ramirez, is here. She arrested Gavin and put him in handcuffs. Carlos is here, too."

A feeble smile greeted her words. "Carlos, here? My oldest friend. Tell him to come here." His head fell back against the stone, and he closed his eyes.

"Can you get up, Mister Gaspar? We need to walk out to the road where we can get help."

He lifted a hand and waved a weak dismissal to that idea. "I can't... can't get up." His hand flailed in the air then landed softly on Millie's knee. "I can go no farther."

Millie pulled a water bottle from her pack, placed it in his hand, and wrapped his cold fingers around it.

He lifted the water bottle to his lips and took a swallow.

"I'm going out to the road, Mister Gaspar. I'm going to tell Robby where you are. She's already called for medical help. They'll be here soon and can help you." Millie began to stand but he grabbed her hand.

"There is something I must say to someone."

She eased back down by his side.

Mr. Gaspar's eyes were wide, whites showing, as if he had seen something frightening. He spoke in a barely audible whisper. "That professor. I want somebody to know the truth. I killed him."

She feared he was becoming delirious. "I've got to go get help, Mister Gaspar. You're going to be okay."

His grip tightened on her hand. "Listen to me. When the professor came to town, he talked to me and Della. I knew what he was looking for. Two days later, *mi abuela* Margarita came to me in a dream and said to follow him." His glazed eyes looked into the sky, as if he was picturing this long-ago vision.

Refocusing on her face, his next words made Millie sway side-to-side. She wished she had pulled away and gone for help, but instead she leaned closer, spellbound. "He was digging up the cross. I knew he almost had it when I heard the shovel hit the little metal box I buried it in. I couldn't let him desecrate the only thing I had left of our beloved Rosalinda." A tear traveled down his cheek.

Millie looked away. She looked at the carved nude's dangling cigarette, anywhere but at what seemed like the face of a dying man.

"I talked to the professor, asked him what he was doing. He started to lecture me on how religious artifacts were brought from Spain. Ha, as if I don't know my own family's history." Gaspar's voice became stronger. "I grabbed the shovel from him. He tried to take it back. He said, 'Don't bother me, I'm onto something important here.' That made me madder."

Again, he gazed into the distance, his face wavering between rage and regret.

"I swung the shovel. I hit him hard. He fell."

Millie recoiled. She relived the moment when she went down into the root cellar and saw the desiccated body. She recalled Robby's words when the medical investigator removed the body: "...we got a good look at the side that had been facing the sod wall. Front of his skull was cracked wide open... I'd never seen a dried-up brain before."

The silence wedged between them was broken by a crashing roll of thunder. Scattered drops of rain fell on Mr. Gaspar's face. A cold drop landed on Millie's neck and slid down her back. With one hand clamped in her landlord's grasp and her other arm pulsing with pain at the slightest movement, all she could do was flex her shoulders.

The cooling drops seemed to slightly invigorate her landlord.

"I am a murderer, too. José killed the bastard that murdered Rosalinda. It needed doing, and so did keeping her cross safe from the professor. I bring shame to our family." He touched his forehead, heart, and both shoulders, making the sign of the cross.

"Tell Della, tell Bailee." With the mention of his loved ones, his lips moved into a smile for a moment. "Once, when I was a child, I killed a little rabbit with a rock. That was the worst thing I'd ever done until I saw that man digging for the cross. Maybe the professor had a family, too. My nightmare is they would never know. You must tell them, so they no longer fret. Tell them I am sorry."

Millie squeezed her eyes shut, but that did nothing to stop the words from chilling her heart. She did not want to be the recipient of this man's confession. Yet her landlord's next words kept her rooted in place, to understand the tragedy that happened at this homestead.

"When I realized what I had done, I carried and dragged the body to the root cellar—to hide, no smell for the vultures."

"You put Doctor Bernnard in the root cellar over by the cabin? By yourself?"

He looked at Millie and answered the disbelief in her eyes. "I was younger then, stronger." He loosened Millie's hand and lifted his arm as if to show he still was strong. But his hand fell over his heart.

"That night, I went to Carlos' house, called him to come outside. I told him what I had done. He knew of the cross. He did not know that I had buried it. He walked back and forth, back and forth. I did not know what he was going to say to me."

Millie eased back, preparing to rise and go for help. Her mind was befuddled. Her landlord, Della's loving husband, friend to all—a murderer. And now that distinguished, gentlemanly Carlos. He was involved, too.

"Once he stopped swearing at me, *amigo* that he is, he agreed to help me the next day. He got rid of that fancy, red Bronco the professor had here. Ever since you found it in the wash, we've been scared that we'd be discovered."

Millie soaked up every word. She would need to relate all this to Robby and Detective St. Claire, and Wirt. Lydia, too.

"I did not know where he hid the vehicle. I was over here. I covered up where the professor had been digging and got rid of the briefcase."

The briefcase, the missing piece related to the professor's disappearance. Millie blurted out, "What happened to the briefcase, Mister Gaspar?"

He angled a thumb toward the massive stone behind

his head. "I hid that leather bag behind here where no-body would find it. I was in a hurry to get rid of it, some things dropped out—a pencil and candy bars and maybe some papers. I don't remember. They were gone, animals I suppose, when I came back later."

Millie recalled the pack rat nest piled up against the sheep pen post and rock cliff, where Lydia found the yel-low pencil. Bits of paper also decorated the nest. Lydia might not be so eager to dissect the nest when she hears why the pencil ended up there.

"But the rose bush I found," Millie had to ask the ques-tion, to refute the rumors once and for all, "is that where Rosalinda is buried?"

"No. No, you heard me say, at my birthday party, that she is properly buried in the cemetery. That Gavin thief, he heard it, too."

The gruffness was back in his voice. This time Millie was relieved to hear it; perhaps he was regaining enough strength to walk to the road.

"I put the rose there, because it is where I buried Rosalinda's beautiful cross. *Mi abuela*, as she lay dying, told me to open the bottom drawer of the dresser by her bed. The cross was there, wrapped in a black shawl, still in the package that José sent to her months after he left. Margarita made me promise to never let the cross leave the Gaspar homestead. The very day we put *mi abuela* in the ground, I brought the cross to the homestead and buried it by the red cliffs that Rosalinda loved. I thought it would always be safe there."

"That's why you didn't want me or anyone to go on that side of the sheep pen—because they might see the rose bush or even the cross carved next to it."

"It took me many days to carve the cross into the rock. Later, I planted one of the roses Rosalinda tended, that the young couple brought all the way from Taos." His voice was weakening. His body seemed to deflate with this effort to tell the truth, to ensure someone would carry his story to the Gaspar family and to Doctor Bernnard's family. "I used to bring water to the rose bush many times during the summer and say a prayer for Rosalinda. Now I just come only a few times a year, but always on the day she died, August tenth. I can't do that anymore. Will you, Miss Millie, will you take water to the rose?"

He began rubbing his bad leg. But even that movement seemed to exhaust him. His head sank back against the rock and rolled to one side.

"Antonio, where are you?" Carlos called in his crackly old man's voice. Mr. Gaspar did not stir at the sound of his friend's voice.

Millie sprang erect and peered down the path that came from the road. About to answer, Millie hesitated, brushed her hair back, and without thinking, traced the scar on her forehead with a finger. *He'll know... he'll know Mr. Gaspar told me what they'd done. What if...*

She looked down; her landlord had not even opened his eyes. She took a deep breath, there was no choice. She shouted, "Here. Here, by the boulder. Come and help us."

34. Rescue

The friend in my adversity I shall always cherish most. I can better trust those who helped to relieve the gloom of my dark hours than those who are so ready to enjoy with me the sunshine of my prosperity.
— Ulysses S. Grant, eighteenth president of the United States, 1869–1877

Carlos rushed to the prone man, dropped to his knees, and lifted Mr. Gaspar's hand. Carlos' tightened brow made his bushy eyebrows bristle even more. Worry, then resolve crossed his face. Without looking up, he said, "Help me lift him. We must get Antonio to a doctor."

Millie's uninjured arm was closest to Mr. Gaspar, so she wiggled out of her backpack and let it fall to the ground. She bent down, lifted her landlord's arm over her shoulder, and let out a grunt as she and Carlos lifted him upright. They steadied the unresponsive man between them, then started toward the road. For the moment, the rain was little more than an annoying drizzle; the gathering dark clouds seemed to be holding off for their sake. After their first tentative steps, the two rescuers fell into a steady pace carrying the shorter man between them. As they reached the road, Millie looked toward where she had left Robby and the handcuffed Gavin by the vehicles. "Thank heavens, the ambulance is here." Relief and a glimmer of hope that her landlord might survive flooded her body.

Robby ran toward them, motioning the ambulance driver to follow.

As the bright white vehicle with blue lettering approached, Millie peered in the opposite direction through the junipers until she could make out the reassuring tan of the BLM Suburban where she had parked it.

One EMT lurched out of the driver's seat and rushed to them while the other opened the back doors of the ambulance and pulled out a gurney.

Robby paced back and forth on the other side of the gurney, reaching out, wanting to help, but letting the EMTs ease the limp body from Millie and Carlos and lift him onto the gurney. They both disappeared inside and began assessing their patient.

Millie clamped her right hand on the ache in her other arm and moved next to Robby. Carlos did not move from the spot where the EMTs had relieved him from the task of carrying his friend. He seemed to be absorbing the full impact of his friend's condition. His trance was broken when one of the EMTs exited, closed the back doors, and ran to the driver's seat.

"How is he?" Carlos called out.

Robby went to the driver's side, exchanged a few words, and stepped away as the engine started. She joined the two other anxious watchers on the side of the road as the ambulance pulled away. She shook her head, having no more information to ease their concern.

Carlos rounded on Millie, peering into her face with angry eyes. "What did that man do to Antonio?" Then he glared at Robby. "Where is he anyway?"

Robby raised her hands in a back-off motion. "Easy, sir, Gavin McIntyre is on his way to county jail. Detective St. Claire and Deputy Begay left a few minutes ago."

Carlos seemed to crumple. "Forgive me. I am so worried about Antonio." He looked down the road where the ambulance had disappeared, then up to the sky. Raindrops mixed with his tears. "I've got to go tell Della and take her to the hospital."

Millie watched him taking long strides back to his vehicle. When Carlos had insisted she call him by his first name that rainy Sunday at the Gaspars', she'd experienced only his charm and gallantry. He'd come to her defense when it seemed like Mr. Gaspar was interrogating her about finding the Bronco in the wash. Now she knew the secret they both had been hiding. Did this shared secret deepen their friendship or just safeguard it? How could she tell Mrs. Gaspar that the man she married was a murderer?

. Robby brought her back to the present. "Normally, I'd welcome this rain, Millie, but today, we're getting out of here. Come on."

Millie pointed down the road. "The Suburban's just over there. I'll follow you. Mister Gaspar told me to park off the road, so nobody would notice I was here alone. I wonder if he anticipated something like this."

"Oh, yeah, now that you point it out, I can just see it

parked in the junipers. No wonder I drove right past it. I didn't even think you were here until I saw Gavin threatening you."

"I was trying to get your attention. When you just drove on by, well, I..." Feeling that moment's rush of fear, Millie tried but could not suppress a whimper.

Robby moved next to Millie's side and reached up to put an arm around her shoulders. "You've been through a lot today, Millie." For a moment, ignoring the increasingly heavier rain, they stood, taking deep breaths. "Now come on, you're not driving with that arm. You're coming with me to the hospital." Robby pointed to Millie's hand clamped over her throbbing arm.

"Ugh, I'm afraid you're right." On the way to Robby's patrol vehicle, Millie veered to the road's edge and, with her good hand, broke off a sprig of sagebrush. She crushed the small, three-lobed leaves and held them to her nose, taking in the reassuring scent of the desert's permanence.

Millie let out a quiet moan as she pulled herself up into Robby's patrol pickup.

"We're going straight to the hospital. Wrong of me to be so focused on Gaspar I didn't have the EMTs tend to your arm."

Millie let out a deep breath, settling back against the seat and resting both hands on her lap. Robby had cranked up the heater to high. It felt good as their wet clothes warmed and began to dry.

"I'm sure glad you came along when you did, Robby. Just before you got here, Gavin was bragging about 'entertaining' his tour group when they tore up the place. Bailee was here, too."

"Back up there, Millie. You're saying Gavin was behind all that vandalism?" Robby asked.

"Uh-huh. His entertainment was getting Bailee to

appear in a wedding dress to act as the murdered ghost bride."

"That's sick," Robby said. "Is this Bailee the volunteer who was with you all when you came across the Bronco in the wash?"

"Yeah. Bailee Fernandez. She was the one that got that thrift store wedding dress we found. And it was Bailee that wanted the fruit tree cuttings. Gavin said she took right off for California to take the fruit tree stock to her brother for his orchards there. He said she wasn't in on the jimsonweed raid."

"You got him to admit all that? How it all happened?"

"He claimed he didn't know they put spray paint on the outhouse door, but it's all his fault. He hyped up that bunch and turned them loose on the homestead."

You're lucky he didn't leave you for dead after he told you all this."

"I'm not feeling too lucky."

After a few minutes, Robby asked, "What was Gaspar's condition when you found him? And how did you know where to look for him?"

"Remember that boulder with the nude? I showed you where the Gaspar name was carved on it? When I couldn't find him, I figured he'd try to go there. I think he was trying to hide from Gavin. He looked terrible when I got there, but he kept wanting to talk."

"Huh, that's just where his friend Lucero said Gaspar would go." Robby glanced over when Millie gave out another low moan and slowed her speed over the bumpy road.

"You said Gaspar was able to talk to you. Did he say anything about what Gavin was grumbling about, the cross he was after?"

Millie took a deep breath, sorting out her landlord's

words. "Yes, he told me about the cross, and..." *Best just to say it.* "Mister Gaspar killed Doctor Bernnard."

"Holy shit." Robby's hands popped up from the steering wheel and slapped back into place. "He said that? He told you he killed the professor?"

"He said he had to tell somebody before... I guess he thought he was going to die then and there."

Robby croaked out, "Hmph, he's going to wish he had kicked off if he actually confessed to murder. That's serious jail time. If the old boy lives, that is."

Millie slumped in her seat. Feeling woozy, she wanted to think the heat was getting to her, but having to incriminate the man who had taken her in and made her feel like family caused her stomach to churn.

A crash of thunder immediately followed by lightning snaking over the Lejos Canyon road released a slamming-down sheet of rain. Robby wrenched the windshield wipers on high, slowed even more, and without taking her eyes off the road, asked, "How'd he do it?"

"When Doctor Bernnard arrived here to continue researching the cross, somehow he put it together that the Peralta site was where to look. He'd met with the Gaspars, so they knew what he was doing. Get this, Mister Gaspar's grandmother came to him in a dream and warned him about the professor. He acted on her words and followed Doctor Bernnard. When he saw the professor digging up the cross, I guess he just lost it. Hit him with a shovel and put the body in the root cellar."

"How'd that old codger manage to do that?"

"He wasn't old then," Millie replied. "The next day, he went back with Carlos Lucero. He covered everything up around the sheep pen and hid the briefcase Doctor Bernnard had with him. He left it behind the Gaspar boulder. He did that while Carlos got rid of the vehicle."

Robby, open-mouth, stared at Millie. "Wait, you're saying Lucero, that old guy here with the shotgun, helped? That makes him an accessory to a murder!" Upon seeing Millie grab for the dash with her uninjured hand, Robby veered back on the road as sagebrush scraped along the side of the pickup.

Millie gulped, drew in a deep breath, and continued. "It was Carlos that rammed the Bronco into the wash."

"Hells, bells. And I just let that old boy get in his pickup and drive off. He's probably not much of a flight risk but I've got to let Sylvia know to pick him up at the hospital." Robby reached for the two-way radio next to the steering wheel.

35. Hospital

To us, family means putting your arms around each other and being there.
— Barbara Bush, United States First Lady, 1989–1993

Millie slid out of the patrol pickup in front of the Wellstown Regional Hospital emergency entrance. As Robby drove off to park, Millie heard someone call her name.

"Millie, Millie, at last you're here." Momma Agnes rushed out of the portico's shade. "Like I told Robby when she radioed in, Wirt's at a conference in Denver, so I came myself. Della is already here. What is happening with my cousin Tony?" As they walked through the sliding glass doors, Momma Agnes cried out, "*Ay, dios mio*, your arm! You're hurt, too."

Della Gaspar stood farther down the hallway, looking terribly alone even though busy hospital staff veered around her. She barely seemed to notice them, just continued staring at the closed door with a No Admittance sign. Momma Agnes gently led Mrs. Gaspar back to the seats in the waiting area off the main hallway. The potted plants and bland paintings did little to soothe the few people who also sat and waited, stirring hopefully and fearfully each time a medic exited from the swinging doors.

Millie sat at the edge of the seat, next to Mrs. Gaspar, with Momma Agnes making encouraging sounds on Mrs. Gaspar's other side. Millie took in the scene. The last time she was here, it had been after midnight. Her bloody face got immediate attention. Now, in the late afternoon, patients being discharged were being wheeled to the exit door and families coming or leaving from visiting relatives passed by.

When Robby came in, she went to the seated trio and extended her hand to Mrs. Gaspar. "I am so sorry we have to meet under these circumstances."

Mrs. Gaspar looked at her uniform and said in a pleading voice, "Why did that other police woman take Carlos away?"

"That was Detective Sylvia St. Claire from the sheriff's department. While Mister Lucero was bringing you to the hospital, did he tell you that your husband was escaping from a man named Gavin McIntyre?" At her nod, Robby continued. "Detective St. Claire came to the homestead and took McIntyre away to jail. But I learned more information about the situation" Robby glanced at Millie. "I radioed Detective St. Claire about that, just before I radioed in to the office."

Momma Agnes laid a hand over Mrs. Gaspar's. "I got Robby's call. When she said that Tony was being taken to the hospital in an ambulance and Carlos was on his way with you, I came here right away."

Mrs. Gaspar shook her head, her uncomprehending eyes shifting from Robby's face to her badge.

Robby's voice was even, but she avoided the distraught woman's eyes. "I'm sorry, we need to understand everything that has happened at the Peralta Homestead. Detective St. Claire will need to detain Carlos Lucero at the sheriff's department for questioning."

At the sound of a phone ringing, Mrs. Gaspar dug her cell phone out of the purse clutched on her lap. For a moment, her face brightened. "It's Bailee. I called and told her that Antonio was in the hospital. I told her not to worry."

Millie caught the name Bailee and gave Robby a wide-eyed look. Robby silently mouthed, "Speak of the devil."

Mrs. Gaspar answered the phone. After a few murmured assurances, the tired woman finished with, "My dear, you don't need to come all that way..." She tucked her phone away and announced, "Bailee loves her Tio Tony. She's on her way back here. Says she'll be here tomorrow morning. That young'un drives too fast."

Millie admired the woman's courage. She made her voice sound as if this were a routine call from her niece.

Robby squatted down and looked straight at Mrs. Gaspar. "I know you don't need any more bad news, but there's something you need to know about Bailee. She was involved in the vandalism at the homestead."

Mrs. Gaspar's hand flew to her heart. "Tony told me something bad happened at the homestead. He was very upset. Was that Gavin fellow involved? I knew he was a bad influence, what he kept saying about a ghost. I told Bailee so, too."

Robby, keeping eye contact, said, "I need to talk to her when she gets here. Will you have Bailee come to the BLM

309

office?"

Through tight lips, Mrs. Gaspar said, "I will make sure she does as you ask." The overwhelmed woman sobbed, "If... if my Antonio is..." Momma Agnes pulled her cousin into her arms.

Robby motioned to Millie, "Now, let's get you checked in and your arm attended to."

Millie took her place in the line behind three clusters of anxious looking people waiting in front of the check-in desk. She appreciated her friend's steady presence at her side. She wasn't sure she could stand up much longer.

When it was finally their turn, Robby stepped up to the window. "Her name is Millicent Whitehall." Robby's voice sounded distant.

The pain in her throbbing arm dimmed the noise, then the bright room seemed to dim, as well. When she wavered at the verge of passing out, she felt a strong arm slip around her waist from the other side.

"I've got you," Ben whispered.

***

Two hours later, Millie stepped through the door held aside for her by a nurse's aide. Ben sprang up from the waiting area couch, rushed to Millie, and started to wrap his arms around her.

"Ouch, stop," Millie shrieked.

Ben jumped back. "Oh, sorry. I forgot. Gee, you sure look better than you did when I first came in."

The aide at Millie's side smiled at the handsome young man and addressed Millie. "You'll feel better as soon as that sedative and the antibiotics kick in. But watch for any sign of infection; a cut like that is nothing to take lightly, Miss."

Ben's face crumpled with concern. "Momma Agnes

called me a few hours ago. She said you were on the way to the hospital, that she'd see me there, and hung up. She took Della home a little while ago. They said her husband was stabilized and there was nothing more to do tonight. Momma Agnes asked me to stay and drive you home."

There was a time when Millie first arrived in New Mexico that she'd felt very alone—far from her family back in New Jersey, in this harsh land, among people that dressed and behaved so differently from what she was used to. Now, even after such a harrowing day, her heart beat evenly. She was among friends, caring friends, who she knew would never let her down.

"I'll walk you to the door," the aide said, "but it looks like you'll be in good hands."

As the aide guided Millie toward the sliding glass exit doors, Ben rushed back to where he had been sitting, scooped up his pile of empty drink cups and fast-food wrappers, and stuffed them into a nearby trash can.

The rain had stopped. Millie breathed in the freshened air, but shivered in the cool night. The windshield of Ben's red Miata reflected the half moon. Ben held the door open, and Millie eased herself into the passenger's seat.

Ben went to the trunk, pulled out a Pendleton wool blanket, tucked it around Millie, and dropped into the driver's seat. "We've got to stop meeting like this, Millie. I hate hospital waiting rooms."

"Sorry to interrupt your evening. I promise I won't do it again." Millie tried to match Ben's irrepressibly good humor, but she was feeling very, very tired.

36. Bailee Almost Apologizes

Every calculation based on experience elsewhere fails in New Mexico.

— Lew Wallace, New Mexico Territorial Governor, 1878–1881

A knock on the front door woke Millie from a deep sleep. Through half-open eyes, she saw Ragged Ear standing alert at the end of her bed. The sound of Lydia's voice caused Millie to push herself upright. She looked down and realized she was still in the clothes she'd had on the day before, except there was a big bandage on her left arm below where her shirt sleeve had been cut off. She ran her fingertips across the wool Pendleton blanket that covered her bed, feeling a warmth that came from more than the blanket.

When Millie opened the front door, Lydia stepped inside, saying, "Wake up, Miss Millie."

Millie mumbled a "good morning" and "why are you here?"

"It's way past morning, Millie. I came because Momma Agnes wanted me to see if you were feeling up to coming in for a meeting in the conference room at two o'clock."

"I mean, why are you back from Santa Fe?"

"Momma Agnes called me last night saying Robby took you to the hospital. I left Santa Fe early, early this morning. I've been at the office already. Momma Agnes told me all about what happened to Mister Gaspar, what Robby said he told you, how Carlos Lucero got arrested, and—"

"Wait, wait a minute. I know what happened, I was there." Millie looked at her watch. "Yikes, it's past noon. Yeah, I'm okay. Let me get washed up. I'll be right back." As she stumbled to the bedroom, Lydia plopped into an armchair. Across the room, Ragged Ear sat on Millie's laptop, appraising the visitor with a fixed stare.

Somewhat refreshed and dressed in clean clothes, Millie re-entered the living room. Ragged Ear had moved over to Lydia's lap and was polishing his whiskers against his new friend's chin. "How did this cat know, Millie? I remember how this sweetie fluffed up at the Gaspars' birthday party. How'd he know that Antonio did such an awful thing?"

"Cats know things that we can't." Millie went over and lifted a reluctant Ragged Ear off Lydia's lap. "Let's get going."

The ride to the office felt almost normal to Millie. Lydia effused almost non-stop about her adventures in Santa Fe, except for an occasional "how's the arm" and "you've got to tell me everything that happened at the homestead." Lydia steered with one hand each time she stuck her wrist in front of Millie's eyes, pointing out one more etching on the thick silver, Navajo-crafted bracelet she bought in Santa Fe. Then she fished a small item wrapped in tissue from her blouse pocket and handed it to Millie.

Millie smiled. The harsh pain in her arm was almost gone, just a slight ache remained, so she was able to use both hands to unwrap the tissue. Puzzlement replaced the smile. She fingered the three-inch object, carved from olive-colored stone, with a flat snout, stubby tail, and splayed feet. "Um, what is it?" She cradled the small figure in her palm; it seemed to give off a sense of life, of energy.

"It's a Zuni fetish, Millie. When I told the sales lady that I was an archaeologist, she said the mole *had* to be my fetish."

"A mole? The little mouse-like mammal that lives under the dirt, eats worms and stuff?"

"Well, I admit, it wasn't the cutest of all the carvings they had there, but the woman explained that these fetishes depict animals that have cultural meanings. She assured me that the ones carried in that shop were made for the tourist trade. Members of the Zuni tribe view the world in six directions, north, east, south, west, and above and below. The mole represents the below—like archeologists, they dig for goodies from the ground."

"If you say so." Millie shrugged, tucked the fetish back into its wrapping, and handed it back to Lydia.

"You didn't spend all your time in Santa Fe shopping, did you?" Millie chided. "How'd it go at the state office?"

"Well, I made good use of the time I was there, let me tell you. I could have spent a week looking through those shops on the plaza and art galleries all around. But talking to the state people was even better. They couldn't stop asking questions about our work at the homestead. They want our documentation reports as soon as possible. I'll tell you the rest at the meeting so Wirt can hear it too."

Millie and Lydia hustled directly to the conference room from the parking lot and found the others already gathered around the meeting table. Millie sat next to the area manager, who was at the head of the table. Lydia took the chair next to her. Across from Millie, Robby was twirling her steno notebook on the table. Next to her sat Detective St. Claire and Deputy Begay.

Millie's eyes widened. "Oh, you found it! Thanks." There in the middle of the table lay her backpack. She reached for the familiar object and pulled it onto her lap even though it was slightly damp.

Wirt cleared his throat. "Glad to see you all in one piece, Millie. And welcome back, Lydia. I've asked Sylvia and Bub to join us to go over what happened at the homestead. Right now, Millie, I'm wishing that I never agreed to let you go back there by yourself."

Lydia settled back in her chair. "I think I'm glad that I missed out on all that, but wait till I tell you what the Santa Fe folks said."

"We went out to the homestead this morning," Robby said, making a gesture to include the two law officers beside her. "I rode out with them so I could drive the Suburban back. I showed Sylvia the damage to the cabin and outhouse on the way to the orchard, where we retrieved Gavin's gun. Then we got your backpack, Millie, over by the boulder. We had to poke around for a while behind the boulder where Gaspar told Millie he hid the briefcase, and Bub found it."

Lydia gasped, "What? Gavin had a gun? Millie, why didn't you tell me?"

Robby took up the story, as much for the benefit of the others at the table as for Lydia. "Like Wirt wanted, I was doing my usual patrol by the homestead. I saw Gavin

McIntyre holding a revolver, forcing Millie toward the orchard. To make a long story short, I got behind them just in time to see Gavin trip and Millie kick the gun out of his reach, giving me enough time to run up and put him under arrest."

Lydia, eyes wide and mouth hanging open, turned to Millie.

Millie winked at Lydia. "You know that piece of twine you laid out so you could find where you hid the pearls? Gavin tripped on it and landed on his face. It probably saved my life."

For a rare moment, Lydia was speechless, then burst out, "My string. Ha, I told you I always carry a ball of string in my pack. Was he after the pearls? Are they safe?"

At Millie's nod, Lydia began to relax, but instead, leaned forward and pointed farther down the table. "What's that?"

St. Claire reached for the leather satchel, pushed it toward Lydia, and said, "This is the briefcase that was among Doctor Bernnard's possession when he went missing. It wasn't in his Bronco when we found it and it wasn't anywhere around the root cellar. This is the missing piece of the puzzle."

Lydia pried the stiff leather briefcase open and poked at the contents, "Yuck, this is just a clump of pulp. I don't think even a good archivist could salvage anything out of that."

St. Claire gave it a push back down the table. "It doesn't matter much anymore. Gaspar told Millie what happened."

"What will happen to Mister Gaspar, if... if he lives?" Millie asked.

St. Claire acknowledged the concern in Millie's voice. "I contacted the hospital just before I got here. Gaspar was awake enough this morning to talk with his wife. He suffered from dehydration and exposure. He'll probably recover, but they're watching him for an irregular heartbeat. We're assembling charges. There's no statute of limitations on murder. But he's what, somewhere in his eighties? This took a lot of piss and vinegar out of the old man. It'll take a long time before going to trial. No telling if he'll ever see jail time."

Momma Agnes stepped into the room. "Are you ready for us now?" A grim-faced Della Gaspar gave her niece a little shove. Bailee Fernandez walked over to the chair next to Lydia, slumped down, and reached for the cell phone in her pocket. At a tap on her shoulder from Mrs. Gaspar, the petulant-looking Bailee clenched both hands in her lap. Mrs. Gaspar lowered herself in the next chair with a grunt, while Momma Agnes filled the next chair.

"Tell them, tell them everything you told me." Mrs. Gaspar commanded, then in an apologetic voice, "I am ashamed of this niece of ours."

Bailee looked up. "It's Gavin's fault. He wanted me to wear that stupid wedding dress and pretend to be the ghost bride. He said he'd pay me a hundred bucks." Bailee glared at Millie. "All I wanted was some of those fruit trees you said were so important. No big deal."

"Sorry, destruction of federal property, graffiti on the outhouse, digging up that jimsonweed, that's a big deal," Robby's tone was icy.

Bailee's eyes went wide beneath her turquoise bangs. "I didn't do all that."

The last thing Millie wanted to do was to come to Bailee's defense, but she had to speak up. "It's true. Gavin told me she got the fruit tree grafts and took off for California before they went for the jimsonweed."

"There, see. The ghost thing, it was just for fun. I bet I

looked just like Rosalinda in that wedding dress."

Mrs. Gaspar gasped. Momma Agnes' face radiated thunder.

More than her drooping shoulders, Mrs. Gaspar's tortured face told Millie that this woman suffered from a greater shock than a misbehaving niece. Mr. Gaspar must have told her himself, what he had revealed to Millie. What a shock it must be to learn your husband killed a man.

"I'm sorry, Tia Della," Bailee sounded almost contrite, "I shouldn't have done it. Especially because that scumbag-cheat Gavin handed me a fifty dollar bill and said that was all he had on him. I told him off and stomped all over that wedding dress."

Wirt rubbed his chin, but not before Millie caught sight of his grin. Bub let out a snicker that he turned into a cough.

"That's enough, Bailee." Robby used her cop's voice that meant no back-talk. "I'm giving you a citation for willful removal of plants or their parts on federal property. I considered adding littering for the trashed wedding dress, but I'll add that to Gavin's tab. I'd like to track down those creeps in his tour group, too, but not having evidence on who did what, it wouldn't get me anywhere."

"A citation, wha... what's that mean?" Bailee whined.

"I'm checking other similar offenses. It'll be either a fine or community service, or both."

Mrs. Gaspar addressed Robby, "She'll do as you say, I assure you." She grasped the table, pulled herself up, leaned down next to Bailee's ear, and hissed, "And not a word of this to your Tio Tony."

Head lowered, Bailee got up in slow motion. She stopped behind Lydia's chair and straightened her shoulders. "So, if I need to do community service or something, can I come and volunteer at the homestead with you guys again?"

A push from Mrs. Gaspar sent her toward the door.

Lydia burst out laughing, breaking the tension in the room. "That Bailee, she's something else."

"Volunteer at the homestead," Millie blustered. "Not while those red sandstone cliffs are still standing."

"You've got that right," Robby said. "With this on her record, she'll have a hard time ever going to work, or even volunteer, for a federal agency."

37. Curse and Blessing

Let sleeping dogs lie.
— Ancient proverb

Momma Agnes scooted next to Lydia and looked over to Wirt. "Is it okay if I stay and hear what happened at the homestead? Della's going to need a lot of help to get through this."

Wirt nodded, "You're part of that family and I just as soon you get the truth of the matter. Those two men are well-known in the community. This will stir up rumors and even more speculation about finding a body in the root cellar. You'll be on the front-lines of protecting the family's privacy."

St. Claire turned to Millie. "You'll need to make a statement about what McIntyre said to you about Bailee's involvement. So far, we're holding him on harassment pertaining to Gaspar and yourself. Robby will provide us with the federal codes for damages to the homestead."

"I can give you some help on that," Lydia said. "I'll put together a damage assessment report to include archaeological value and cost of repair and restoration. There are clear guidelines for compiling a damage assessment analysis, as a result of past ARPA related court cases."

"Gavin deserves every charge," Millie said. "He pretty much admitted he's been stealing artifacts for years from digs he'd been on and getting away with it." She hoped she'd never see Gavin's face again. Whatever happened to him wouldn't restore damage to the orchard.

St. Claire continued, "My priority is handling Gaspar's case. When we picked up Carlos Lucero at the hospital, he seemed almost relieved to get the matter off his chest. He gave us a formal deposition last night. I need yours as soon as possible."

"Take whatever time you need to assist in this case, Millie, and to take care of yourself," Wirt said. "Robby told me that you said Gaspar did the deed way over by the sheep pen and carried the body to the root cellar himself. But why'd he do it?"

All eyes turned to Millie. She shrank from the attention. She just wanted to go back to the first days at the homestead, when she walked among the orchard's venerable heirloom trees and the only noise was Lydia's humming coming from the cabin.

Millie looked down at her hands resting on the table, selecting her next words. "Mister Gaspar wanted Mrs. Gaspar and Bailee to know the truth about what happened, and for Doctor Bernnard's family to know, too. It was because he was protecting the cross at the Peralta Homestead." She let out a long breath and said, "It's the silver cross. The cross is real, not a legend. It's at the center of all of this. There was a cross attached to the rosary that came with the Peralta family from Spain. It all makes sense now."

Millie spread out her fingers on the table and began. "Lydia, you'll remember the birthday party where Mister Gaspar told us about how Rosalinda was killed at the cabin. He was mainly passing the family tragedy onto his niece Bailee, but you and I heard it, too. So did Gavin.

"José Peralta, Rosalinda's husband, had an older sister who also homesteaded in Lejos Canyon. José got home one day, found his wife dead, took her body to his sister's place, and went after the murderer. Whoever killed her also stole the cross. José tracked him down and mailed the cross back to his sister. José never returned. The sister was Mister Gaspar's grandmother, Margarita Peralta. She loved Rosalinda like one of her own daughters. She held the cross dear, keeping it in the Peralta family."

"Uh-huh," Momma Agnes said, "I've heard Tony say that. Tony always seemed to know that José killed the man."

Millie glanced at Momma Agnes and began making small circles on the table with the palm of one hand. "Just before his grandmother died, Margarita made Mister Gaspar promise to never let the cross leave the Peralta Homestead that Rosalinda loved."

"Uh-huh," Momma Agnes said again. "We always suspected that is why Margarita never married Alejandro Gaspar, the good man she tended the homestead with for most of her life and raised children with. It was to keep the Peralta name attached to that property. At the time, it was a dishonor to the family that they never had a proper church wedding. She went by the name Margarita Peralta all her life. But the children took their father's name,

Gaspar."

Lydia moved out of The Thinker pose and turned to Millie. "Why, Millie, you knew all along there was something out of order on the homestead filing papers. You saw there was a mix-up with the initials."

"Yes, the name on the filing claim for the one hundred and sixty acres was José Manuel Peralta, five years later the patent deed had M. J. Peralta." For a moment, Millie felt good that the anomaly she'd discovered was born out through family accounts. "After his grandmother's funeral, Mister Gaspar buried the cross near the sheep pen."

"That's what Gaspar told you, *near* the sheep pen? That doesn't narrow it down very much," Robby said.

Millie didn't respond. The image of Doctor Bernnard's map appeared in her mind. He had penciled in something like a T, with a question mark next to it. Now she knew it was meant to be the cross location. The professor must have encountered the out-of-place rose bush beyond the sheep pen and maybe noticed the cross carved into the cliff. He made a guess about the cross' location. He never got the chance to verify his guess.

Millie knew exactly where the cross was buried, between the rose bush and the cross carved into the cliff. But she remained silent. She hadn't thought to mention coming across the rose bush to Robby the day they discovered the jimsonweed stolen. Out of respect for the family's privacy, she saw no reason to say more now.

Lydia sensed Millie's apprehension. "Yeah, could be anywhere. I suppose somebody could spend a lot of time going over the area with a metal detector, but to me, it's just plain wrong to go digging up family relics, even if," she scrunched up her face, "that's something archaeologists have been known to do."

Momma Agnes laid her hand over Lydia's. "Thanks,

dear. If that was Margarita's dying wish, the cross should be left buried."

Bub had said little but now his voice was firm, compelling. "For us Navajo people, it is wrong to take things from the dead."

Wirt tipped his chair back, rubbed his eyes, and dropped back down with a thump. "Two murders occurred at the Peralta Homestead because of that accursed cross. I believe the legend of the silver cross should die right here, in this room."

Silence filled the conference room, followed by solemn nods.

St. Claire stood up to go but leaned back against the table. "I get a thirty-year old cold case dumped in my lap. Millie connects the Bronco to the professor, so we get an ID on him. Then she gets a full confession from Gaspar. You ever think about going into detective work?"

Robby gave the detective a high-five. She followed St. Claire and Bub to the door and said, "Thanks Sylvia, Bub. I'll be in touch."

Robby returned to her seat, saying, "Yeah, Millie, you've solved a thirty-year-old crime and helped capture the perpetrator of an ARPA violation for federal property damage. All in a day's work for a botanist, right?"

Wirt turned his attention to Lydia. "How's it look for getting that site on the National Register?"

"They're all for it, Wirt. As soon as they get our documentation, they'll do their part and support BLM in sending the nomination in to Washington D.C. I described all the features of the site and told them about the ruin within walking distance of the cabin, and the Navajo and Puebloan rock art, and that the Old Spanish Trail passed through there, and..." Lydia stopped to take a breath. "And here's the clincher, I showed them copies of the handwritten letters that I got myself from the state archives about the pearl rosary handed down through the family. They see all kinds of potential for making the Peralta site a showcase for the layers of cultures that New Mexico is famous for. I can't wait to get out to the homestead and do a proper job of securing those pearls."

Millie wished she could share Lydia's enthusiasm. Of course, she would finish the recording and documentation of the site, but it would never feel the same. Every time she would pass by the outhouse or enter the orchard, damage, terror, and sadness would accompany her. Yes, those responsible would be punished, but will putting the site on the National Register help or hinder protection?

Lydia slapped her hand over her mouth. "Oh, oh, maybe I shouldn't have told them about finding pearls from the rosary."

Wirt's brow angled down toward his nose for a moment, then he smiled. "You two found the pearls doing authorized work. If the pearl rosary helps get stronger protection for that site, I'd say that's all to the good."

Momma Agnes added, "The rosary is a blessing. That cross was a curse. There's no need to mention any silver cross, right?"

"Right," said Robby.

"Right," Wirt repeated.

"Never heard of a cross," Lydia said.

Millie just smiled. She'd ask Ben to borrow his Grandfather Sageman's pickup for Saturday. She needed to take water to that thirsty rose bush.

38. Rest In Peace

...May she ever walk in beauty.
— Adapted from Navajo Chant

Millie sat on her front steps, a three-gallon plastic container of water at her feet. Next to it was a big cooler that Lydia had unloaded from her car's trunk before she went to call on Mrs. Gaspar next door. Millie didn't know what Lydia had in the cooler, but figured it would be an over the top lunch for the three of them.

Lydia returned and joined Millie on the steps.

"How's Mrs. Gaspar managing?" Millie asked.

"I feel sorry for her, Millie, she's so sad and confused. She can't get a straight answer from the hospital when Antonio will be released and doesn't know what will happen to him then."

"Yeah, she looked awful last night when she and Bailee got back from the hospital. I spent a few minutes at their house. Good thing Momma Agnes was there to head off prying questions from the folks that stopped by. There'll be more people coming by today." Millie looked toward the Gaspars' house. Even the row of rose bushes seemed droopy and forlorn. Earlier that morning, Millie had clipped the prettiest blossom from the rose bush that her landlord had transplanted from the homestead.

Ragged Ear pushed his way between them, sat down, and joined the conversation with a soft purr.

"Ah, good, here comes Ben." Millie waved and stood up. "I'm glad he could get his Grandfather Sageman's pickup. That Lejos Canyon road would shake my little car to pieces."

"Thanks for inviting me along," Lydia said. "I know we'll be working back at the homestead next week, but I've just got to check on those pearls. Hope I'm not intruding on a day with your boyfriend."

Millie barely got out a "He's not my..." when Ben hopped out of the faded blue Chevy pickup. He put the water container and cooler in the back and held the passenger door open.

"Wait, we can't all fit in the front seat," Millie said.

"I told you we'd be a little crowded. Grandfather took out the back seat years ago when he had to take a sheep to the veterinarian. He never got around to putting it back."

Millie, squeezed in the middle, decided she liked the feel of Ben's leg against hers and having her friend Lydia at her side giggling at Ben's tales.

He was recounting some of the knotty escapades he'd been involved in while dealing with problem wildlife. First was having to coax a skunk out of tribal headquarters. "That was a dicey one, I tell you. If that skunk had let loose, no telling if our department would get any budget the next five years. Then there was that black bear in the school yard."

She didn't even mind the occasional bump that pressed her sore arm against Ben. Millie reveled in the moment, letting the tension of the previous days' turmoil fade away.

When Ben seemed to run out of stories, Lydia interrupted Millie's relaxed state. "What do you think would have happened if Robby hadn't seen you and if Gavin hadn't tripped on my string?"

"I don't know. Gavin seemed determined to get the silver cross, no matter what. If Robby hadn't come by just when she did..." Millie's voice trailed off; she didn't want to dwell on how easily things might have ended otherwise.

"Gawd, you could have been killed." Ben squeezed her knee.

"Sorry, I shouldn't have brought up what a terrible time you went through," Lydia said, "but I told you so, trouble always comes in threes. Could have been three murders at the homestead."

Millie elbowed her partner. She wanted to hang on to the good feeling of their day together. "Come on, Lydia, you're just trying to make a dumb saying fit something that didn't happen. I'm still here and I'm just glad we can get back to work now."

As they neared the homestead, Ben asked, "What's in that cooler, Lydia?"

"You'll see," Lydia teased.

Ben pulled into the small parking area, went to the back of the pickup, and let the tailgate down. He lifted the water container to the ground, and pulled the cooler closer so Lydia could reach it. When she opened the cover, the aroma of fried chicken filled the air. She brought out a plate, partially unwrapped the tin foil cover, and swirled it under Ben's nose. Ben's eyes followed the plate as if he were gazing at the Holy Grail. He reached toward the plate.

"Un-uh," Lydia said, "first we do what we came here to do. I'm going to check on the pearls, and Millie's got water for some kind of plant, I suppose."

Ben's face crumpled. "Okay, I don't know what you're going to do with that water, but I'll carry the container over to the cliff for you, Millie." He turned to Lydia, "Maybe just one piece?"

Lydia couldn't resist a hungry man's plea for food. She pulled a drumstick from under the tin foil.

Ben's thanks was mixed with smacking lips. He took a breath and said, "Is it okay if you show me those pearls that used to be the rosary?"

"Sure, I'll be looking over the cabin until you get back." Lydia tucked the tin foil around the plate and put it back in the cooler. "Then we'll have lunch."

Acting as if it weighed a ton, Ben used both hands to lug the water container through the junipers and gave out a fake put-upon grunt when he sat it by the sheep pen.

Millie went to the corner and unhooked the dipper that she was pretty sure had hung on its peg since Mr. Gaspar planted the rose bush and began bringing water on a regular basis. She took a few steps back to Ben and spotted the sharp pointed wire that had ripped her arm. The crazed look in Gavin's eyes and the blazing pain flashed in her mind. The dipper fell from her trembling hands.

Ben grabbed her shoulders, turned her to face him, and pulled her body into his arms.

Millie couldn't help it. She let out the terror of that day in tears that wet Ben's shoulder. He held her tight until her body calmed. She leaned her head against his, quieting the tears.

"It's all right, *ayoo aniinish'ni*."

"I'm sorry," Millie whispered. "It was all so awful."

She stepped back, but let their clasped hands hang between them. "Ben, I know I'll be okay—with you in my life."

His moist eyes held a smile. He leaned close for a tentative kiss.

They stood in a tender embrace, until a rumble from Ben's stomach caused them both to laugh.

"You go look at the pearls, Ben. There's something I need to do here by myself, a promise I made." She waved off his protest. "I won't be long. Lydia's waiting for you. I saw a pecan pie in that cooler, too."

With that enticement, Ben started back toward the cabin, looking back three times with a lopsided grin before disappearing in the junipers.

Millie picked up the water container and dipper and walked to the rose bush. She rested the palm of her hand on the warm rock cliff, tipped the container, filled the dipper, and dribbled water around the base of the cherished plant. She repeated this process, soaking the ground in a two-foot diameter around the stem.

Then Millie knelt on one knee between the rose bush and the cross carved into the rock wall. She pulled a day pack around from her back, opened it, and lifted out the blossom she had clipped that morning from Mr. Gaspar's rose bush. She laid the pale yellow flower on the sand and whispered, "Rest in peace, Rosalinda. Your cross is safe. Rest in peace."

Millie drifted back to the sheep pen and hung the dipper back on its wooden peg. She gazed along the top of the red cliffs. She did not see the raven, but knew she would on some other day. Taking long strides, she headed to the vehicles, hearing Ben and Lydia's laughter even before reaching the road.

Ben sat on the tailgate, dangling his legs, and munching on a chicken wing. Laid out next to him was the outdoor feast Lydia had extracted from the cooler. Upon seeing Millie, Lydia poured a cup of lemonade and handed it to her.

Lydia drew a small object from her shirt pocket. "Millie, I've got something for you. I got this in Santa Fe."

Millie unwrapped the tissue and a smooth, tawny-colored stone fell into her hand. "Oooh," Millie cooed, "it's a mountain lion." She held it up in her palm for Ben to see.

Lydia smiled. "Knew you'd like it. When I saw the little sign by it at the store, I thought it was just the right Zuni fetish for you. The mountain lion represents north, like you come from farther north, and it's known for courage and solitude."

"It's beautiful." Millie wrapped her fingers around the gift and held it near her heart.

"So what's next for you two after you're done here?" Ben asked. "You make a pretty good pair the way you, ah, *unearthed* the history of this place." He winked at Lydia.

"We do make a good pair," Millie agreed, meeting Lydia's fist bump.

Millie looked toward the red sandstone cliffs that reached into the bluest of blue skies.

What came next, she knew, would include her friend Lydia, and she admitted to herself, her boyfriend, Ben.

Author's Notes

The idea for this book came from a field trip some years ago in celebration of New Mexico Heritage Preservation Month. Jim Copeland, Bureau of Land Management archaeologist, led the field trip to see early homesteads, a stage stop, and a cemetery in northwest New Mexico. One comment he made germinated in my mind until it grew into this full-blown story. He mentioned there had been occurrences of grave-robbing in the old cemeteries. I was aware of the devastation of 'pot hunting' for Ancestral Puebloan artifacts, but it was news to me that grave-robbers had been at work violating Anglo and Hispanic cemeteries.

In addition, I wanted to incorporate the continuum that rock art reveals of human occupation in this region. Rock art messages left by the overlapping cultures reveal human history stretching back for hundreds of generations. For me, rock art inspires wonder. Who made this? Why in this exact spot? Was someone looking over his or her shoulder directing placement of each element?

I want to acknowledge the wonderful experiences I have enjoyed on field trips sponsored by the Northwest New Mexico Site Steward program and the San Juan College Encore program. I especially want to recognize the many hours spent visiting rock art sites with David Casey and Luanne Crow. David's research brings life and meaning to these symbols on rocks. Luanne's good nature makes these trips always enjoyable.

Many people helped shape this story. I wish to thank my publisher, Geoff Habiger, for his insightful editing, his patience in bringing this book to fruition, and his knowledge of what makes a good mystery.

I want to thank my Tuesday afternoon Zoom pals, Vicki Holmsten and Terry Nichols, for making every chapter better. Members of my critique group, San Juan Writers, provided much thoughtful help.

I am grateful to Patty Tharp, San Juan County Historical Association and Julie Bell, author of award-winning historical novels, who reviewed the manuscript for accuracy of homesteaders' lives. Cindy Yurth, retired Navajo Times reporter, Elaine Benally, retired San Juan College Director, and Angela Watkins, Aztec Library Director, helped shape cultural references. Kristie Arrington, retired BLM archaeologist, reviewed references to archaeological work with an experienced eye. It takes a considerable amount of time to review an entire manuscript and I sincerely appreciate their help.

My thanks go to Scott Graham, Cindy Yurth, and Kristie Arrington for kindly reading the manuscript and providing testimonials. Their words aptly express my intent for the story.

My artist friend, Trudy Farrell, contributed the handsome images at the beginning of chapters.

Most important of all, I thank my husband, technical advisor, and best friend, Jim Ramakka, retired BLM wildlife biologist, for continuous support and our many adventures.

Lastly, I wish to recognize those who study, revere, and protect our cultural heritage sites. Keep up the good fight.

About The Author

Through photography and writing, Vicky Ramakka shares her love of the southwest in local, regional, and national magazines. Her articles have won awards from the New Mexico Press Women and SouthWest Writers. Her first novel *The Cactus Plot, Murder In The High Desert* won the New Mexico-Arizona Book Award for cozy mystery and reached best seller on Amazon.

She credits attending conferences and workshops, plus networking with other writers, as important contributors to her writing success. She is a member of San Juan Writers, Women Writing The West, New Mexico Press Women, and SouthWest Writers.

Vicky and her husband reside in northwest New Mexico. She volunteers as a Site Steward to monitor a Rock Art site and enjoys every trip to the nearby canyons and archaeological sites.

BISCOCHITO COOKIE RECIPE

6 Cups flour
1/4 Tsp. salt
3 Tsp. baking powder
1 1/2 Cup sugar
2 Tsp. anise seeds
2 eggs
2 Cup lard
1/4 Cup brandy*
1/4 Cup sugar
1 Tbsp. cinnamon

Sift flour with baking powder and salt. In separate bowl, cream lard with sugar and anise seeds until fluffy. Beat in eggs one at a time. Mix in flour and brandy until well blended. Refrigerate 2-3 hours. Turn dough out on floured board and pat or roll to 1/4 or 1/2-inch thickness. Cut into shapes (the fleur-de-lis is traditional). Dust with mixture of sugar and cinnamon. Bake 10-12 minutes at 350° or until browned.

*The author uses Sangria instead of brandy.

About the New Mexico State Cookie:

The New Mexico Legislature adopted the biscochito (bizcochito) as the official state cookie in 1989. This act made New Mexico the first state to have an official state cookie. The biscochito is a small anise-flavored cookie, which was brought to New Mexico by the early Spaniards. The cookie is used during special celebrations, wedding receptions, baptisms, Christmas season, and other holidays. It was chosen to help maintain traditional home-baked cookery.